Enjoy!

VIKING STORM

SUSAN K. KEHOE

Susan K. Kehoe

 FriesenPress

One Printers Way
Altona, MB R0G 0B0
Canada

www.friesenpress.com

To Melody and Allison. Impossible to thank you enough for all
your comments and suggestions. Your unbiased opinions have been
invaluable in directing my writing endeavours, correcting my spelling
and creating order out of chaos in tenses, POV and grammar, not to
mention my erratic typos.

I must also thank my team at Friesen Press for their support and
patience through edits and revisions, formats and the promotion
process. Hopefully, I'm more computer savvy now.

ISBN
978-1-03-916086-6 (Hardcover)
978-1-03-916085-9 (Paperback)
978-1-03-916087-3 (eBook)

1. FICTION, HISTORICAL, MEDIEVAL

Distributed to the trade by The Ingram Book Company

For the reader's information: I have endeavoured to use accurate historical details in this Viking/Celtic story, but for simplicity, I had used terms such as Norway, Sweden, and Denmark for ease of reference, although those places were governed by multiple-clan kingships and were not formally countries until after 905 CE. This also applies to names such as the Atlantic, North, and Irish seas, and measures of weight and length. All the characters are figments of my imagination. Real historical places and people are used fictitiously.

ACKNOWLEDGEMENTS

To Melody and Allison. It's impossible to thank you enough for all your comments and suggestions. Your unbiased opinions have been invaluable in directing my writing endeavours, correcting my spelling, and creating order out of the chaos in tenses, points of view, and grammar, not to mention my erratic typos.

Also, I must thank my team at FriesenPress for their support and patience through edits, revisions, formats, and the promotion process. Hopefully, I'm more computer savvy now.

OTHER BOOKS BY SUSAN KEHOE

Tango

Nuggets: A Tale of the Cariboo Gold Rush

Ireland: Snapshots in Time

GLOSSARY OF NAMES & TERMS

Name	Meaning
Aoife	Female Irish name pronounced Eefa.
Berserker	A warrior typically wearing bearskins who went into a frenzied fighting state, biting his shield and killing indiscriminately, possibly induced by the psychedelic herb henbane and/or alcohol. Berserkers were often used by kings as elite troops. Did not qualify as warriors for Odin's armies.
Drengr	Warrior, bound by honour to fight to the death for any insult to his person and family. Destined to die in battle and become one of Odin's warriors in Ragnarök, the battle of the gods and antigods, wolves, and serpents at the end of the world.
Erse	Danish name for Irish or Gaelic language or culture.

Far	Danish word for father.
Feoh	A Futhark rune indicating good luck and wealth derived from hard work, often related to farming, fertility, and cattle. Looks like an upright stick with two right-sided branches.
Freyja	God of fertility and prosperity. Commanded the rain and the sun. Had a magical ship named Skidbladnir, built by dwarfs and was fast, capable of holding all the gods of Asgard.
Frigg	Wife of Odin and Queen of Asgard. Mother of Baldr and Hod. Advised Odin in decision making for Asgard. The only woman allowed to sit on the throne. Spun clouds on her spinning wheel. Associated with mistletoe. Had twelve maid servants.
Frithir	Gaelic word for a seer of omens.
Futhark	An ancient alphabet of Indo-European origin, sometimes found on tombstones. Old Futhark had twenty-four letters; later Young Futhark had sixteen.

Knarr	A Viking cargo ship, similar in clinker-built construction to a longship but deeper, allowing an open compartment to carry livestock. Also powered by oarsmen and one large sail.
Kone	Danish word for wife.
Loki	An anti-god shape-shifting trickster, son of giants. Shape-shifted into many forms. Had sons, including the wolf Fenrir and the serpent Jormungand who would be part of the final battle of Ragnarök. His daughter was the goddess Hel who ruled the world of the dead. Played many tricks on the gods and humans.
Longship	A Viking war ship built of overlapping riveted planks with a very shallow draft, powered by oarsmen with one large sail and a wooden rudder. Very effective for travelling up rivers and landing on beaches.
Midgard	Middle earth, the land of humans.
Mjolnir	Thor's hammer. A magical weapon with crushing power that would return to him once thrown. Often depicted on silver pendants worn by warriors for good luck.

Mor	Danish word for mother.
Njord	God of the sea and the wind. Guardian of the sea, wind, fire, fertility, wealth, and abundance. Related to good fishing and boat building. Was married to Nerthus and had twins Freyr and Freyja.
Odin	Pronounced *Othin*. King of the Norse Gods, created the world from the body of a giant he slew. Was part of the pantheon of gods in Asgard, the Aesir. Often depicted as a bearded old man with one eye. Was capable of shape-shifting into other beings or animals. Was the god of victory, magic, war, hunting. Had a spear named Gungnir, which would return to him after it was thrown. Rode an eight-legged horse names Sleipnir. Was often accompanied by two ravens or two wolves. Was married to Frigg but sired many sons with other women, some of whom are anti-gods or giants. Sons included Thor, Baldr, and Hod. Lived in Valasjalf (Valhalla). Had multiple other names. Only accepted warriors into his army who have died in battle while attacking the enemy.
Ogham	Pronounced *Owam*. Ancient Celtic alphabet supposedly of Druid origin.

Onkel	Danish word for uncle.
Ragnarök	The battle between good and evil, the gods and antigods at the end of civilization when all earthly life would be wiped out.
Tante	Danish word for aunt.
Thor	All-important Norse God, son of Odin and goddess Jord. He was the god of thunder, storms, strength, valour, victory, fertility and was a protector of humans. Wore a special glove, Jarngreipr. Rode in a chariot pulled by two goats which he could kill and eat but could later resurrect from their bones. Was married to Sif. Also had multiple children with other women including anti-goddesses.
Thrall	Slave
Valkyries	Virgin warrior women who served the god Odin. They wore armour and could fly. They brought the dead heroes from the battlefield to Valhalla to fight with the gods in Ragnarök. Could be seen as ravens over a battlefield, choosing who to take to Odin.

CHAPTER 1

The Irish Sea off Scotland's northwest coast, 905 CE

The Viking longship skimmed into a surging sea that drenched Gunnar and his fellow oarsmen, despite the tarps. The snarling dragon-headed beast on the prow almost disappeared into the foamy wash, then reared its fearsome head at the next curling wave. The wind picked up, scudding clouds into a dark grey mass, obliterating the horizon. Long ago, the crew had hauled in the sail as fierce westerly winds clawed to drag them back. Automatically, he matched his speed with his rowing partner Olaf. His shoulders ached from the constant hard pull.

"These cursed Scottish headlands and islands are the worst part of the trip," Olaf spluttered, spitting out a mouthful of seawater.

Gunnar glanced over his left shoulder and could see the rest of the crew were just as wet and disgruntled as he was. Finn, one of the biggest and strongest warriors, was bracing his legs against the wooden rudder, keeping the ship heading into the waves.

Somewhere behind them in the roiling waters, Gunnar's older brother Thorkell, was captaining the fully laden trading knarr. Although the bigger ship was out of sight, he prayed to Njord, god of the sea and his nine daughters who ruled the waves, to keep both ships safe.

Five years ago, Gunnar's father Ottar decided to build a longship to protect his trading knarr from Norse pirates. Memories flooded back. As a twelve-year-old Gunnar had followed Ottar out to the woods, they'd searched for that one perfect oak—straight and hundred-feet tall, now the keel beneath his feet. Steinn, his oldest brother had shared responsibilities with Ottar in running both their farm and trading business in Hedeby. Thorkell, as the middle son, had helped to fell trees, particularly in the wintertime when he was not at sea. The three of them had hauled logs and Gunnar often straddled their dun-coloured pony as it dragged the timbers down the hills to the shoreline. Thorkell was skilled at sawing the logs into the wedge-shaped boards used in clinker-built ships. The local shipbuilder did all the trimming and shaping of the support beams, thwarts, and braces supporting the mast and decking.

Meanwhile, Gunnar had run errands, fetched nails from the blacksmith, and held planks in place while the others hammered. He'd sharpened axes and saws, too. His least favourite job had been picking oakum, the scrap wool and fibre caulking that reduced his fingers to bloody blisters. Once the oakum was tarred and wedged between the planks, the ship was seaworthy for at least five years.

Olaf scanned the horizon for any signs of land or Norsemen. "I hope we get as much plunder as we did last summer," he said. "My spoils sold for enough to buy clothes and shoes for my whole family. We didn't go hungry last winter, either."

"Trading's been a lot more profitable than farming, especially since Onkel Bersi moved his trading post to Dublin," said Gunnar. "My father's spending more time in Hedeby and less time on our farm these days. Mind you, we run a lot more risks with this coastline and the Norse."

"The weather's better on the southbound route round England but there you're against the currents and the winds. There's no getting slaves on the Saxon coast—too well defended in most places. We got good coin for those Irish girls last year. The more the Norse settle on the Scottish coast and outer islands, the less chance we have."

Gunnar looked at his partner with respect. The older warrior had been his mentor for the past three years. His scarred hands, missing teeth, and wind-seared skin attested to a hard life at sea. *I've spent more time with him than my family. He's taught me so much from stars and tides, and how to fight. I'm amazed he's survived. He must be at least thirty-five,* Gunnar thought, looking at Olaf's balding head.

Finn yelled, "Land to the west."

All eyes focused on a ridge emerging from the mist, sea, and low cloud. There was a collective sigh of relief. As they approached the coast, Gunnar had a clearer view of the cliffs, sheer imposing black rock walls hundreds of feet high, with white surf relentlessly tearing and exploding into foam. Finn altered course to parallel the shore. Gunnar wondered if he'd choose the same cove as last time, with its small beach and freshwater spring.

Sure enough, when the promontory came in sight, the ship changed course. Finn yelled orders and their rowing slowed as the ship angled into the narrow bay, avoiding the half-submerged rocks. All hands clambered out, pushing the ship onto the sand and pebble. Gunnar and two others began gathering driftwood.

They kept a small box of beeswax-coated mullein heads on board to light their fires. Sparks from two flints were enough to ignite the spiky plants. Snaps, crackles and a rising wisp of smoke promised not only a well-earned meal, but would be a signal fire to alert the knarr to their location.

Finn pried the lid open on the barrel of salt beef. A shout from Snorri, the huge, hairy Norseman, had all eyes searching the horizon where the top of the sail on the knarr became visible. As the bigger ship came closer, Gunnar watched twenty-year-old Thorkell guide the vessel into the sheltered shallows. With a full cargo, her keel was too deep to bring her closer.

The lowing of cattle chained in the cargo compartment echoed around the bay until the knarr crew pulled tarps from the fodder supply and fed them. Gunnar noted crates and boxes were still tied in place, undamaged by the rough seas. He joined the other hands in filling the water barrels by the bucketload from the spring.

Harald, another youth from Hedeby, tried jostling him, but Gunnar dodged. The hostility between their families went back generations and continued with the boys. At seventeen, Gunnar was getting taller and stronger, so there was little difference in their fighting skills. *If I can handle Harald, I can handle a Norseman or a Celt.*

Briefly, he ducked his head in the stream, running his hands over his face and neck, feeling the increasing thickness of the stubble on his chin. It pleased him immensely to finally be growing a beard. After all, he was already a man.

The combined crew of fifty gathered on the beach. Some men cooked chunks salt beef and stale bread on an iron grill over the open fire. Others speared chunks of meat on the tips of their knives directly into the flames. Gunnar looked around at the crew, mostly Danish with a sprinkling of Swedes and Finns. They were all tired, yet remained watchful. So far, they hadn't encountered any pirates or the dark spirits of the Celtic woods, similar to the Viking anti-god trickster Loki at home. There were no bears, serpents, or wolves on Ireland's rocky shores, either.

The wind died as they squatted around the fire. Gunnar always sat with Thorkell. He watched the giant, Snorri, cleaning his sword and compared it to his own. Snorri's sword was magnificent, a rare steel from the distant, exotic city of Damascus in the Mediterranean. Complex wavy patterns in the steel ran up and down the blade. Even their own blacksmith who made very serviceable weapons couldn't duplicate the steel. He had told Gunnar that no one had discovered the secret ingredient of the makers, supposedly a family from the Indus Valley, wherever that was. The sword retained its edge and, unlike his, rarely needed sharpening. The elaborately carved and sculpted pommel, added by the Frankish armourers, was another luxury detail. Snorri often told the tale of killing the Islamic warrior in Iberia, claiming the sword as his own. He had been with a squadron of berserkers at the time, but travelled alone now.

As night fell, Gunnar curled up on the beach, wrapped in his cloak with his sword beside him. He slept, dreaming of battles, plunder and women, and awoke to squawking, keening gulls. Clouds in the east were stained pink and gold as the sun peeped through the retreating cloud cover, revealing a horizon empty of sails. A few of the knarr crew, including Thorkell, were already checking the cargo and the bulls.

Within the hour, the knarr was manoeuvring around the rocks and eddies out of the bay, heading south. The longship crew pushed their ship off the sand until she floated, then clambered on board. Gunnar checked that his round shield was still tight in the rail rack. He opened the port and shoved his oar in place. Matching Olaf's pace, they set the tempo for those sitting behind. Finn manned the rudder again and steered them out of the bay, taking advantage of the tide. The dragon led them into the open sea, away from the cliffs and the dangerous foaming, swirling currents around them.

Even though the wind was not constant, they raised the large, red woven sail, which billowed sporadically. *Good; not so much rowing.* Soon, they overtook the knarr and cruised ahead. Gradually. the cliffs diminished in height as steep, emerald green slopes reached down to stony beaches. He watched for sheep grazing on the high slopes or any tendrils of smoke from a hidden village, but none so far.

Gunnar could feel the tension building. Every man wanted a good fight. The Celtic warriors always gave it. He wanted plunder and women. Dublin's market attracted traders from Britain, the Frankish lands, and even the Mediterranean. While the Franks were seeking young boys for farms and armies, the Islamic traders ruling Iberian lands were their best customers, paying premium prices for virgins and children, harem bound. It was their silver currency, the dirham coin, that was used throughout the trading world. The crew would loot for jewellery, weapons, and even clothing, anything that would sell in Dublin's market.

They reached the river delta at midday. On the broad expanse of mud flats, gulls fought over small crabs and molluscs. Old Olaf pointed to the charred remains of several cottages. "When we were here two years ago, we didn't go further up river. Do you want to check inland?" he yelled to Finn. The crew discussed it and all agreed, taking in the sail.

One man scrambled ashore onto the bank. "This path's been used recently. There are footprints and horse droppings not more than two or three days old," he announced, climbing back on board.

"Right then; let's see what we can find," Finn said. Glancing behind them, he waved to the knarr, indicating the longship was heading upstream.

Gunnar watched as Thorkell waved them on, preparing to anchor the knarr in the shallows to wait. The river was winding but still deep enough for them to row upstream. The land was relatively flat, yet densely wooded with mature oak, ash, beech, and pine. A line of hills rose to the north and west. The river narrowed the closer they got to the hills. Several tributaries emptied into the main channel. Finn dropped his stone-weighted rope over the side and pulled it out wet to the depth at four to five feet. On testing in the tributaries both were shallower. They continued on the main channel until Harald broke the silence. "There's smoke over there," he said pointing to the hill.

"We've only got three feet of water," Finn replied, hauling in his weighted line. "We'll leave the ship here."

Gunnar opened the sea chest he'd been sitting on, taking out his helmet, leather vest, and chain mail. The pointed metal helmet covered his head with a facial visor to protect his nose and eyes. He laced his leather vest in place. Its five-layer thickness had proved effective in the past, bearing multiple slash marks from previous fights. Gunnar slipped on the chain mail over his shoulders.

Buckling on his sword, he checked the knife in its scabbard, grabbed his shield, and climbed the bank to join his shipmates. Some carried swords; others wielded double-edged axes.

For big men, they moved quietly, their leather shoes making little noise on the forest floor as they strode quickly in single file with Snorri leading. Gunnar avoided stepping on the masses of acorn shells. The trees had huge trunks and canopies. The element of surprise would be an advantage.

Snorri stopped, raising his finger to his lips. Everyone came to a halt and listened. They were in a valley with smaller trees and dense undergrowth. Gunnar could hear children's voices calling back and forth. Slowly, the men fanned out, dodging from tree to tree. Three youngsters were in a clearing, playfully gathering firewood, ignoring their surroundings. Three warriors crept up on them, then sprang with their knives drawn, each grabbing a child from behind. Big hands muffled the sounds from small mouths as they each slit a child's throat.

"Too young to sell," said Snorri, dropping the small body to the ground and wiping his knife clean on the youngster's shirt.

Gunnar could smell peat smoke now. The trees were thinning and a beautiful sight met his eyes—a palisaded village of six thatched, round houses with open fields and meadows running down to the river. Cattle and sheep grazed in the fields. Men, women, and children were working everywhere. A man was plowing with a team of ponies. A movement in the marshy area caught his eye and held it.

The girl was young and slim. Her long, dark auburn hair, tied back with a ribbon, hung down to her waist. She was knee deep in water, her dress kilted up as she gathered plants from the reed bed. She had her back to them, oblivious to their presence. Gunnar moved away from the others as the crew split up. He continued watching her as he moved stealthily through the undergrowth. Soon, he was with fifty feet of her.

A piercing scream from the village ruptured the air. The attack was on. Dropping the plants, the girl sprang out of the water like a doe, cutting across the field, her bare feet skimming the ground. Gunnar sprinted after her, surprised she was heading for the village. She took one look at him and ran even faster.

CHAPTER 2

The raid

Fiona was working her way through the reeds, cutting the three-foot-high stems and bundling them together. From time to time, she stopped and looked around her. The crows were quiet; the wind was calm. Her youngest sister Aileen and mother Aoife were up the hill with many of the village girls, gathering nettles and coltsfoot as well as hawthorn flowers and other plants for the herbal liniments, ointments, and tonics she and her mother prepared for the whole clan.

Several days ago, her mother had warned her of an unknown danger and had dreamed of a ferocious storm the previous night. Nothing seemed out of place, but somehow it didn't feel quite right either. Both Aoife and Fiona were sensitive to their surroundings. Fiona's back was to the village when she heard the scream. Immediately, she dropped the reeds and ran for home.

The air was punctured with shouts and the metallic clang of weapons. Footfalls pounded after her and she glimpsed a warrior— blonde, muscular and armed— gaining ground.

Men were fighting, blades flashing. Women and children were chaotically dodging the fighters. Bloodied bodies fell, men flailed and grappled with each another. She caught glimpses of her brothers Kian and Marven fighting hard. Breathless, she leaped over a downed body, seeking her father, Carraig. She caught sight of him battling a giant and saw the split second when he doubled over, a sword right through his belly. The giant wrenched the sword free in a spray of blood and swung again, ripping through Carraig's throat as he fell.

Fiona exploded in rage. With her little knife still in hand, she took a flying leap onto the giant's back, clinging with her knees and left arm as she stabbed his throat over and over again. Arcs of crimson gushed forth. He dropped his sword, clasping his throat, staggered and fell in a thrashing heap across Carraig's feet. Fiona was flung off, landing hard beside her father.

Before she could get her breath, strong hands pinned her down. She looked up at the helmeted man straddling her. All she could see was a pair of startling blue eyes, long, ash-blonde hair, and a grin. Fiona tried to raise her knife, but his weight on her wrist forced her to drop it. He promptly bound her hands and rejoined the battle.

Carraig lay beside her, his life force gone. She watched in horror as the blonde warrior made short work of one of her cousins, easily dispatching the youngster. *No chance of survival.* The tapestry of corpses grew and the sounds of clanging metal swords began to subside to shouts of laughter from the invaders, weeping and screams from the survivors, and moans from the dying. It was over.

Her blonde warrior vanished inside the palisade to appear a short time later, a trussed-up boy over his shoulder. He dropped her ten-year-old cousin Ailin next to her, then went back inside, returning with swords, sheep skins and hides, which he piled beside them.

When he was occupied stripping the fur cape from the giant's body, Fiona rolled and wiggled closer to her father's corpse. Although her hands were tied, she managed to remove the silver torque from his mutilated neck and slip it around her own. His knife, though, remained out of reach.

Fiona heard the warrior laugh. She looked up to see him staring at her. He strutted over and removed Carraig's belt, scabbard, knife, and sword, putting them on his prize stash, away from her. Gazing across the carnage, she could see the victors methodically killing any wounded and knew her brothers Kian and Marven were among the dead. She couldn't see inside the palisade from where she lay. *Had any of my family survived?* she wondered. *Eogan and Darrin had been out hunting.*

Were my older brothers safe? Surely now my grandmother was dead and likely Evelyn's young baby, too. My mother and youngest sister were in the woods. She prayed. Very few had been spared.

Fiona was too numb to cry. Killing Carraig's murderer was her only consolation. She rocked back and forth, wailing the keening death song, not just for him but for all of them.

A short time later, the invaders exited the palisade gate, carrying bundles of goods, then stripped the corpses of necklaces, torques, pins, and armbands. A few survivors emerged, herded together, their hands tied. She counted nine other young women and ten older children, including Ailin. One of the women was Evelyn, her oldest sister.

Fiona watched in horror as two men held a screaming, struggling Evelyn down while half a dozen men, including her warrior, raped her. *Dear God! What now? I don't want to be next.* Poor Evelyn! As a sixteen-year-old virgin, Fiona knew full well that being violated would ruin any chance of ever being married. Being an unwanted single woman for the rest of her life was a terrifying possibility. No decent man would want her. She had no family now to protect her. It meant poverty and loneliness.

A gathering of cawing crows circled the battle field corpses and echoed her black mood as the warriors torched the houses. The flames spread rapidly, devouring the thatch.

CHAPTER 3

Rewards

Gunnar was jubilant. *I fought and killed three men! Now, I've got the young girl and boy. I've got a great pile of booty, too. I even had sex with a woman.* It was impossible to find a woman in Hedeby. All the wealthy men in town had multiple wives and slaves, leaving single, poorer men with none.

His captives were sitting where he'd left them. Gunnar looked at the girl. She was pretty enough to sell to the Islamic traders; her hair was loose with no cap, so she had to be a virgin. *By the gods, she was feisty.* It was hard to believe she'd killed a seasoned warrior like Snorri with her tiny two-inch blade. By the laws of Thor, Snorri's belongings, including the sword, were hers. But now that she was his thrall, he owned everything.

Rolling Snorri's body over, he unpinned the chained silver clasps and removed the bearskin cape as well as the decorative metal bands around the inert, massive, tattooed arms. Gunnar picked up the sword with reverence, running his finger over the razor-sharp edges still stained with blood. He held it up and swung it. The elaborate pommel fit his hand well and the weight was right. The scabbard itself was beautiful with a Viking eagle etched down its length. Gunnar removed his own sword and strapped on Snorri's. The sense of power overwhelmed him.

The crew gathered round and assessed their own. They'd lost three men, including Snorri and Olaf, and had five injured. Despite the element of surprise, the Celts had fought hard. Gunnar had a few cuts and his shield had some damage. He'd been lucky; some of the crew had more severe injuries.

While several warriors set fire to the houses, the others dug graves for their fallen crewmen. The dead sailors were placed in the earth with their weapons by their sides. Gunnar set his old sword in Snorri's grave as was custom, but he was going to keep the better one. A warrior who died in battle always needed a sword in the afterlife. He said farewell to Olaf, feeling the loss. Olaf had made a warrior and a sailor out of him, teaching him fighting, sailing, and everything about trading that he knew. His partner had been a good man, but it was his time, and he'd died with honour. Gunner could visualize a Valkyrie swooping down and flying Olaf back to Valhalla to the hall of Odin, a perfect way for a *drengr* to die, joining Odin's select army of fallen warriors in the battles against the anti-gods for the final battle of Ragnarök—the end of the world.

Gunnar put on the cape, fastening it with the silver brooches, then rolled up the spare swords in the fleeces. The rest of his plunder went in a burlap sack. Finally, he was able to heft it over his shoulder. He hoisted his captives to their feet and pushed them ahead to join the snaking line of thralls on the path through the woods, heading back to the ship. The girl looked around and his eyes followed hers to the crackling, flaming houses inside the palisade.

It was a good piece of property, much like his home farm. The fields had been cleared and stumps pulled. The hills were well wooded. The river ran around the base of the hill and further inland. Other than the marsh, the drainage looked good. The fighting had scared off the livestock, but somebody would find them. Normally, they would have taken the horses or cows, but the knarr was already full. He could hear several of the crew commenting on coming back here with their families to settle, but he knew full well that farming wasn't for him.

Gunnar was definitely interested in the girl wearing the torque. First, the man had worn it and now she did. *The dead man must have been her father.* The torque was pure silver, worth a lot of money. He'd get a good price for the boy, too. The youngster, about ten, looked healthy.

It took nearly an hour to reach the ship and get everyone on board. Gunnar loaded his two thralls, seating them mid-deck near the mast. He switched his rowing position to Snorri's place and shifted the sea chests, filling his with the bag of booty. He didn't take the time right then to look at the contents of Snorri's chest, which he stored under the deck planks.

Some of the men were seriously injured and were tended to with bandages and slings. Finn juggled the rowers accordingly, moving Harald up front. As Harald moved past him and saw Snorri's sword on his hip, he punched a fist in Gunnar's chest.

"You have no right to that!" he said belligerently.

"My slave killed him, so I have the right to all of it," Gunnar retorted, standing his ground. He was about to challenge Harald for the insult, but Finn interrupted.

"Settle down, you two. We've got enough wounded. Get your work done," he said and went back to untying the ship. Harald glared at him, fists clenched, then turned and headed forward. The longship sat deeper in the water now with the heavier load of people and cargo. Several times, they had to get out and push her through shallow areas but finally made their way downstream with the current. By late afternoon, the trees thinned and the delta came into view. The knarr was sitting offshore, waiting.

CHAPTER 4

Present day, Haithabu, Germany—formerly the ancient Danish trading town of Hedeby, a UNESCO World Heritage site

Professor Jon Jorgenssen wiped the black soil from his hands and stood up, stretching his back and shoulders from the cramped position he'd been in. He looked at his four students. *It's going to be interesting to see how well these four will work together on this project.*

Tall, slender Helga was crouched in the trench, carefully working her trowel through the dried peat. Lars was standing at the specimen table, beckoning him to inspect a tiny hard fragment he'd just found. The stocky young man was peering through his thick glasses, in deep concentration and removing soil with a tiny paint brush. Miles and Gena were twenty feet away, diligently screening bucketloads of dark, crumbling earth. *At least those two worked well together. Lars and Helga, not so much.*

The professor had committed his entire archaeology career to study the Viking Age and its history still excited him. Reports from the scanner had identified more than seven hundred anomalies in Hedeby's cemetery. Excavated graves so far had been dated from the early 800s to 1066 CE when Hedeby was destroyed. Only a small percentage of the graves had ever been examined.

It had taken over two years to get his application approved and the official licence to dig. Now the five of them had just three months to excavate the site. The previous week, his team had carefully removed all the sod and stones, then measured and marked the area identified on the scan. Lars had noted that this grave was on lower ground in the cemetery, away from the older chamber graves higher up.

"The chamber graves would have filled up over time and families would have been forced to move burials either downhill or beyond the palisades," Jon explained. Photos had been taken to establish the dimensions of the work area before the test trenches were dug to determine the strata they were working in.

His students were competitive with each other and some days it showed. Blonde Helga, the quiet one, preferred to work alone. All four students were working on their PhD theses. Work was predictably slow as each strata had to be exposed and documented. So far, the soil was undisturbed other than the grave itself and that was promising, allowing accurate dating and for actually finding undisturbed grave goods. Their patience so far had been rewarded with a few broken pieces of curved, coloured glass that looked like a bottle or vase, and a small piece of a delicate woven material. The gender of the occupant was unknown.

Jon briefly looked at the view to the north, a vista of low wooded hills, flat marshy land, and the river that formed the Schlei fjord, the narrowest part of the Jutland peninsula. His eyes scanned the marshy river around the ancient semicircular defensive walls called the Danevirke that stretched around town to disappear into the countryside. In the late 800s and early 900s CE, they'd been thirty feet high, twenty feet wide, and topped with wooden palisades—if the stories and sagas were accurate.

As he had often lectured his students, it had been an overland crossing point for traders, leaving the Baltic loaded with furs, amber, carved walrus ivory, leather, candles, live cattle, hides and slaves, meeting with merchants from all points south and west, including Russia, France, Ireland, Britain, Spain, and Africa.

It had already been established from previous digs that southern merchants carried silks, wine, spices, rich clothing, glassware and, often, Damascus-made swords—the ultimate Viking weapon. All Vikings whether Norse, Dane, or Swede often portaged their longships across the eight miles of swamp land to reach the Treene River that merged into the North Sea, avoiding the much longer and hazardous route around the Jutland peninsula and its many islands infested with pirates.

Lars was working at the table under the tent extension. "Professor, look what I found," he said and showed him the hard fragment

Jon gently cleaned the two-by-three-inch piece with a soft brush and examined it under the microscope. The black soil had flaked off, showing a rust-coloured fragment of metal. In cross-section, it was thicker in the middle tapering to finer edges on both sides. It was badly corroded.

"This could be part of a sword. It's the right width and the tapering is equal. Where did you find it?"

"It was in the last bucketload where Helga is working."

Meanwhile, Gena, her short dark head bowed over the table, was preparing a numbered label for the specimen in her tiny, precise writing and entered it in the finds book and on their map. She had the camera ready to take closeups of the fragment and exactly where it had been located, a small ruler showing its exact size and placement. Jon was impressed with her meticulous documentation.

They lowered themselves into the trench. Helga moved out of the way. "It came from this layer, right here. Come, I'll show you," she said, pointing to the precise spot where the dirt had been removed.

Jon tried to divide his attention between them equally. *They needed to learn to work together, but it was early days yet. Sometimes their competitiveness got in the way.*

CHAPTER 5

Captive

Fiona had never seen a ship before, let alone board one. It was huge. Sitting on the deck with her tied hands in her lap, she stared in awe at the lofty prow with its intricately carved designs of a fanged beast. *It must be one of their gods,* she thought.

She listened to the warriors talk. Most of it was in a language she couldn't understand, but occasionally they spoke a strange form of Gaelic. Looking at her captor as he removed his helmet and vest, she realized he was probably the youngest of the crew, with a light blonde fuzz on his chin. He couldn't be much older than her, but he certainly could handle a sword. She'd watched him examine the sword of her father's killer. From the way he handled it with such reverence, it had to be something special. The muscles in his arms rippled as he rowed. *That's where his strength came from, just like the blacksmith at home.* Home. The word plummeted her into despair. Here she sat, one of the captives, crammed into the narrow walkway with oarsmen either side. No chance to escape, surrounded by an empty expanse of water.

Fiona looked at the captives ahead of her, recognizing each one. They knew each other intimately, having lived together all their lives. Her sister Evelyn was looking pale, her dress torn and bloody. She'd lost her baby, her husband, their father, and grandmother. The other girls hadn't been raped—yet. Fiona shivered.

"What are they going to do with us?" Ailin whispered, looking up at her, putting on a brave face.

"I don't know," she said, still numbed by the speed and violence of the raid.

"Are you scared?" he asked in a small voice.

"Yes," she said, wishing her hands were free. "Did you see my mother at all?"

"No. She was still up in the woods with the girls."

"Good. What about Eogan and Darrin? Did they come back from hunting?"

"I didn't see them come in," he said.

At least a few of the family might have survived. Aileen, her youngest sister, had been with their mother's group up on the hill. They would likely walk to the nearest village, where Aileen's betrothed lived. At sixteen, Fiona knew it would be difficult to find a husband for herself. She was too much like her mother, a seer and an apprentice healer, shunned to a certain degree but grudgingly respected by the clan. It was unlikely a family would want her as their daughter-in-law, despite Carraig's status as chief. The potential rape situation would make it even worse.

The sun was sinking in the west when the scenery changed. The trees diminished to shrubs, then the landscape opened up. The few shoreline trees were twisted into leaning shapes, sculpted by the onshore wind. The river widened and suddenly the land gave way to the sea. She was awestruck at the vastness, never before seeing so much water.

Out in the bay was another ship, even larger than the one she was on. It was impossibly big. On the deck, more men were cheering and yelling at the longship's crew. Waves gently rocked the boat, slapping the wood against her thin legs. That scared her, but she watched as her captor stood up, like the boat wasn't rocking at all. *What if I fall overboard?* A familiar odour assailed her nostrils. *Cattle? Here?*

The longship gently ground to a halt as the oarsmen ceased rowing, the prow nosing into the soft mud. Fiona's captor lifted both of them to their feet and dropped them over the side where he joined them. Men on the other ship were climbing overboard and moving through the water to meet them. Several were floating small barrels, which they rolled onto the beach. They all seemed alike, tall and fair. The crew of the bigger ship had hair cut shorter than the fighters with their flowing hair and beards either braided or tied back. Many were tattooed. Few were older with shorter hair.

The captives bunched together and were told by two men speaking a heavily accented Gaelic to sit down. Her family obeyed. Fiona wanted to get closer to Evelyn and managed to wiggle beside her. She gently leaned against her. They looked at each other, and Fiona wiped the blood from Evelyn's face with the hem of her dress, examining bruises on her neck and arms.

"Sorry, Ev. I can't help you much," she said.

Evelyn nodded, wiping the drying blood from her badly bruised inner thighs.

Fiona started checking everyone within reach. Mostly, it was cuts and bruises. They sat and waited, watching the seamen on the beach. She quietly sang the blessing song to calm them. All shared the same stunned silence. At least they were still alive. She was very hungry and very thirsty.

No fire was lit that night. Snippets of conversation from the men revealed concern for other raiders—Norse they called them. Her young captor separated her and Ailin from the others and squatted in front of them.

"I'm Gunnar," he said in fractured Gaelic. He gave each of them of a chunk of beef and slices of bread.

She looked back at him, pointed to herself, and said "Fiona," then at her cousin, "Ailin." It was quiet for a few minutes as they ate. Satisfied, Gunnar rejoined his companions.

The meat had been salty but good. It would have been easier to eat if she'd had her knife. She wiped her greasy fingers on her dress. With his heavy foreign accent, his Gaelic had been hard to understand.

Now, she was thirsty. Looking at all that water, she got up and walked not ten feet away where little wavelets repeatedly crept over the rock-strewn sand then slid away again. She bent over, cupped her hands and swallowed a mouthful of water. It was so salty, she coughed and gagged, spewing it back out. She heard a gale of laughter from the men, then Gunnar was behind her, putting his hand on her shoulder.

He was laughing heartily and shaking his head. "Don't drink—salt water," he said, sweeping his arm across the full vista of the sea. "I'll bring water." He led her back to sit with Ailin.

Fiona watched as Gunnar and several other men walked back to the trees, carrying leather buckets. Shortly, they returned and passed the water around for all the captives to drink. When he handed the bucket to her, she let Ailin quaff down his share, then took long slow mouthfuls, finally handing it back to him. He drained the rest.

The one Gunnar called Thorkell was probably only a few years older but leader nonetheless. A few of the knarr crew returned to their ship, carrying water for the cattle. She wondered if Gunnar and Thorkell were related. They looked very much alike with broad foreheads and cheekbones, straight noses, and the same fair hair, although Thorkell's was trimmed shorter. They always sat together.

As the light faded to a darkness, she brushed a depression into the sand, then curled up with Ailin snuggled beside her. The breeze was cool and she shivered, wishing she was home with a warm blanket. Eventually, Gunnar joined them, put his sword on the ground, then spread his cloak over the three of them.

Fiona feared having a man close like that. *Is he going to rape me?* He settled on the ground, his back to her. She was glad of that but so far, he hadn't made a move. *Was there something worse in store? Would he seek revenge for the giant's death? Was death preferable to rape?* Fiona could smell his stale sweat and hear his breathing, which initially had been rapid and irregular. He was close enough she could feel his movement. It seemed forever before his breathing slowed and he was snoring. Slowly, she let the panic subside, remembering Aoife's chants, mouthing the words silently until the tension slowly ebbed.

Ailin was asleep by then, and there she was, sand-wiched between the two. Gradually, she was warmed with their body heat and dozed off, listening to the constant, rhythmic murmur of the waves lapping on the beach, a few night birds calling. Normally, those would have been calming, but it was broken by the occasional cries and whimpers from the girls as some of the other men took their pleasure.

Her thoughts moved to her mother and the life she was leaving behind. For her whole sixteen years, she'd been her mother's apprentice, gathering and working with the herbs to help the sick. She knew if plants were edible or not, which ones to use for specific ailments, and how to make the many creams, ointments, tinctures, and tonics for the clan. She'd only just begun helping the midwife birthing babies. Some clan members con-sidered her mother a witch, but Fiona had never seen her cast spells or use her knowledge for anything but good. Aoife was treated with a cautious respect, even by the men and the Christian monks. Her mother had taught her all the chants, prayers, and blessings to help people heal.

As she lay on the sand, listening to the snores of the now sleeping men, she tried to sense her mother's pres-ence, but only felt a heavy void. Aoife had gone into the oak grove alone the previous week for her private time with her gods. Their ancient clan myths described

Druid priestesses in such places and tales suggested her mother was descended from one. When she'd returned from the grove, she'd been troubled and warned Fiona of a mysterious approaching darkness. She'd told her, "Be brave." Fiona had no doubt this was the darkness her mother had foreseen. *Was this the beginning of a mystic journey?* She felt helpless, numb and confused. *How could that be? Women didn't make mystic journeys, only warriors did.*

CHAPTER 6

Dublin (Dubh Linn)

In the darkness, Gunnar lay beside the girl. He thought of her standing on the beach trying to drink seawater. Obviously, she'd never been out of her village. The look on her face had been priceless.

He'd seen her gazing at the prow and everything around them, with those wide blue-green eyes. As he rowed, he continued to watch. She was still wearing her belt with small pouches and spindle attached. A few crushed plant stems hung limp from the top of a pouch. He'd seen her checking the other captives and singing to them. She had to be a healer of some kind. It made him think of old Runa, Hedeby's healing matriarch who had lost her apprentice to a dysentery that had swept the town the previous winter. Maybe the girl could be a useful replacement. He'd discuss that with Thorkell.

Gunnar loved the colour of her hair. It was so dark an auburn it almost looked black in some light. It hung down to her waist. There was no doubt in his mind he wanted her. His body throbbed for need of her.

Gunnar debated bedding her. If he took his pleasure now he'd never get her virgin price from the Islamic traders from Cadiz. If he married her, he could claim the sword, since she had legal right to it as Snorri's killer. He could have it all, including the silver torque.

He had felt the tension in her body when he'd first laid beside her. The boy on the other side was already asleep. Eventually, the noise in camp settled. Some of Gunnar's comrades were sating their lust. It was a temptation to snuggle in closer, but he didn't trust himself. Her breathing was quiet and even. Eventually his body allowed him to sleep.

Morning found them preparing once again to put to sea. He decided to untie his captives' hands. Gunnar was sitting now with another seaman, one of the Swedes. He missed his old partner, Olaf. "We've got another storm coming by the look of it. Can we make Dublin before it hits us?"

"If Njord is willing," the Swede said, a man of few words.

Gunnar quickly lifted Fiona and Ailin on board. "Storm," he said, pointing to the dark gathering clouds and visible sheets of rain. It would be rough going. "Stay sitting. I don't want you falling overboard."

The knarr was already on the move. The men pulled down the tarps to shelter the crew and captives. Once the longship was beyond the rocks, Finn and three others dropped the sail, which caught the gusts, billowing right over the heads of the thralls.

Both the currents and the winds were tricky. Finn had to steer close enough to the shore to catch the southerly current but not too close or they'd hit the rocks. If they went too far east, they'd be caught in the northern current on the British side. Gunnar wondered how Thorkell managed with the knarr's deeper hull.

Finn yelled and pointed behind them where other ships were now visible. *Merchants or raiders?* The whole crew kept a watchful eye on them. The wind was picking up in the darkening sky with waves higher, foam blowing from the crests. They were moving well under sail, so the crew shipped their oars.

Glancing at Fiona and Ailin, Gunnar could see them clutching each other to steady themselves. No sense of balance yet. He could hear someone retching behind him. Waves washed over them but the tarps deflected most of the wash.

Later, a single longship passed them, leaving plenty of room between them. They too had captives on board and the gaps at the oar spaces meant they'd lost men on their raid as well.

The coastline was blurred in the blinding rain, but he could see the hills had diminished in height, quite different from the northern coast. Dublin was not far off. They passed several heavily laden cargo ships. The knarr was maintaining a steady pace under full sail not far behind them. Finally, the cloud cover lifted, the rain stopped, and the tip of the peninsula and bay emerged where the river Liffey opened into the sea. The bay extended many miles upriver into a forested lowland with cultivated fields marked by hedge rows.

The longship entered the estuary first, followed closely by the knarr. Strong hands began hauling in the sail in unison. The longship navigated among six other ships into the narrowing waterway, avoiding the outgoing ones fully loaded with northern goods and slaves. Heading south, their massive size dwarfed the locals out fishing.

Dublin itself was on a curved, raised area at the base of a hill on the south shore where the river Poddle joined it. He could see the palisade walls and the thatched rooftops of Viking houses. The oarsmen slowed as the river became more congested. Finn expertly angled the ship into the narrower tributary.

It took Gunnar a moment to remember which dock belonged to his uncle, but Finn never forgot those details. They were moving very carefully, only oar tips apart from other ships as they crowded into the small channel. Traders were shouting to one another. Strange ships with two or three masts were also tied at the docks. They were clinker-built too with their planked sides much higher than the knarr and raised cabin areas fore and aft. He knew from last year that these were oceangoing slavers from Iberia. Their below-deck cargo holds would soon be filled with the captives from the longship.

The river Poddle curved and opened into a large pond the locals call The Black Pool or Dubh Linn, giving the town its name. Several longships were fully beached on their sides, being repaired. Finn docked the longship onto the shore, leaving room for the knarr to anchor beside them. As the prow ground into the mud, the men shipped their oars. Gunnar assisted Fiona and Ailin to their feet and dropped them over the side into the shallows. Once again, he tied their hands and led them to the pathway outside the wooden palisade. The captives huddled together, waiting.

CHAPTER 7

Dublin's market

After Gunnar put them ashore, Fiona stood against the palisade wall and watched the activity around the other ships. She was both fascinated and appalled. Near the biggest ship were a group of short, stocky, dark-skinned men dressed in long robes with shoulder-length head coverings held in place with headbands. With their hooked noses and jet-black beards, they were a contrast to the blonde warriors and traders.

Right there on the dock, they had gathered a group of several naked women and children whose clothes were piled on the ground. The man in charge was examining a young woman who was trying to cover her nakedness with her hands. He walked around her, looking at her body, her hair, and the inside of her mouth. Fiona was horrified. *Carraig would have looked over a horse like that!*

The trader and a blonde warrior, just like Gunnar, haggled back and forth, finally reaching an agreement. The foreigner nodded and signalled the women and children to get dressed; his cohort herded them on board the ship. He removed a handful of something small, shiny and metallic from his pouch. It clinked as he counted. The warrior counted them too and placed them into his own pouch. He walked away, looking pleased.

Thorkell shouted "Mohammed," from the deck of the knarr, and the senior man responded by waving back, calling "Thorkell" before he boarded his own ship. Mohammed briefly eyed Fiona's family clustered against the palisade and nodded.

Fiona had the blinding realization this was their fate. They were going to be sold to the foreigners. That man had done business with Thorkell before.

This was reinforced when two older men, obviously locals, walked past them, looked them over, and said to each other in the local Gaelic dialect, "Look at these poor devils; may the good Lord save their souls. I hate seeing Irish folk being sold like that."

The market was humming with activity. The outer palisade walls were packed with booths displaying clothing, hides, furs, and weapons. Vendors were shouting to attract customers to their wares, some with barrels of beer and mead, or were holding up swords to prospective buyers. There were foreign merchants selling shiny glass mugs and piles of exotic fabrics, even musical instruments.

Ordinary people in plain woollen clothing were leading horses and pigs along the path. They too were speaking Gaelic although their accent was different from hers. A steady stream of people flowed through the palisade gate. She'd never seen so many in her life. Listening to the Irish conversations Fiona heard comments about ongoing skirmishes between the Leinster Irish and Mide Irish. *They must be local clans.* Further conversations indicated the Danish Viking king and his army had been driven out. Apparently, the local Irish Leinster king, Cearbhall was allowing the Viking traders to stay because of the trade they brought to Dublin. *Was her captor a Dane?* It seemed likely.

Gunnar returned to check on her and Ailin. "Stay here," he said. "Don't go with anyone else. I'm still trying to find my uncle."

The crew were helping the wounded men, carrying them and their belongings across the mud to the palisade. The knarr crew were going through the complicated process of unloading the cattle. The bellowing animals were huge. It took two men with halters and ropes to pull each one out of the cargo compartment, then down the ramp to solid ground. The four bulls were beautiful, glossy reddish-brown animals with grand sets of horns, sleek and well fed. They soon drew a crowd as Thorkell extolled their virtues as fine sires for both meat and milk cows.

Fiona caught sight of Gunnar with an older man and two servants approaching on the path. The man was Carraig's age, but taller, his blonde hair neatly cut short, well dressed in a shirt and trousers of fine linen, covered by a calf-length coat. He wore a beautifully tooled leather belt with many dangling pouches as well as a knife scabbard. Even his high leather boots were stitched and laced. She'd never seen such finery. The life force pulsed strong around him.

The man stood there for a few minutes, scrutinizing the captives, then gave instructions to Gunnar and the retainers. Quickly, he moved on to talk to Thorkell. The retainers took command of the bulls, driving them toward the pastures outside the gates. The rest of the crew began unloading goods from the ship.

Gunnar approached and in his broken Gaelic said, "That man is my uncle. You're going to his house. Follow me."

He led the group into the town. She could feel the stares of the townspeople, which was unnerving. She felt so unkempt. The bloodstains on her dress were very evident and her hair was a windblown tangle. The sheer size of the town astounded her. It was bigger than her whole village, including the fields. There were hundreds of houses, but they were rectangular, not round. Most of them were wooden plank with thatched roofs. *Hundreds must live here!*

The street wound its way between the houses, intersecting with many other paths, finally coming close to the northern edge of the palisade where there was one large house, two smaller ones, and a blacksmith shed as well as a small fenced paddock. An older woman stood on the doorstep proud and erect with two younger ones subserviently standing behind. The thralls were conspicuously shorter and darker-complexioned than their mistress. Fiona watched as the older lady greeted Gunnar warmly in his language. She was tall and big boned, wearing a long frock covered with a linen over-dress. Her greying blonde hair was topped with a white cap just like the ones married women at home wore. The silver pendant around her neck had a symbol Fiona didn't recognize, but the quality was obvious. The other necklaces were amber and brightly coloured stones. This was a wealthy, powerful woman.

The woman looked at the captives and directed Gunnar to take them to the smallest house. Turning to the two female thralls, she gave orders in trader's Gaelic. The skinny, redheaded one went back into the main house, while the younger brunette followed Gunnar as he shepherded the captives to the smaller dwelling.

It was rectangular, high and airy with large, horizontal crossbeams spanning the inside, notched into the vertical posts. Bed benches lined the perimeter walls, just like the houses at home. Light only came in through the open door and a hole in the roof over the fire pit in the centre. A huge cauldron of water was simmering.

The thrall spoke to the captives in Gaelic and told them to sit on the benches. Gunnar ordered their hands released, spoke to her very briefly, then left the house, closing the door behind him.

Fiona sat on a bench beside Evelyn. They hugged each other for a long time. Ailin joined the other boys further down. She was pleased to be on dry land, not swaying with the waves. She watched the dark-haired thrall untying the ropes to free each person. The group was very subdued.

"Me name's Ainsley. Mor Frida will give you food shortly. All of ya look like you could use a good wash," the thrall said in Gaelic, eyeing their torn and blood-stained clothing. "There's soap, towels, and buckets of water. That door there goes to the outhouse. Help yourselves while I find ya some clean clothes."

One of the boys opened the door to the "outhouse," whatever that was, but the smell gave its purpose away. He used it and closed the door. *That was a convenience they hadn't had in the village.*

Meantime, Ainsley was going through some sea chests and handing out clothing. Fiona was glad to see Evelyn get a fresh dress. Most of the girls had their combs in their pouches and started working through their tangled hair. She scrubbed her face and hands with the coarse soap and warm water, then her legs and bare feet.

Ainsley beckoned to her, holding up a dress. "This should fit ya. Would you be Fiona?"

"I am," Fiona said, stripping off the old dress and slipping into the other one. It wasn't new, having a few neat mends, but at least it was clean.

"Gunnar said you'd be the woman with the silver torque. He asked me to find out if you knew anything about plants and medicines. He noticed plants in your pouch. He doesn't speak Gaelic very well as you've probably noticed," the girl said.

"What language is he speaking?"

"That's Danish, from some place beyond Britain. Most of the traders speak some form of Gaelic as well as their own tongue. It's how they trade with each other."

"My mother was the healer in our village," said Fiona. "We made all our own remedies from local plants. We both took care of the sick, injured and dying." She somehow needed to prove to somebody that she had skills. *Ainsley should understand that.* For a fleeting moment, Fiona felt her mother was alive. *Was it wishful thinking?*

She could see Ailin and his companions looking bright and curious, ready to get into trouble. "I'm afraid they'll be sneaking off."

"Trust me, they won't get far. You're Christian then?" Ainsley asked.

"Well, yes, we are, but we only see the abbot once or twice a year because we live so far from his monastery. We still follow the old ways some of the time."

"Aye, I know what ya mean. Us Irish folk need to help each other out. I'll pass all that on to Gunnar when I back to the main house. In the meantime, let me take these dirty clothes. I'll wash them as best I can. Now all of you sit and wait, especially you lot," she said with a voice of authority, looking directly at the boys. Carrying the huge bundle of laundry, she closed the door behind her, leaving the room in semi-darkness.

It felt so good to be clean and sheltered from the sea. One of the boys opened the door, took one step outside, and promptly jumped back as an aggressive volley of barking erupted.

"There's a huge dog out chained out there," he said wide-eyed.

Evelyn spoke up. "Ainsley meant what she said. Just sit and wait."

It was the first time since the raid that Evelyn had showed signs of being her normal bossy self. Later, Fiona heard voices outside and the two thralls brought in a bag with enough bread for all of them and a wooden platter heaped with slices of smoked pork and fish. Everyone grabbed a share. Still just fingers, no knives.

Fiona sat on the bench beside Evelyn. There was no rush. Ainsley returned shortly with several buckets of water and two tin mugs. "There's water here if anyone's thirsty. You'll be spending the night here, so settle in as best ya can. You've got blankets." They nestled together, eventually falling into deep troubled sleep, awaiting the future.

CHAPTER 8

*Present-day Germany, Hedeby
cemetery archaeological dig site*

Miles was in the trench, brushing a particularly stubborn piece of dirt. He'd worked around it with a dental pick, trying to free one edge. Finally, the dirt flaked off, revealing a small rounded white surface. His heart raced. *Bone?* He used the brush again over the upper surface, restraining the urge to work faster, feeling the tremor of excitement in his fingers. *Helga seemed to have all the luck finding stuff; now it's my turn.*

Another small piece of dirt loosened, revealing part of a tapered bone, about half an inch in diameter. Carefully, he continued clearing minuscule amounts of soil until the object was visible. It was approximately an inch long. He let out a yell. "Professor, I found a bone!"

Jon scrambled into the trench, followed by Helga, Lars, and Gena. "Let's see. Where?"

"It looks like a finger bone—tapered," Miles said, stepping aside so he wasn't blocking the light.

Jon kneeled and stared at the piece still half embedded in the wall. "You're right. Lars, get some photos of this. Miles, keep working on it. When you get it out, continue to work to your left. The rest of the bones should be there if they haven't eroded. The pieces of metal from a sword were on his right, which makes perfect sense if he was on his back with his sword by his side. Some burials on Birka Island in Sweden have warriors sitting with their back to the wall, but any we've worked here have been on their backs; Christians too for that matter, though they never have grave goods."

Lars photographed the bone *in situ* with the ruler showing size, capturing the strata using both closeups and several views of the whole trench.

By the end of the day, with all four students scraping, several more phalanges emerged. Each was filmed, numbered, bagged, and recorded. Jon looked at the bones and compared them to his own. They were as large as his, if not larger, and the right pinkie had a slight curve to it.

"I think these are probably male from the size, but I can't rule out a large woman. I'll take them back to the lab to clean them properly. We've done exceptionally well today; only the distal phalanges have disintegrated. Finding those shards of a shattered gravestone bearing faint scratch marks was a bonus. If we can put it back together, we might be able to find out who he was. Those marks might be Old Futhark runic writing, but it's too early to tell yet."

"It'll be like putting a jigsaw puzzle together. It must be in a hundred pieces. You have to wonder if it was deliberately smashed," Gena said.

Physical tired yet mentally invigorated, they covered the trench with a tarp for the night and put their gear in the car. Jon dropped them off at the university and drove straight to his lab to secure the bones and organize the work schedule for the next day. The box of shattered stone would have to wait for now. By the time Jon got home, his wife Elsa would be in bed. These digs and his absences had created problems with his marriage. Thankfully, his boys were teenagers and as independent as his wife was. Jon sometimes wondered if they missed him at all.

CHAPTER 9

Keep her or sell her?

Gunnar left the thrall house and hurried back to the gates. He needed to talk to his uncle about Fiona and retrieve his sea chest. He didn't trust Harald, so he'd taken the precaution of removing a bag of silver coins from Snorri's sea chest and lacing it to his belt. He hadn't had time to go through it yet and was most concerned that Harald would challenge his right to the sword and possibly steal the silver.

He worked his way through the crowds and found his Onkel Bersi bargaining with a customer for tanned hides. Bersi's two sons were showing several buyers fine woven goods. Many customers were rooting through the bins and displays.

"Did you get them settled?" Bersi asked.

"Yes. Tante Frida sent them to the small house. Ainsley was taking care of them when I left. I need to talk to you."

"Oh? Why, what's going on?"

"There's a thrall I'm interested in. Her name's Fiona. I think she's a healer. I asked Ainsley to ask her and find out. You know my Gaelic's not good. During the raid, Snorri, one of our men, killed her father. I was chasing her at the time and almost caught her when she leapt like a cat onto Snorri's back and punctured his throat with her knife. He bled out."

"She killed a warrior? Unbelievable!"

"I like her. She's brave and a virgin and she's wearing her father's silver torque. I don't know whether to sell her to the Muslims at virgin price or keep her for myself."

"Uh huh. so that's the way it is."

"I'm concerned because she legally has rights to Snorri's sword and his belongings. He's got no family. I want that sword. Harald is going to challenge me for it, even though Fiona's my thrall," Gunnar said, removing the sword from the scabbard and showing it to his uncle.

Bersi paused for a few moments, examined the weapon carefully and handed it back. "The workmanship is magnificent. It's very valuable. It would be worth killing for. If he challenges you, could you defeat him?"

"That's a good question. Being a year older than me, he's bigger and stronger, but I've grown over the winter and my skills have improved over the past year. I killed three men on the raid. One was a good fighter, the others not so much," Gunnar said.

"You realize that you could sell her and take what you want anyway."

"I know that but I could have it all—the woman, the sword and the torque."

"You'd be giving up at least four silver dirhams for her, five for the sword, and probably three or four for the torque. Can you afford to lose that much coin?"

Gunnar jiggled the coins in both his and Snorri's pouches. "I could."

"You could always marry the girl if you like her and it would be yours anyway."

"That had crossed my mind," Gunnar said with a grin. "The other thing is that she's a healer of some sort. She was gathering plants. Could be useful back home."

"I need to meet this young woman," Bersi said. "The Muslims are only in port for another couple of days. Meet me at the house once we close the booth and I'll look at her," Bersi said, eyeing a customer looking at hides.

"I've got a couple of hides, sheep skins, and several swords from the raid to sell you, so I'll go back to the ship now, and talk to Thorkell," said Gunnar. "He's busy getting the cargo ashore. We've got a really good assortment of amber for you this time."

With that, he walked through the market towards the knarr. He joined Thorkell's crew, hauling crates and chests from the deck until the sweat was pouring down his back. The shore was stacked with goods. Onkel

Bersi's men started moving them along the path to the booth and storage shed.

Within three hours, the deck was cleared. Thorkell sat down on a sea chest and exhaled, looking tired. "I'm glad that's over. I'll wait 'til the men come back, then I'll give Bersi Ottar's lading bill. We should make good money on this shipment. It's gone well this time, and your crew will get a hefty haul from the sale of the thralls."

"Thorkell, that's what I want to talk to you about," Gunnar said, sitting on the chest across from him. "I've taken a fancy to the thrall I captured," he said, repeating the whole story. "I don't know if it's better to sell her and take the loot or marry her and have it all anyway."

"So, Harald wants Snorri's sword and it's hers. Are you prepared to marry her?"

"If she's a healer, we could certainly use her in Hedeby. Old Runa must be close to sixty years old. It would be a shame to waste those skills. If I marry her, is there room at your house for the two of us to stay until I can find my own place? Mor and Far's house is crowded with his extra wives," he said, watching the expression on his brother's face.

Thorkell thought for a moment. "There's no space at my place either, with twenty of us there. What about Old Runa's house?"

"You know how it goes with me being the youngest. I have to find my own place and there's no land available in Hedeby or nearby even if I had to money to buy it. I could join the war with the Franks but I want to be rich enough to have a wife and a couple of concubines. What would I do with her if I'm away? Onkel Bersi offered me a job. He can't keep up with sales at the booth, even with his two sons helping. I probably wouldn't be much of a merchant. The land Fiona came from was a good spot, and several of the crew are thinking of taking their families back there, if the Norse don't get there first. I'm no farmer, either."

Thorkell got to his feet. "We need to hire more crew to replace the dead and wounded. We'll start cleaning the manure out of the cargo hold tomorrow, but for now I think we should go to Onkel Bersi's. You've got me curious now. I really didn't pay any attention to the captives back there when we were at sea. I want to see this Fiona for myself. There has to be a benefit in selecting a wife. You know, trade connections, land, or money. I hope he's got a barrel of mead handy. I could use some."

Gunnar checked his sea chest to see if Harald had taken anything, but it was undisturbed. He removed the hides, fleeces, and swords to sell to Bersi. Hoisting the bundle on his shoulders, Gunnar joined Thorkell on the path to town. The torque and sword were worth more than Fiona's slave price.

CHAPTER 10

Bersi's choice

Fiona was sitting on the bench after the meal, wondering what would happen next. Evelyn stayed beside her. Although her sister was badly bruised, she seemed a little brighter now she was clean, sheltered, and fed, as did all of them, even the boys. Fiona listened to the noises from the town as it settled into evening. Laughter, the low hum of voices, occasional barking of dogs, curses—all the sounds of home except for the squawking of sea birds. It made her sad and reminded her of her father. Carraig's smiling face drifted through her thoughts with a startling clarity, as it had been the early morning of his death.

She still wondered if her mother and her youngest sister Aileen were safe. Aileen was a delicate, gentle soul and wouldn't have survived this. She gave thanks to the Lord that Aileen had been with their mother. Fiona felt a calm settle on her that felt like the warmth of Aoife, but very far away. She just had to be brave and deal with whatever was to come.

It was after dark. Loud male voices came from close by. The dog barked, its chain clinking. The door opened. Three men came in carrying torches. She recognized them: Gunnar, the captain, and the merchant.

The merchant walked slowly around, making each captive stand up, appraising them from head to toe, feeling the muscles in the boys' arms, watching them move. She didn't understand a word the men were saying. It was no different with the girls. When it was her turn, she felt the nervousness return but was determined not to show it.

"Get to your feet, girl," the merchant said in Gaelic, standing there with hands on his hips, thoroughly eyeing her from all angles.

She got up, stood straight with her head high looking back at him, meeting his scrutinizing gaze that lingered on her breasts and hair.

"Gunnar tells me you are the daughter of a healer and have learned her arts. Is that true?" he asked.

"Yes, I was her apprentice. I helped her make the medicines and take care of everyone in my village." She glanced at Gunnar, who was watching closely. The captain stood silently in the background, just watching and listening, keeping the torch high.

"Did you kill the warrior Snorri during the raid on your village?"

"Yes. He killed my father and I avenged my father's death." She could feel her heart racing and breath quickening.

There was a pause, then a tiny smile crimped the corners of his mouth. "Does the torque you wear belong to your father?"

"Yes," she replied, not wanting to reveal how old it was or that Carraig's grandfather had passed it down through three generations. It was valuable.

He fingered it. "I think that's all I need to know," he said. A torque meant kingship. The girl had come from worthy stock. The three men walked out leaving them all in darkness.

Fiona heaved a sigh of relief and sat down. All the girls huddled together for a few minutes. Murmurs circulated around the room as they visited the outhouse, came back to their benches and snuggled together under thin woollen blankets.

Nestled beside Evelyn, she lay there trying to feel the energy. She didn't feel anything negative, dark, or evil in the room. So far, they had been well treated. The following day might prove otherwise.

Early morning, when it was barely light, the crowing of a few roosters woke Fiona. She listened to town sounds–jingle of harness, the rattle of wheels and low voices on the pathways outside. Although it had taken her a while to settle, she'd actually managed a few hours sleep. She stretched, feeling Evelyn's warmth. The boys were still sleeping, just a jumbled heap of arms and legs. The dog's chain rattled. There were more footsteps and murmurs from the main house.

As the sun rose, everyone got up. Fiona took some water from the bucket and wiped her face and hands, then braided her hair after combing it thoroughly, as were everyone else.

She heard Gunnar outside talking to someone. Then there were a lot of male voices. *What now?* He opened the door and entered, followed by the longship crew. They each gathered their captives and led them outside. Gunnar took a firm grip on her arm, then grabbed Ailin, escorting them outside. Even without his helmet, he was more than a head taller than she was and a lot stronger. His aunt and the two thralls were watching them.

"Fiona, go with Tante Frida. She will look after you. Ailin, you're coming with me," he said, pushing the boy into the exodus of captives moving along the town path towards the gates and awaiting ships.

Fiona gave him a surprised look but he nudged her forward. She walked to the lady, who nodded to her.

"I am Frida, Gunnar's aunt," the woman said in fluent trader Gaelic. "Ainsley, take her into the house and keep an eye on her until Gunnar returns."

"Are they selling my family to the foreigners?" Fiona asked.

"Yes," Frida said, looking down at her. The woman was as tall as Gunnar and almost as big boned.

"Am I being sold?"

"No. Gunnar has other plans for you when he gets back," she said.

Too scared to question further, she followed Ainsley into the house. *Plans? For what?*

It was a sturdy post and beam house with plank walls, the same as the smaller building. Here, though, there were richly dyed blankets on the benches in sumptuous reds, dark greens, and yellows, and large pelts covering the walls. Wooden panels separated the bench areas giving some degree of privacy. The fire pit was elaborate with a large metal frame for searing meats, bearing the iron cooking pots and water cauldron. Another woman, much older than the others, was baking bread. From her clothing and subservient manner, Fiona took her to be a thrall. The main area was divided into two sections by wicker panels, separated by a door.

"Follow me," said Ainsley. "This door goes to the garden and our outhouse."

Fiona could see the separate family outhouse. Another slave was winding up a bucket of water from the stone-lined well. She noticed the pacing dog eyeing them from the end of its chain. A fence separated the house and garden from the neighbours.

Since they had their own well, they didn't have to go to the river like the poorer folks, she thought. The high palisade blocked easy exit from the town so there was no chance of escape. The thralls were in the midst of the daily laundry and the redhead was hanging Evelyn's dress on the clothesline. It was cleaner but still tattered and the faint remnants of blood stains were still visible despite lye soap and the scrub brush. Just like the memory that would never really go away.

"Ainsley, why have I been separated from the others?" Fiona asked, failing to keep the fear out of her voice.

"The men talked for a long time, last night after they had seen you. It's not my place to say. I see you've still got a spindle on your belt. Do you weave?" she asked in hushed tones, in her native Gaelic.

"Yes, I weave."

"Come back inside. You can work on the loom until Gunnar returns. He can explain it to ya."

Fiona sat on the bench and looked at the loom. *How had it been strung?* A three-foot-wide piece had already been started. She examined the warp and weft threads on the framework, the shuttle and the basket of wool skeins, recognizing the simple, plain one over, one under pattern. She rolled a strand of wool between her fingers, feeling the fine texture. Trying to put her mind at ease, she threaded the shuttle and went to work. Before long, she was totally engrossed in what she was doing, working with a steady rhythm, threading the shuttle through alternate threads and tamping them down.

As she sat there, people came and went behind her but it was just background noise. She had to admit, weaving was calming. Nobody bothered her. The cook was kneading bread dough by the hearth and preparing a meat stew in a large iron pot. Occasionally, she could hear Ainsley and the redhead talking outside.

It was nearly midday when Gunnar returned. He was carrying two sacks of goods, handing them to Frida and speaking in what Fiona now understood was Danish. She had completed about an inch of finished material when he walked over to her.

"Fiona, come with me. I need to talk to you," he said in his Gaelic, stumbling over some of the words.

She stopped weaving, put the shuttle down, and stood up, looking up into those fierce blue eyes. She was nervous. Up close, Gunnar seemed even larger, such big hands and wide shoulders.

"Come sit with me," he said, leading her over to one of the benches. "I've decided to keep you for myself. Tomorrow, you will become my wife. Onkel Bersi and Tante Frida have agreed to marry us here, in this house—just a small ceremony. I'm taking you back to my home in Hedeby. We need a healer as ours is very old, and she needs a helper."

She sat there for a moment, trying to understand what he'd said. "You're going to marry me?" wondering if she'd misheard.

"Yes," he said with a lascivious grin.

For once in her life, Fiona was speechless. She looked at him and nodded as the reality set in. She had no idea how she could be a good wife to the man who had raided her village, killed her relatives and sold the rest into slavery. He'd raped Evelyn. *Did she have a choice?*

"What do you think of that?" he asked, not understanding her lack of response.

"I don't know your language. I have no dowry to offer and no family to give me to you." *Marry a murderer? Surely refusal would mean death or slavery.*

"Don't worry about the dowry. You're wearing your father's torque and I have your father's sword."

"Will your family accept me as your wife?"

"As the youngest son, I have some leeway. Far Ottar arranged Steinn and Thorkell's marriages, but it won't matter for me. I do well crewing on the longship and getting the plunder I've collected on raids. Thorkell is willing to stand with you. Show me the torque."

Reluctantly, she removed it and handed it to him. It was heavy with twisted cords of silver, terminating in rounded ends heavily decorated with animal motifs. Years of use had eroded some of the detail.

"I don't think you should be wearing this in public. It's valuable, worth at least a cow. Instead of me giving you your bride price, I'll let you keep the torque. In towns like this, there are thieves everywhere who'd kill you for it. I'll put in my sea chest, along with your father's sword, for safe keeping once the ceremony is over," he said, giving it back to her.

"I'm Christian. Who will marry us?" she asked.

"There are Christians in Hedeby, more coming in every year. Still, most of us follow the old Danish gods. Traditionally, we stand in a circle and join hands. A ribbon is tied around our hands, and my uncle will make a tiny cut on our palms so our blood runs together. It is our blood bond. Then we feast and honour the god Thor and Goddess Freyja for fertility, love, and beauty. I've ordered a barrel of mead. It's coming this afternoon."

"Our marriage ceremony is similar, joining hands. Hand-fasting we call it. We don't do the blood bond. We usually wait each year for the Christian abbot or monk to visit for any marriages to be performed. I didn't know Thorkell was your brother. He's captain of the other ship, isn't he?" she asked, hoping her interpretation of his garbled words was right. *She had noticed the two men looked alike but now he'd confirmed the relationship.*

"Yes, he is. Let's have our morning meal and I'll go back to the ship to help him. He's got the crew cleaning out the cargo hold. He'll be wanting to head home in two- or three-days."

After a quick meal of fresh bread and oatmeal, Gunnar returned to the ship. Fiona went back to the loom and wove for the rest of the day, numbed to the core. She fought off the tears, her hands going through the motions, unseeing, uncaring.

Gradually, her mind and breathing calmed. Household noises became sharper. Ainsley brought in a dried stack of laundry from the garden. A cart rumbled down the path later that afternoon, drawn by an elderly horse. Two burly drivers rolled the barrel of mead down the plank from the back of the wagon and right up to the front door step. Tante Frida directed them to move it to one side. There was much laughter as they got it upright and went on their way.

Onkel Bersi returned late in the day with Thorkell and Gunnar in tow. Gunnar was carrying a small sea chest. She'd seen it on the longship. He placed it on the bench and opened the lid then lifted out Carraig's sword, offering it to her. She took it from him and looked at it for a long time. *While the offering of swords was often part of a wedding ceremony, especially in higher ranked families, was this an attempt on his part to show trust?* She didn't know. Wiping the dried blood from the blade, she carefully gave it back.

The men ate their evening meal. Fiona sat beside Tante Frida, mostly watching them. Much of the conversation was in Danish. They looked at her periodically and she wondered if they were talking about her. *This was unnerving.*

If she kept calm and concentrated, she could vaguely see the aura of light around each person. All different. The colour and extent of the light were clearly visible. Dark colours meant evil things; lighter colours were good. Broad bands of light emanating outward showed power. Narrow bands close to the body meant holding secrets.

As a seer, her mother had taught her all these things. She was the only other member of the family who had the "sight." Even the colours themselves had meaning. The purples, blues, and greens were calming, healing, and honesty, while the reds were strength of will, and yellows were calm and caring. Black was evil, deep and hidden. White was purity. Right now, the light was good and that was confusing as she didn't feel evil in them, yet Gunnar had killed her family.

The supper stew had been tasty, rich in beef and vegetables. The bread was exotically twisted in figure-eight pieces and had been drizzled with honey. *Yum, tasty.*

"I've never seen bread made that way. It's so good," Fiona said as cook cleared away the wooden trencher;

her serious face momentarily broke into a small smile, as if surprised by a compliment.

Thorkell and Gunnar left to spend the night on the ship. Thorkell remarked that there was always a risk or theft or damage if he left it unattended. "Many of the crew sleep on board too. Not that I trust them much either," he said.

Tante Frida directed her to the bed bench beside hers and Bersi's. The tapestries on the wall were rich and colourful. Fiona sat there, just watching the activities. Bersi was the only one to go down to the door at the far end. He searched through the keys on his belt and found the right one. He disappeared inside the mystery room, carrying a full pouch of clinking coins, returning empty handed.

That night, Fiona lay on the bed, her mind swirling with thoughts of the next day. She'd have a husband. She didn't even know the man, though that was customary with arranged marriages. Gunnar's strength frightened her. *Make the best of it,* she told herself. *It was better to be married than sold into slavery. It has to be my destiny for these events to happen.*

She knew about mating from watching farm animals. Many a night at home, she'd lain in bed, listening to the newlyweds as they paired for the first time. A meeting of strangers. There were whispers as clothing was removed and thrown on the floor. Awkward moments, comments, and giggles. The creaking of the bed frame. Some girls cried out as if in pain, while others only moaned. Often, there was laughter afterwards or ribald remarks. With the man's groaning completion, there were the footsteps of the parents rustling through the reeds on the floor as they confirmed the union. She didn't want to think about what Gunnar would do to her, picturing how he was with Evelyn. She fell asleep praying for guidance from her gods.

The following morning, Fiona awoke when the thralls got up. Ainsley was getting the fire started and the redhead was filling the cauldron with water. She stayed where she was until Tante Frida and Onkel Bersi stirred.

Tante Frida spoke with Ainsley, telling her to heat the bath water. She was going first. Seeing Fiona awake, she said in trader Gaelic, "Bersi will be going to the booth until midday, then he'll come home and prepare for the wedding. You and I shall bathe and get dressed."

Meanwhile, the cook had already started grinding the wheat into flour and preparing the dough, lots of it. Already the rich yeasty aroma was filling the room.

Not knowing what else to do, Fiona sat at the loom and started weaving again. About an hour later, Tante Frida emerged, looking crisp and neat in a rich russet linen dress, her cap and overdress pristine white. *That purple-brown colour could only come from wild plum.* Fiona had only seen that once before, on her abbot's robe.

Ainsley took her to a curtained space with a table and stool. Heat was rising from the large ceramic bowl, brimming with hot water.

"Take your clothes off then," she said.

Fiona reluctantly stripped off the dress, dropping her belt on the floor.

"Just sit there and I'll give you a good scrub," Ainsley said, adding a few drops of a fragrant oil to the water.

Closing her eyes, Fiona inhaled, immediately recognizing the sweet essence of honeysuckle. *Aah.* Some of the tension flowed away. Honeysuckle was a fragrance noted for helping her recognize the true path from a false one on her journey.

Ainsley rubbed the soap through her hair, washing it thoroughly, then poured several jugs of rinse water over her. After that, she scrubbed her back and shoulders with the soap; Fiona washed her face and hands.

"I made this batch of soap myself," Ainsley said. "It's good for the hair, too."

"Do you use the water from wood ashes?"

"No. This one's from horse chestnuts, ground up and soaked in water."

"You'll have to tell me how you made it. It's lovely. What sort of wedding ceremony do they have?" Fiona asked.

"For you and Gunnar, it'll likely be a simple version of their Danish ritual. For an elder son, it can be grander, especially if the bride's parents are rich landowners. They exchange swords, the dowry, and bride price. It will just be the blood-bonding ceremony befitting a youngest son. According to their customs, the bride and groom must remove all old clothing and bathe, then dress in new clothes so they have a new beginning. Tante Frida has a dress and shoes that'll fit ya," Ainsley said as Fiona towelled herself dry.

How strange it felt being bathed by someone else. At home, it had been a bowl of water, a bucketful, or even a dip in the river.

Ainsley return a few moments later with the dress over one arm and a pair of shoes in the other. It was a simple dress of plain wool with the usual full-length sleeves, a slight gather at the waist, flowing down ankle length, in a lovely shade of pale blue. *That had to be a woad dye, if I remembered mother's story correctly.* Woad didn't grow in their area. There was a plain white linen pinafore overdress to cover it. The weave was tight and very fine. Fiona got dressed and was about to put her belt on when Ainsley put it aside.

"Leave it off for now. It would spoil the look of it. Put your shoes on, then I'll do your hair," she said, seeming comfortable in expressing her opinion to a fellow Gael as she combed Fiona's long, dark tresses. She gathered a few strands of hair around her ear, braiding it right to the ends, which she tied with a ribbon. The braid was three feet long. Then she repeated that on the other side. Binding the two braids together, Ainsley now had the mane contained, hanging damply down Fiona's back.

She inspected her work, checking her over from top to bottom. "Let me look at your hands," she said, inspecting the short, torn nails. She frowned, then trimmed them with a tiny pair of bronze scissors, smoothing them as best she could.

Fiona looked at the shoes. They were real shoes— shaped leather stitched to a thick leather sole with fine leather lacing, so different from the one-piece leather ones with bindings at home. They fit reasonably well.

"Out ya go. Grab a piece of bread, then just wait at your bench," Ainsley said, moving her into the hall. Fiona picked up her belt and followed the girl back into the main room.

Tante Frida looked her over and smiled. She held up a white cap. "Once you are married, you must always put your hair up and cover your head." Placing it on Fiona's bench she said, "You and Gunnar will sleep here tonight."

Fiona nodded, looking at the cap. The custom had been the same at home. Her hands began to tremble. Fiona muted a sob and turned away from Frida, trying to control herself.

Frida took her by the shoulders and turned her around, a look of concern on her face.

"I watched him rape my sister. I'm afraid. He's so strong." Fiona couldn't continue and stood there with her head bowed, her breath coming in sobs, eyes downcast.

Frida moved her to the bench and sat quietly with her until the tears stopped.

"Pull yourself together child, before the men come back. Marrying Gunnar is a better choice than being sold as a slave to the foreigners."

"My sister's on that ship," she whispered.

CHAPTER 11

The union

At his cousin's house, Gunnar scrubbed himself clean, doing his best to remove the ground-in grime accumulated on his hands, arms, and feet from weeks at sea. Exposure to seawater alone hadn't removed it. Thorkell had bathed earlier. It was generous of his cousin to let them use his house.

Sitting there gave him time to think about the last few days. Onkel Bersi had been an absolute godsend. He'd taken the time to look at Fiona and had apparently liked what he'd seen. The fact that she had healing skills, was daughter of a chieftain, plus she had the silver torque all made her valuable.

When they'd gone back to the main house after seeing her, Thorkell told them that Harald was still angry about the sword and intended "to do something about it."

Bersi suggested a quick marriage to establish the legitimacy of Gunnar's claim but also warned him to stay out of Harald's way. "You could crew on the knarr on the way back."

"I have no intention of crewing on the knarr," said Gunnar. "I want to be on the longship, where I'll get my chance to fight and get my share of plunder." They had to be battle ready at all times. Without the cattle in the knarr's hold, there would be room for Fiona, and Thorkell could keep an eye on her. Gunnar was sure he could handle Harald.

He rubbed his chin. The stubble was a bit thicker. He was impatient for it to be long enough to braid. The warriors who wore it that way looked fearsome. Warriors didn't cut their hair, either, unlike the merchants. Gunnar dunked his head in the water and washed his hair. He liked the soap that made it look blonder. It hung down his back. With some of the money he'd received for the boy, he'd bought himself new clothes— a long-sleeved shirt, trousers, and shoes—all new as tradition required. Trading had gone well. Mohammed was buying virgins for five to six dirhams, roughly the price of a cow, and the boy had gone for three. The boys were highly sought after as eunuchs in the harems.

Gunnar had had time to sort through Snorri's sea chest and found more than two hundred silver coins. He'd keep her father's sword as part of the marriage exchange. Fiona had a certain look about her when she handled the torque. At least for now, they would be safe in Bersi's house, away from Harald. Their family feud had gone on for so long it was just ingrained.

Gunnar fingered the golden hammer of Thor pendant around his neck. It was a magic hammer that would return to Thor after being thrown. Thor called it Mjolnir. With luck and Mjölnir he'd never lose his weapon. Gunnar had claimed the pendant the previous year from one of the Norse he'd killed. Putting his sword and belt on, he was ready and sought out Fiona. When he'd told her about their marriage, she'd had a strange look on her face, so quiet and distant. *Marriage to me would be a lot better for her than being sold as a thrall for some foreigner's harem.*

Gunnar entered Bersi's house. Cook was busy at the fire pit, stirring a pot of stew. Tante Frida was sitting on the bench deep in conversation with Fiona. His uncle was out of sight, probably still having his bath, so he rejoined Thorkell.

"Onkel Bersi sold two bulls already. You know his daughter's married to an Irish earl who owns a manor house a couple of hours away. The day we arrived, he sent a messenger to let them know about the bulls. His steward arrived this morning and bought two. It won't take long for the other two to sell. Father will be pleased."

"How much did he get for them?" Gunnar asked.

"Eight dirhams each."

"Father and Bersi will split the profits."

"I wouldn't be surprised if Bersi keeps one for himself. He owns several fields beyond the palisade. He's got cows and sells milk to the townsfolk and raises the cross-bred calves for meat," Thorkell said.

Onkel Bersi appeared in the doorway, dressed in his good clothes, looking like the successful merchant he was, adorned with gold chains and rings. "Go on in, Thorkell. I want to have a word with Gunnar."

Thorkell nodded and went inside.

Bersi put his arm around Gunnar's shoulder and they walked a little way down the path away from the house. "Gunnar, Frida asked me to speak to you. Fiona saw you take the female thrall the day of the raid. That was her sister. To put it bluntly–she's afraid of you. It might be prudent to be gentle with her tonight."

Gunnar looked at him, stunned. "As a warrior, it was my right. I wanted the experience, and I took it. There are few opportunities back in Hedeby."

"I know that. I'm just telling you. No hurry. When she's your wife, she'll be available any time you want," Bersi said.

Gunnar nodded. "Well, she is a virgin. Her sister wasn't. She must know what people do."

"Yes, but she is a small woman, and you are a strong, lusty man. Sometimes we men have to consider the woman if we want any peace in the household, you understand," Bersi said with a knowing look on his face. "It's time we go inside."

Given what his uncle just said, Gunnar decided it might not be a good idea to give Fiona a knife yet. *If she could kill Snorri, she could kill anyone, including me.*

Bersi's two sons, their wives, and a dozen children were coming down the path towards them. The women were bearings pots and platters. The children were carrying gifts. The dog barked at them. "Are we all ready, then?" Bersi asked once everyone was inside, getting their attention as the room filled.

Pots and gifts were placed on the table. As the noisy circle formed, the wives pulled the children into place. A girl of about six took the lid from the pot she'd been carrying and started to scatter white hawthorn petals on the floor. The fragrance immediately wafted through the room.

Gunnar saw Fiona sniff the air. *She knows that smell,* he thought. Tante Frida and Fiona arose from the bench to join the circle. Gunnar walked over and stood beside her. He looked down at her, taking in the vision before him, a young slender girl, barely a woman. Gunnar gazed at her long, flowing dark-auburn hair, slim and delightful figure not fully developed, and healthy unblemished skin. Wearing a blue dress, she looked so different from the thrall he'd captured just a few days ago. He'd chosen well. However, she was small-boned. *I hope she'll bear me sons.*

When Fiona finally looked up at him and their eyes met, Gunnar could see she was calmer. Thorkell came forward and turned the pair to face each other. He took Fiona's hand and placed it in Gunnar's. Covering their hands with his, he said, "In the absence of Fiona's parents, I, Thorkell, stand in for them, in giving her in marriage to my brother Gunnar. Their hand-fasting and co-mingling of blood will bear witness to this union. May the Goddess Freyja look kindly upon them, bring them prosperity, a long life, and many sons." He then stepped back.

Onkel Bersi moved out of the circle, took his knife from the scabbard on his belt, and nicked the skin at the base of their palms, allowing the blood to mix. She didn't flinch. Bersi then bound their hands together with a coil of bright-green ribbon.

"I, Bersi with my wife Frida, stand before the Goddess Frigga, mother of Thor and wife of Odin, as witnesses to the union of my nephew Gunnar and Fiona. The blood and hand fasting joins them as husband and wife," Bersi said, stepping back.

Gunnar untied the ribbon and raised her hand to his lips. The circle broke up and the noise level increased as the crowd mixed and mingled.

He stood there, watching her as his oldest cousin presented an iron cooking pot and two carved wooden spoons with intricate Celtic designs on the handles. Fiona turned to him and asked, "How do I say, "thank you" in Danish?"

"*Tusind tak*," he replied putting his arm around her waist.

"Look at the carvings—they're beautiful," she said, shyly stepping forward to thank the couple who smiled at her.

"Both my cousins are Danes from Hedeby and have adapted well to living here as traders. They came with Bersi when he first set up his trading booth."

The younger cousin and his wife presented them with a small wooden chest and offered it to Fiona. She accepted with her thanks and opened it. Her mouth dropped open in amazement as she gently removed a small stone mortar and pestle carved out of a polished, pale-green marble. Also in the box were six small leather pouches. Each one she opened had dried leaves and flowers.

Gunnar could see she was almost in tears as she put the pouches down and took the wife's hand. "Erin, I don't know how to thank you—that's the most wonderful gift I've ever had. Even my mother, who was a healer, didn't have one as good as this."

Erin, gave Fiona a big hug and a very Gaelic reply that Gunnar could barely decipher as meaning that she was Irish, too. She'd found the mortar and pestle in the market and it was an appropriate gift to give a healer. Erin turned to him and said, "You're a lucky man, Gunnar. Take good care of her."

Gunnar thanked his cousin in Danish. "Now we've both got Irish wives."

"She'll have you trained as a husband very quickly. Believe me, I know," the man replied with a laugh, looking at his wife who nudged him hard with her elbow. "Worth it, mind you."

"Maybe tomorrow Fiona could join me. I need to go to the market to shop for fish and flour so I can show her how money works," Erin said.

"Would you like that, Fiona?" Gunnar asked. *It had never crossed his mind that she'd never been in a town and never used coins.*

Fiona smiled and nodded.

Practical Thorkell presented them with a woven, woollen blanket in a plaid pattern of rich yellows and reds.

Onkel Bersi gave Gunnar a game board with ivory pieces. "It's about time you had your own board. See if you can beat me this time," he challenged. Gunnar was delighted. The wooden board had been skilfully made with alternating squares of light and dark wood. The playing pieces were carved walrus ivory of warriors and kings.

"Thanks; I've always wanted one of my own. Thorkell, do you remember when we were younger and we used to play on father's board all the time?"

Thorkell grinned. "We were supposed to be working and he caught us. Got a good thrashing for that."

Tante Frida came forward and handed Fiona the white cap, identical to her own.

"Tusind tak," Fiona said. She'd have to learn Danish quickly to fit in but he needed to learn the trader's Gaelic as well. They'd have to teach each other.

The meal was casual with everyone taking what they wanted, including the children who were running around, playing games while the adults talked. Cook had provided not only the stew and bread but a number of sweet treats, buns sticky with honey and topped with a rust-coloured powder, which had everyone licking their fingers, looking for more. Finally, the cousins, spouses, and children went home, leaving the place a lot quieter and less chaotic. The level of mead in the barrel had dropped substantially.

"I'll come and get you mid-morning," Erin said as she was leaving. "We'll go shopping."

Gunnar watched Fiona say goodbye. He was pleased to see she and Erin were getting along. At least they both spoke Gaelic. The three men spent the rest of the evening sitting at the table with Onkel Bersi telling stories, taking turns playing the game board.

Fiona sat quietly beside him. From time to time, in between mugs of mead he pulled her close and kissed her on the lips. Gunnar felt her tense between his arms but she didn't pull away. *Onkel Bersi was right, she was afraid.* He was looking forward to their time in bed but would have to slow down as Bersi had suggested.

"Can I wash this blood off my hands?" Fiona asked. "I don't want to offend your god."

"Go ahead, the ritual's over," he said. He'd been waiting for this all evening and now he wasn't quite sure how to handle it; here in Bersi's home, it wasn't the same as taking a woman in the heat of battle.

CHAPTER 12

*Present day, archaeological
dig site, Hedeby*

Dr. Jon Jorgenssen looked down into the trench with satisfaction. The team seemed to be working together better. Helga as usual, preferred to work alone and was sifting soil. Miles was carefully brushing dirt away from the right side of the skull and chest cavity they'd unearthed, while Miles and Gena tackled the feet up. Most of the right radius and ulna arm bones were exposed. One of the wrist bones and three finger tips were missing, eroded away. The shoulder joint was partially exposed, showing the socket of the scapula and the tip of the clavicle as well as a fancy piece of decorative rusted metal that looked like links of chain mail.

Lars was at the table, meticulously brushing dirt from a piece of fine woven wool, like a shirt but, he also had a piece of fur the skeleton seemed to be wrapped in. "Professor, it will be interesting to find out what kind of fur this is. It looks like bear. I need to clean this up before we send it off to the lab," he said, as Jon nodded in agreement.

After a group lunch break, Gena was carefully plotting all the finds on a map in minute detail, keeping track of each item and photographing them from dirt to cleaned, padded specimen container.

Jon had concerns. Although the dig was going very well, it could not be rushed and time was a problem. He only had a few months to work on this excavation before his permit ran out and the bad weather set in. Classes resumed in September. His students were working hard and doing a superb job of it, despite the personality clashes. At one point, he thought Lars would leave, but they had discussed it and the young man had decided to stay. Jon needed all their skills. *It was worrying.* Some nights he worked alone long after they'd gone. He had managed to have chain-link fencing installed around the site, but even with locked gates and tarps, he was anxious about the security of the project. He could hire more students, but the site was small and tight with other anomalies close. Lars had been very competent with ground-penetrating radar and interpretation of the data, but right now it was the dirty work he needed done.

Jon was confident in these four, and didn't need any more complications. He was often up past midnight doing ministry paperwork. While he would have preferred to be actively doing more of the dig himself, it wasn't going to happen. He missed seeing Elsa and the boys. By the time he got home, they were already sleeping. It had become a matter of leaving notes to each other. Hardly good for any marriage. He sometimes wondered if his job was worth the price of his family. Elsa had known full well what she was getting in for before they were married as her father had been an anthropologist at the university. Still, he sensed her frustration.

CHAPTER 13

Becoming a wife

Fiona was fascinated at the intensity of the men playing the chess game; contemplating a move, then the explosive reaction when their opponent won, almost coming to blows. Finally, Thorkell decided to go back to the ship, while he was still sober enough to walk. Gunnar had beaten him twice. *Grown men playing a game didn't make any sense.*

She was so glad Gunnar's cousin had an Irish wife. Erin seemed to know just how to handle a Danish husband. Fiona needed all the help she could get and wondered if she really was married in the eyes of God without the Christian ceremony.

Ainsley was picking up the last of the platters and trenchers. As she passed, she said, "Your old dress is nearly dry. I'll hang it on your bench. I got most of the blood stains out of it. It'll do you for around the house.

At least it's wearable. I darned the tears," she said, showing her the stitching.

"Thank you, Ainsley. Another day or two and I'll be back on the ship. No point wearing good clothes for that. My goodness, these stitches are so small; I can barely see them. You do good work."

Seeing the girls work dawn to dusk reminded her it could very easily have been like that for her, if she hadn't married Gunnar. As it was, she was at the mercy of the mistress of the house. Tante Frida though, had been kind and generous, giving her the dress, shoes, and cap.

The hour was getting late, the fire dying down. Gunnar staggered to the outhouse to relieve himself of the gallons of mead he'd imbibed. She went to the bench. First, she removed her overdress, then the blue one, which she coveted for its beautiful colour and the fineness of the weave, hanging them on the back wall. There was no choice but to be bedded by her husband. She loosened her braids, letting her hair cascade over her body, climbed onto the bench, and pulled the blankets around her nakedness, waiting.

A short time later, Gunnar bade his parents good night and came over to their bench. He took off his sword, placing it on the floor, then sat beside her, mead fumes wafting over her. His strong hands pulled her to his chest as he kissed her. She tentatively ran her fingers over his muscular arms and looked at him. He nuzzled her neck and ran his fingers through her hair, sliding them over her breasts.

"I can't believe we are married and you are my wife," he whispered. He stripped off his shirt and pants, dropping them on the floor, then pulled the blanket away, fully exposing her. Her first instinct was to cover herself. He was solid muscle. His blonde hair almost as long as hers, draped over his shoulders and chest, framing him. He was watching her every move, his breathing increasingly ragged, and nostrils slightly flaring.

Kneeling over her, he pushed her down onto the bench. She could feel his weight and his hardness. Her own heart was pounding. Gunnar's kiss was now hungry and forceful. She was so tense, pinned beneath him, it was hard to breathe. He ran his rough hands over her, fondling her breasts, sliding down to her thighs, groping.

Finally, the heft of his body came down on her. It hurt. He groaned. It was over and he was dead weight on her. Two faces appeared—Onkel Bersi and Tante Frida. Gunnar glanced at them.

"It's done!" he said, with a tremendous grin on his face. "You've witnessed it. It's legal now."

Bersi and Frida nodded and returned to their bench. Without further comment, Gunnar rolled off and lay beside Fiona. He brushed the hair from her face, pulled up the blanket, then smiled and closed his eyes until sleep claimed him. The house was quiet. Either every-one else was sleeping or listening.

So much for that, Fiona thought, wide awake. *He got what he wanted.* Now she knew what it was all about. It reminded her of the big ram at home, chasing a ewe. She thought about the harmony between her mother and father and the love they gave each other, her mother's sighs and soft moans of pleasure. It had been mutual and unhurried. *Will I ever have that with Gunnar? Would it ever be pleasurable or will I just have to tolerate it?* She lay there, his arm still around her and eventually fell asleep.

The following morning, Fiona wriggled out from beneath him, grabbed her dress, and got up, noticing a small blood stain on the blanket and smears on her thighs. The thralls were already preparing the morning meal, grinding wheat and oats, and lighting the fire. She went out to the garden, grabbed a pail of water, and washed her face hands and the blood smears on her legs. She decided to keep her old dress for the ship and her blue dress for special occasions. *Today was market day with Erin.*

It was raining lightly, so she sat inside near the fire pit and combed her hair, coiling the braids around her head and pinning them in place. The cap could wait until later. Tante Frida and Onkel Bersi were getting up. A sleep-tousled Gunnar emerged from their bench, put on his clothes, and strapped on his sword. He sat beside her and kissed her on the cheek.

"Good morning," he said with a big grin on his face. "You're up early."

"You were sleeping and I didn't want to wake you."

"That's too bad. I was hoping we could have a little more time in bed."

"We'll have plenty of time for that tonight," she said, trying to distract him.

Fiona needed to keep busy so she pulled the trunk out from under the bench. Carefully, she put away her blue dress and overdress on top of Carraig's sword and torque. She wrapped the mortar and pestle and the cooking pot and spoons in an old blanket before putting them inside, then slipped the trunk back under the bed. After straightening out the blankets on the bench, she glanced at Gunnar. He was looking at her with a slight frown.

Fiona sat beside him. "Gunnar, I'm going to the market with Erin today. Please explain to me about coins."

He pulled several silver dirhams from his pouch. Trying to find the right words, he said, "This piece of silver is one dirham. It's an Islamic coin, but it is used everywhere on our trade route. In Hedeby, we don't make our own coins so we use theirs. It is a coin with a set value but it is also a weight," he said handing one to her. "If you are buying a small thing, this would be too much, so we often cut them into four pieces which we call hack silver."

She looked at the coin. It was round and shiny with strange wiggly lines.

"What do the lines mean?" she asked, giving it back to him.

"That's Islamic writing. I can't read it. We do have our own written language in Denmark, called Futhark. It's a very ancient language used on things like tombstones and runes. When we get back to Hedeby, I'll show you. I can read it but have difficulty writing it."

"How much silver would you get from selling slaves?"

"Mohammed pays us two or three dirhams for a boy or a girl, maybe four for a young woman, and five for a virgin. Same as a cow. The bulls we delivered sold for eight."

So, if she hadn't married him, she would have been sold for four or five pieces of silver and Ailin for three.

"Erin's very good at bargaining so she gets things at a lower price. She'll show you how it's done. Townsfolk buy everything, flour, fish, clothes, whatever they need. That's the way here. Nothing is grown in town. There's no space. Farmers raise the livestock in the country and bring the animals to town. The butchers buy them, kill them, and sell the meat to us. We do the same thing in Hedeby."

Cook was preparing bread for the next meal. Fiona went over and thanked her.

"The sweet buns you made yesterday were very good. What was the brown powder on them? I've never tasted anything like that."

"That's cinnamon. The foreigners bring it from their land over the sea. It is very expensive. Sometimes Mor Frida wants it on regular bread, too. It looks like little curled sticks when we get it and I grind it into a powder," she said, showing her a pouch of it.

Fiona smelled it and handed it back. "Thank you. I'll remember that."

The morning household routine continued as usual. Onkel Bersi was organizing the goods he was sending back to Hedeby and itemizing each item on his list. Fiona was fascinated watching him write with a bird feather on a piece of calfskin, dipping the tip into a small container of black liquid. The writing looked like angled twigs on a bare tree, more complicated than the Ogham script her mother Aoife could write.

"That's Futhark; it looks like a tree," Gunnar told her. "He'll mark down how many of each item is in stock. See—he has seven rolls of silk," he said holding up his fingers. "Then he writes *sjau* beside it. Sjau's seven. Beside that is the price he paid for it —*fjorir*, four dirhams. That way Ottar knows how many and their cost. He will charge *fimm,* five dirhams in Hedeby to make his profit. Bersi gets the best price he can for our trade goods. We bring in the hides, amber, bulls, and take the exotic things back."

From the locked storage room, Onkel Bersi brought out bolts of material. Fiona looked at them in wonder. She'd never seen such rich shades of blues, deep reds, rusts, greens, yellows and purples. Some were a silky texture with a high sheen. Other bolts were fine like netting; she could see her hand right through them. They were very light. Gold thread glittered through a few of them. The weaving was unbelievably fine. There were also boxes and small barrels smelling of fragrant herbs and spices stacked by the doorway, awaiting transport.

Bersi looked at Gunnar. "I'll need you to escort the cart back to the knarr. Wrap each bolt in calf hide for me. They must be stored in a chest. They'll be ruined if they get wet. The spices need to be kept dry, too. There's gold jewellery to go but I'll wait until the day you're sailing before I give that to Thorkell. Far too much temptation for thieves. Eyes will be watching the ships day and night. There's also a crate of Italian glassware— beautiful stuff." He opened a crate, pushed the straw packing aside, and brought out a clear blue jug with matching drinking glasses. "The rich folk in Hedeby are going to love it. Once everything's on board, Thorkell won't leave the ship," Bersi explained.

Fiona was fascinated with the fragility of a clear blue glass bottle, small enough to fit in her hand. She watched as Gunnar laid out a hide and place a bolt of material on it, rolling it up tightly and tying string around each end. Soon all the bolts were protected. He went out to the shed and came back with a crate big enough to accommodate them, packed them inside, and nailed the lid shut. Both men went back into the store room.

Tante Frida took Fiona aside. "Are you alright?"

"Tusind tak. The first time isn't easy. I wasn't expecting it to hurt so," she said.

Frida took the new cap and put in on her head, adjusting her braids so it fit comfortably for her.

"There. Now you look like a Danish wife. Erin should be here soon. Gunnar tells me you've never been in a town before, so you'll find the market interesting."

Fiona was going to have to get used to wearing a cap whether she wanted to or not. It would have been the same if she'd married at home.

A short time later Erin appeared on the doorstep. "Good morning, Mor Frida. Is Fiona ready? Ah, I see you are, with your cap on. Come along then. Here, Fiona; you can carry this basket for me," she said grasping her by the elbow and steering her out the door. Away they went down the path, towards the main gate.

"Erin, I had Gunnar explain money to me this morning. Can you tell me what it's like living in town?"

she asked as they strolled arm in arm with Erin telling her about the houses and businesses they were passing. She could see the blacksmith's forge, the local butcher shop with pig and goat carcasses hanging on hooks, and the local inn and pub.

"Gunnar told me you were from a very isolated village, so this is your first time in a town?"

"Yes, there were only six houses, all family members with no strangers, except when one of our lads married and brought his new wife back and, of course, our girls left our village when they married a boy from outside. All this is new to me."

"My goodness, no wonder you're amazed at everything."

"Well . . . like this morning. Onkel Bersi was writing with a feather on a piece of calfskin. I'd never see the like of it. The only person I know who writes is our abbot and we only see him once or twice a year. None of us read or write Latin. My mother wrote Ogham but she used a stick."

"Fiona, how old are you?"

"I'm sixteen," she said, changing the subject. "I need to talk to you about their language. How long did it take you to learn Danish and what's the best way for me to learn it? Gunnar's taking me to Hedeby."

"My husband just started pointing at things and giving me the Danish names. We've been married for six years, but it took me about three before I became reasonably fluent. There are still times I don't understand what he's saying, especially if he's talking to another Dane. Sometimes I think he deliberately speaks Danish if he doesn't want me to know something. But that's a husband for you. It's best to forget Gaelic if you can and just keep trying the Danish."

Fiona looked around. "You don't grow your own food or hunt?"

"No, my family are merchants, too. We buy and sell by barter and coins. There's no space to grow food inside the palisade. Some of the townspeople are fishermen, so they have small boats and fish in the bay to feed their families, then sell the surplus. Many of the local Irish live beyond the palisade in the surrounding countryside and raise vegetables and grains like wheat, rye, and oats. They also raise pigs, goats and sheep. The local Irish lords have big estates and enough land to raise cattle and horses as well. They have slaves to work the land."

"I overheard Thorkell saying Onkel Bersi might keep one of the bulls. He seems to be into a lot of different things."

"He has cattle of his own on rented pasture. He sells the milk and meat in town. He hires farmers to look after them. Most of the sailors from the ships come to the inn and drink the local beer; others drink mead. He's into brewing, too. There are a lot of community water wells but like Bersi, we have our own well beside the house."

"When we were waiting outside the palisade that first day, I heard an old man saying that you are ruled by an Irish king."

"That's true. The Danes ruled here for two hundred years but King Cearbhall and the Leinster Irish defeated them not long ago and took over Dublin. They tolerate us Danish traders because we bring so much business to the area. Most of those ships out there are foreign. You'll see his soldiers patrolling, especially at night to stop the drunks and thieves. They keep an eye on us traders but generally don't interfere. The Irish tribes squabble amongst themselves often enough."

They walked through the gates and into the market where the booths were set up. It was very busy with women and children swarming the tables. Fiona eyes grew wide as she watched Erin and the fish monger barter back and forth for six fresh silvery fish. He was asking one price and she would counter with a lower one. Back and forth, back and forth, until finally they reached a compromise. Since the merchant was speaking Gaelic, it was easy to understand and she now understood the process of haggling.

Erin pointed out all the trays of fish, displayed under the awning. "There are different kinds of fish. Look at the size, the shapes, and the colours. Here, you've got fish from the freshwater river; those are from the sea. Each taste slightly different. I just bought cod, which is a sea fish. Those over there are flat fish from the sea. I believe they live deeper, on the bottom."

Fiona did a double-take: the fish was indeed flat with two eyes on the top. *What amazing things!*

"You notice he's also got sea creatures that live in shells, like these clams," Erin said picking one up and showing her. "You pry the shell open to get the meat out, and they're very tasty but quite expensive, too, so we don't have them very often. I see you're knife scabbard's empty. You'll be needing a knife for your household chores like gutting and scaling the fish. Ask Gunnar for one. Those long skinny fish are eels."

Further down the row of booths a farm couple were selling vegetables. Fiona easily identified the cabbage, parsnips, carrots, and pod peas, but there were other things as well. Erin bought three cabbages, peas, and carrots, placing them in Fiona's basket. She also bought cream-coloured honey that the old woman ladled from a small keg into a ceramic jar. Bargaining took place with every transaction, and Fiona paid close attention.

Another booth had woven blankets and linens suitable for ordinary folk, not like Bersi's booth with wares for the rich. That was surrounded by well-dressed customers buying the materials and spices, keeping Bersi and his two sons fully occupied. Money was changing hands quickly. She saw Erin glance at her husband. He nodded to her over the heads of the customers he was serving.

Fiona scanned the bay and saw Gunnar and the knarr crew loading goods from the cart. Thorkell was on deck yelling instructions. The longship floated at anchor beside the knarr, ready to go. She could see barrels already aboard both ships. They were preparing to sail again.

Dozens of poorer families were gathering shellfish on the mud flats now the tide was out. Their clothes were ragged, none wore shoes, and their hair was wild and unkempt. Babies were slung across their mothers' backs in sacking. In the distance, Fiona could see cattle in the fields, the waving heads of growing wheat, a forester loading his horse-drawn cart with kindling, and tendrils of smoke from unseen houses in the woods. Carpenters were building a frame house across the river. *In my village, we'd done all those things ourselves.*

"Erin, I'll be needing some moss for my bleeding time. Can I get that here? I used to collect it myself back home, as well as the plants my mother needed. I'll need some herbs, too."

"I've got some at home you can have. I get it cheaper than the merchant here who sells it. A couple of women I know gather it. We'll stop in the healer's home on the way back."

Fiona noticed two soldiers lounging around the palisade gate, watchful of the Danes and talking to the local fishermen. They were short, powerful-looking dark-haired men, armed with swords and shields emblazoned with the symbol of the stag. Two horses were tied to rings further along in the palisade wall, with saddle cloths bearing the same markings. She assumed these were the king's men. Ships continued to come and go in the harbour, including another slaver. Her sister's ship was gone. Thankful she'd escaped that fate, Fiona closed her mind, not wanting to think of Evelyn and her cousins.

Enroute to Erin's house, they stopped at a small house on a side street. The door was open and an elderly man with a long, grey, braided beard was busy sorting through green plant leaves. Fiona sniffed the air, immediately identifying the scents and shapes. The voyage ahead was a journey into the unknown and would likely be violent. She would need a supply of herbs for coughs, colds, pain, and wound care.

"Erin, I'd like to get some of these, but I don't have any money. Can you buy them for me and I'll have Gunnar repay you?"

"Alright."

"What will you be needing?" the man asked, looking at her sharply when she rattled off the names: coltsfoot, meadowsweet, mullein, and yarrow. He pulled bins from the shelves and offered each one to her. She removed the lids, smelled them, and took a small pinch of each, rubbing them through her fingers, making sure they were fresh. Fiona was aware of his critical look. She opened the jars and checked the ointments that which had been prepared just the same as she would have done under Aoife's watchful eye.

Erin said to him, "Her mother was a healer, so she knows what they're for."

He nodded and filled small pouches for her, as well as several prepared ointments and tonics. Erin did the bartering. A quarter dirham exchanged hands.

"She has the look about her," he said to Erin as they were leaving.

Fiona glanced back at him, wondering what he meant, but then she saw the light pulsing around him. He had the aura of power, just like her mother. Most people would not have been able to see it. Erin didn't. It was the healers and witches who had that talent.

CHAPTER 14

The voyage continues

Gunnar spent most of the day wading through the shallows, hefting cargo from the cart to the knarr. He wanted to go home, show off Fiona, and find a place to live.

Thorkell was on deck, deciding where each barrel and crate would be placed to balance the load. The barrels of salt beef were heavy to move, needing four men to lift. Once on board, they were firmly secured on the aft decks of both ships. Two sailors had worked for several days filling the water barrels, refilling and hauling smaller kegs repeatedly from the community wells.

Gunnar noticed a new, tarp-covered shed in the cargo hold where Thorkell had stored the fabrics and spices on raised shelves so they wouldn't be awash in seawater during a storm. The odour of cattle still lingered.

"This shed will provide better shelter than the main deck," Thorkell said. "I should have thought of it before. There's enough space inside for Fiona to sleep on the lower bench. It's safer away from the men, and I can keep an eye on her."

"Thank you, brother. Were you able to hire more sailors?"

"No problem. Lots of experienced seamen around here. They'll stay with us at least to Bruges. I think some are planning to sign on as mercenaries against the Franks. So, how'd it go with Fiona?"

"How'd you think it went?" Gunnar retorted with a grin on his face and a swagger in his step.

"You look pleased with yourself."

"I am. It's a whole lot different bedding your wife at home than taking a woman in a raid. She went shopping with Erin this morning. She needs to get used to living in town."

"She's going to buy stuff and will be asking you for money."

"I never thought to give her any. We even discussed coins this morning. She wanted to know what they were."

"Fiona will catch on quick; you'll see. Seems a bright young thing. I've seen her looking around, always watching. You made a good choice. Tomorrow, we'll sail on the morning tide," he said, slapping Gunnar on the back.

Then it was back to work, carrying sacks of flour. Finn was ready to load another barrel of beef onto the longship. Gunnar joined the others, adding his strength to the lift. Suddenly, another pair of hands were on the barrel. It rose over the rail to roll onto the deck with comparative ease. The sides of the longship were considerably lower than the knarr's.

Gunnar looked up to the biggest man he'd ever laid eyes on. He was ever taller than Finn.

"I'm Gunnar. You must be the Norseman Thorkell told me about."

"That I am. Ivar Forkbeard's my name," the man said, looming over him, hands on hips.

"You made that easy," Gunnar replied, assessing every detail—the height and width of him, the quality sword, the light chain mail, over his shirt, and his hand-tooled leather belt with a beautifully worked knife scabbard. The man had battle scars on his tattooed arms and a jagged one across his forehead, slashing down onto his cheek, completed with an opaque left eye, giving him a sinister look. *Obviously, a seasoned warrior.*

"Good to have you aboard, Ivar. Were you in Normandy?"

"*Ja*, there and many other places. I've just come from Iberia. Time for me to go home. I've been away three years."

Most of the original crew were back, including Harald who looked at Gunnar and frowned, seeing the sword on his hip. Knowing he was safe from any legal challenge, Gunnar ignored him and checked his sea chests. His spare sword, helmet, and shirts hadn't been touched. The bearskin cape was still there. His shield was in it proper place on the shield rail.

As a group, they had a brief discussion and elected Finn as their leader for this voyage. It was different on the knarr where some of seamen were traders, who'd paid their fare to sell goods in Dublin. A lot of the knarr cargo belonged to them. Thorkell was the captain, but Steinn and Ottar owned the ship.

Gunnar assumed the crew had spent their days ashore at the inn or curled up on the beach at night and once again were out of money, having spent all their silver on beer, mead, and the local street women. A few were sporting black eyes and bruises. One was missing a few front teeth.

With the cargo loaded, Gunnar headed back to his uncle's house. He found Fiona working the loom. She got up when he entered and returned his smile. He gently took her by the shoulders, pulled her close, and kissed her. She stiffened but didn't pull away.

"Gunnar, I need to repay Erin. She bought my herbs and showed me how to barter."

He handed her two quarters. "You keep one quarter for yourself. Give the other one to Tante Frida so she can pass it over to Erin. We'll be leaving early in the morning."

"Can I have my knife back? I need it to work with herbs and wool. With all those men on board, I'd feel safer if I had one."

"I'll get one for you. Is there anything else?"

"I need to learn to speak your language as quickly as I can, so please tell me the Danish name for things. How do I count in Danish?" she asked

"We'll start with the easy ones. Uncle is *onkel* and aunt is *tante*. Yes is *ja*; no is *nej*. One is *ein*, two is *tveir*, and three is *prir*," he said using his fingers.

"Good. You'll have to put short phrases together." She was so childlike and trusting, stray auburn strands of hair escaping the confines of her cap and those blue-green eyes mesmerized him. He stood there for a moment holding her, overwhelmed with a feeling he couldn't define, but whatever it was, he liked it.

"Come, show me what you're doing," he said, leading Fiona to the loom. He examined her work. The threads were tight, well-spaced, and even. It looked just as good as his mother's. *No reason she couldn't join the weavers at home and make a living that way if the healing didn't work out.*

He spent the evening playing the board game with Onkel Bersi, who won. Fiona sat with Tante Frida and was ripping an old linen dress into strips for bandages. *She was thinking ahead. They could easily run into trouble on the way home.* Her attempts at Danish were amusing his aunt.

"Gunnar, have you got my knife yet? I need it for cutting the wool. What is the Danish word for knife?" Fiona asked.

"Knife is *kniv.* I couldn't find yours. Onkel Bersi, do you have a small knife with a two- or three-inch blade? Fiona's wanting one," Gunnar asked.

"I've got some in the storage room," Bersi replied, disappearing down the hall, jangling the keys. He emerged a few minutes later and showed one to him.

"How much do you want for it?"

"One dirham," he said.

Fiona jumped to her feet and ran over, looking very excited. "Can I try bargaining with you for that? I need the practice," she asked, looking eager.

Bersi looked at her with a tiny smile crinkling the corners of his mouth. "I couldn't possibly sell it for less than one. Look how it's made—fine steel and the blade will stay sharp for a long time. I've got a sick wife at home and my children have no food to eat. One dirham it is," he said getting in the spirit of the occasion, morphing from successful merchant to grovelling trader.

"Well," she said, looking it over thoroughly and trying to be serious. She handed it back to him, put her hands on her hips, and said, "The trader four booths down, has one just like it, and he's selling it for half of that. I'll give you two quarters."

Now Bersi was enjoying himself. Putting on a sad face, he looked over the knife again. "Well, I don't know what my family's going to do, but I could go to three quarters."

She took the knife and examined it again. "I don't think so," she said handing it back to him and turning to walk away.

"Alright—two quarters then. You drive a hard bargain," he said and burst out laughing, then all of them were laughing, including Tante Frida.

"Ja," Fiona said and took the knife, looking pleased with herself.

Gunnar looked at his uncle, still grinning and paid him the two quarters. Fiona slipped the knife into her scabbard and tied it on her belt.

Bedtime came and everyone settled on their benches. Gunnar undressed and sat on the bed watching her. Fiona was still very shy with him, her back turned to him as she slipped her dress over her head and undid her braids. He ran his fingers through her hair until they formed a dark cascade. He pulled her down on top of him so he could see her framed in hair, her breasts touching his.

"Gunnar," she whispered.

"Hmmm," he murmured, nuzzling into her neck.

"Please be gentle; it still hurts," she said not making eye contact with him.

"I thought I was," he said, feeling the silky sensation of her skin under his fingertips. *Maybe the husband's way was different from the warrior's.* He slowed down.

Gunnar was awakened by the sounds of Bersi getting up. Fiona was still sleeping. He rolled over and put his arm around her, nibbling her ear. She opened her eyes and blinked.

"Come on, sleepy one. Time to get up," he said.

"Could you get my sea chest out? I'm going to wear my old dress," she said.

He pulled it out and set it on the bed, leaving her to dress. The thralls were up and Cook had come in, lighting the fire in the pit for hot water and preparing the bread dough.

Onkel Bersi unlocked the storage room and beckoned Gunnar to join him. He was holding a small box made of carved ivory inlay in mahogany wood. There was a fine brass latch.

"Gunnar, take this to Thorkell. Keep it hidden." He lifted the lid, displaying necklaces of gold, finely worked with inlaid red and green gemstones. There were gold medallions and arm bands with scenes of the gods and animals. He closed the lid.

"I don't have to tell you how valuable these are. They're worth at least fifty dirhams. Don't even tell Fiona. There isn't a man on the knarr or the longship who wouldn't kill for that. Here's the bill of lading for Ottar," he said, handing him the scroll.

"I'll put it in Fiona's sea chest. It should be safe there until I can give it to Thorkell. He must have a hiding place on board," Gunnar replied.

"He does. We've done this before but this is the largest shipment I've ever sent. Take care of it. Not a word to anyone."

"I understand." Gunnar realized the enormity of the responsibility and trust Bersi was placing on him.

Folding the scroll inside the box, Bersi wrapped the box it in a piece of felt and handed it to him.

Stepping out of the storage room, Gunnar looked around for Fiona but she wasn't in sight, probably out back. He raised the lid on her sea chest and slipped the box under the blue dress. He took his game board, which was on the table and rolled it in woollen fabric for protection, putting the game pieces in a pouch, setting it inside the cooking pot where it wouldn't rattle around. He closed the latch.

Tante Frida and Fiona came in from out back. Fiona was wearing a thigh-length hooded woollen cape with sleeves in a dark rust brown colour. It closed with a bronze shoulder pin. She took her cap and put it in the sea chest.

"I think it'll be too windy to wear it on the ship. Look Gunnar! Tante Frida's given me this wonderful cloak. I'll be warm and dry if there's a storm." She turned and gave Frida a hug, thanking her in Danish.

Cook gathered a package of bread and cheese, handing it to Fiona.

Gunnar took Fiona by the arm and led her to the door. "Come, it's time to go. Many thanks to both of you. You've been so good to us with the wedding and making us welcome in your home. I really appreciate all you've done."

"You're welcome, Gunnar. If you ever change your mind about being a warrior, there's a place at the trading booth for both of you here," said Bersi.

Gunnar hefted the sea chest up on his right shoulder. It was heavier than he expected. Of course, it now contained the mahogany box, the iron pot, Carraig's sword and torque, plus all Fiona's pots and herbs. She trotted along beside him. It was still early and the town was not awake. Few people were out and about, mostly fishermen. As they went through the gate, he saw Fiona look back and wave. Bersi and Frida returned the wave from their front step.

In the harbour, the knarr and longship looked ready. Some of the crew were already on board while others were wading through the shallows to join them.

"Fiona, wait here for me. I'll put the sea chest on first," he said, splashing through the wavelets. Thorkell's face appeared over the rail. Gunnar quickly climbed the rope ladder, being careful to balance the chest, then passed it to him, his eyes darting briefly to the chest. Their eyes met. Thorkell nodded, getting the message. He was expecting the secret cargo.

"I'll bring Fiona on board now," he said, climbing back down to get her.

"Here," she said. "You haven't had any breakfast," stuffing a packet of cook's goodies into the front of his shirt.

Laughing, he scooped her up and carried her to the ship to keep her dry, accompanied by whistles, whoops of laughter, and ribald comments from his crew mates. She blushed, clinging tightly to him. Positioning her feet on the ladder, the basket slung from her arm, Gunnar passed her over to Thorkell.

She turned and looked at him as he waded over to the longship, swaggering to his shipmates. Many of the old faces had returned. He nodded to the Norseman who was sitting aft. Two faces were new. He found his sea chest and sat on it, opened the oar hole, and slipped the oar in place. *Back to sea.*

CHAPTER 15

*East coast of Ireland, south
of Dublin, 905 CE*

Fiona stood on the deck of the knarr watching the crew manoeuvre the ship out of the harbour. The longship had forged ahead of them. She clung to the mast to watch the longship's crew expertly coordinate their rowing. The ship seemed to glide out on the water. She couldn't make out which one of the oarsmen was Gunnar. *Distance was not a bad thing.*

On board the knarr, Thorkell was shouting orders to the crew, who were backing the ship away from the dock and turning towards the sea. It was fascinating to watch as one side of oarsmen paused while the other side rowed and the ship changed course, as the crew angled the sail to catch the wind.

She watched Thorkell standing with feet braced, sword by his side, looking very much in command. Although he was only a few years older than Gunnar, he was in charge. The crew were obeying him and they obviously respected him. She thought most of them were from Hedeby, a mix of sailors and merchants. They worked so well together, it was obvious they had done this before.

Thorkell was responsible for so much—the ship, the cargo, the sailors—compared to Gunnar who only wanted to fight. She didn't understand how two brothers could be so different. She wondered how they knew where they were going, once at sea.

An older man sometimes handled the rudder. Sun and wind had darkened his skin, weathering it into deep, squinting creases. His attention was focused on the way forward, avoiding other ships in the harbour and watching the longship ahead.

Fiona was pleased with the little shed in the open cargo bay. Her bed was the lower shelf of several, just the right size for her with her sea chest underneath. The shelves above held the precious fabrics and glassware in their crates as well as an assortment of other chests. She sat down on her bench and ate the remaining bread and cheese, pondering what she was going to do to pass the time.

She felt the ship rise as it hit the waves of the open sea. The knarr moved differently from the longship. It didn't ride on the waves but into them. Her balance was off when it rolled, so she clung to the rail. The crew loosened the ropes and the sail dropped, gradually filling with the light wind, billowing above her over the cargo hold. Squawking, soaring white and grey gulls followed them, gliding on air currents.

Soon enough, they were out of the bay and turned south, leaving the sea birds behind. It was cloudy, but the sun still shone through the eastern sky revealing moderate seas. Fiona noticed they were following the coast with the current now.

Thorkell walked over to her. "Good morning, Fiona. We'll make good time today with this light wind." The men were not rowing now but coiling the ropes on the anchor line and doing other chores.

"How do you know where to sail?"

He chose his words carefully, his Gaelic far better than Gunnar's. "There are many things—the direction of the sun, where it rises and sets, the direction of the wind, usually from the north and west here, the direction of the waves, and the coast line itself, if it's visible. At night, we use the stars to guide us. I've sailed this before and so have the crew. The man at the rudder knows where the shoals are and how deep the water is by the way the waves break."

"So, you know just be looking at the land, the sky, and the water where you are?" she asked in disbelief, thinking of the miles of coast line they'd already passed. "What is that land?" she queried, looking at the distant blue hills and mountains, their peaks ringed in cloud on the eastern horizon.

"In answer to your first question, if you've done the trip a few times, you remember the coast. That country is Wales, a part of Britain. It has the roughest seas and coasts, as well as Norse pirates. I stay well away from there," he said, clearly amused at her curiosity.

"I need something to do. Do you have any fleece on board? I could spin."

"Let me see what kind of work we can find for you. Sit where you are so you don't get in our way. You'll find your balance after a few days," he said, moving easily along the deck to adjust a rope on the sail.

Fiona was baffled at how they could remember all those different places. She realized the cargo bay was the main storage area. It's eight-foot depth was really just a deeper section of the main deck. The pervasive reek of cattle still clung to the wood despite the thorough cleaning Gunnar had described. The main deck too had some cargo, tied down with rope, including the barrels of salt beef and water. The knarr's prow was plain sculpted wood—no dragon to lead the way. The men slept under deck tarps. She felt lucky to have her own bench. The longship remained ahead of them, its red sail full and the oars still.

Thorkell opened a chest or two, finding a burlap bag of washed fleece. "Here you are. You can spin that."

"Tusind tak. What's 'wool' in Danish?"

"It sounds the same, 'wool,' but it's written differently," he said and left her to her work. She sat all morning removing bits of dried grass and seed heads from the fleece, then separated the fibres with her comb until she had a fine roving. As she twisted and spun the drop spindle clockwise for this batch, her fingers twisted the handful of hair thinner and thinner into a yarn. She compared it to the fibres in her dress and the ones she could see in Thorkell's shirt. His shirt fibres were even finer. By midday she stopped. *Enough of that for now.*

The crew were frequently adjusting the sail, taking advantage of the wind. The Irish coast retained its high hills with green forests and rocky escarpments. Occasional small bays with pebbled beaches were tucked inside promontories of weathered, layered rock, where waves were crashing and foaming. They'd passed several tiny villages and small boats with one or two fishermen. Occasionally, bigger ships passed to the east heading north. *Probably going to Dublin,* she mused.

It was a long day, as she settled into a routine, spinning or watching the crew at work. The rolling motion of the waves was becoming normal. Day passed into evening, the sun slipping behind the hills on the coast. The longship changed direction and carried them into a small protected bay. She watched the crew edge the ship onto the beach and clamber out. She could pick Gunnar out of the crowd now.

Why am I so interested? Good question. Maybe because in this environment. I need him to protect me. She could name a few crew members by now. The knarr crew hauled in the sail, firmly tied the ropes and dropped anchor. Fiona wondered if he wanted her to go ashore or stay on board. She watched and waited.

The crew of the longship were prowling the beach, gathering driftwood, and checking the woods. From her vantage point, Fiona couldn't see any other people around—no signs of villagers. There were no other ships visible, either. The helmsman pried open the barrels of beef and water. Thorkell hooked a piece of meat with his knife. He beckoned her over, and snagged one for her, too. She took a long drink from the communal water mug. The crew lined up, basically ignoring her and that was fine by her, not wanting any trouble.

Each ship had its own beef supply. After they'd eaten, most of the knarr crew went ashore. Soon, Gunnar waded across and climbed the ladder to join Fiona. As the three of them sat together, the two brothers talked. Those on shore sat around the fire and as darkness fell, they put out the fire and most slept on the deck. The men were tired but took turns on watch. The longship crew always had their swords. Only a few on the knarr carried them, but weapons were readily available in the storage hold if needed.

"Well, how did you do today?" Gunnar asked as they climbed down to the shed and sat on the bench together, his arm around her, lifting her face with his fingers to kiss her.

"I spent most of my time spinning. Thorkell explained how he guides the ship using the sun, the wind, the stars, and the waves. I didn't know any of that. You look tired," she said.

"We didn't do a lot of rowing today with the wind blowing south, but it's still a long day," he said, slowly pulling her down on the bench. "There's enough room for both of us here. I'll stay the night and go back in the morning," he said.

Their coupling wasn't as rushed but still rough. She was embarrassed doing it, the lone woman on a ship full of strange men. He was slowing down and not so noisy as they whispered to each other. Fiona didn't want the crew to hear the sounds of their mating. She fell into a deep sleep, snuggled into the warmth of Gunnar's body and the protection of his arm around her in their cramped quarters. That didn't change the ambivalence she felt about him.

Fiona awoke several times during the night, hearing the wind pick up and the waves slamming hard on the shore. She dozed until daybreak when she heard Thorkell and the crew come alive on deck. Gunnar kissed her then slipped over the side to get back to the longship.

The sky was overcast and the wind blowing fitfully. Out to sea the waves had white caps. She counted the days by the number of skeins she spun . . . one . . . two . . . three, or ein, tveir, prir.

Few ships were on the horizon but Thorkell was watching one in particular, a single longship barely visible yet always there. Several times he signalled to Finn, pointing in the direction of the potential threat. Once, the two ships pulled close together, shouting distance apart, and discussed strategy. She didn't understand any of it, only picking up their concerns from their expressions, and gestures.

As evening closed in, they chose a small cove to spend the night. Fiona could see why they'd selected it. The cliffs around the bay were vertical with no easy access up or down. There was a rocky shoal allowing only one ship at a time to enter and there was enough depth for the knarr to anchor within the shallower water. No fires were lit. She saw the knarr crew now arming themselves with spears and axes; a few, like Thorkell had their swords. They looked grim.

There was a very obvious difference between the two crews. The longship crew were younger and more aggressive—the warriors, the raiders, the protectors. The knarr crew were older—sailors and traders still capable and warlike to look at but not so aggressive. Many bore the scars of old wounds.

Gunnar climbed on board and sat with her while they ate their beef.

"Are they pirates? Will they attack us during the night?" Fiona asked.

"Not likely until dawn but we can't risk it. Likely Norsemen. They've raided both sides of this coast for years. Some of them live in Ireland; others in Scotland. They are after our cargo. They'll kill us and take the knarr if they can," he said, giving her a hug, then returned to the beach.

Fiona could see the excitement building in him. He was so eager for battle! He wanted to fight. It made her blood run cold and her pulse quicken. Here she was watching as he disappeared along the headland where the Norse would land. *What am I supposed to do? Just sit there and wait? There will be no sleep for any of us tonight.*

Fiona went into the shed and opened her chest, looking at Carraig's sword. It was a good thing he'd recognized it in his stash and not sold it. She held it in her hands, feeling the weight of it. It wasn't too heavy but she didn't know how to use it, so she put it back.

She sorted through her herbs and bandages. If they survived, there would be wounded. That she could help with. Fiona unsheathed her knife. The edge was razor sharp, allowing her to defend herself if she had to. *How will I differentiate between our crew and pirates in the dark? They'd all look the same.*

Lying on the bench, Fiona listened to the night, the wind, and the waves. She wondered why she could see the auras of darkness or light around people but it just happened. It didn't come if she asked for it. She needed to know who to trust. Thorkell seemed a trustworthy man; his aura was bright. There were even traces of light around Gunnar at times. She wished Aoife had taught her those things. Later, she dozed off but was awakened by the call of an owl.

CHAPTER 16

Pirates

Gunnar left Fiona in Thorkell's care, climbed down the rope ladder, and waded ashore. The seamen in the knarr crew came down as well, to support the longship crew; the traders stayed on board to defend the cargo. The ladder was pulled up behind them. Ivar and Harald were heading for the promontory marking the entrance to the bay where the shoal was visible at low tide. He decided to go with them. The best way to protect the knarr was to stop the pirates from entering the bay.

The encroaching darkness made it hard to see, but Gunnar heard a splash and a curse as Ivar slipped on the wet rocks, so he followed the sound. There was little cover, except for huge, fallen boulders at the base of the cliff. He found the pair crouched there, ready to spend the night on watch. The clouds obscured the moon and stars. It was difficult to even see their own ships. Gunnar pulled his bearskin cape around him, settling down in the sand. The rest of the crews were scattered on the beach.

He nodded off to sleep from time to time but it was a long night. He thought of Fiona. Thorkell had managed to extract the jewel box from her sea chest before she'd gotten on board. Gunnar had no idea where it was hidden. He had to protect his wife at all costs and prove himself a warrior.

Near morning, before the soft light of the sun even broke the horizon, Gunnar heard a muffled splash. The three men were instantly alert. There was another small noise and muted voices quickly hushed. Harald puckered his lips and sent out the hoot of a lonely owl, their warning to the crew.

A dark prow emerged from the low-lying mist, grinding onto the shoal and ghostly forms, deceptively large in the fog, armed with swords and axes, climbed onto the rocks.

"Wait," whispered Ivar. "Let them come ashore. They don't know we're here."

Gunnar and Harald nodded, willing to follow the more experienced warrior. They hunched behind the boulders, swords ready. When all the raiders had disembarked, the pirate leader took stock of the "sleeping"' men on the beach, raised his sword, then let out a bellow, echoed by the mob behind him and charged the beach. The men who had been feigning sleep promptly jumped to their feet and met the attackers in the shallows.

"Now!" Ivar shouted and the trio broke into a run, leapt over the rocks into the water, attacking from the side. Gunnar faced a stranger and saw the glimmer of metal as a sword arced downwards. He swung his shield up to divert the blow, slashing with his right. Grunting and shoving, they pushed each other apart, jostled by the fighting pairs on either side. Gunnar and his adversary exchanging blows, equally matched and equally determined. Seeing a body directly behind the man, Gunnar lunged forward again with renewed vigour, bellowing like a bull. The man took a step backward and toppled over the corpse. Gunnar hit him with his shield and gutted him. He finished with a downward slice to the man's exposed throat. The sword fell into the sea from lifeless hands.

Gunnar glanced around, catching sight of Ivar cutting his way through the fighters, mowing them down like wheat. He surged into the fray, slicing left and right until it became a blur of screaming faces and flashing blades. The curses, grunts, and shouts were deafening. All he had was a fraction of a moment to identify his opponent. *Friend or foe?* A moment too soon and he'd have killed one of his own; a second too late and he'd be dead. On it went.

Just as the first rays of the sun pierced the horizon, the battle was over. An overwhelming silence came over the bay. Gunnar stood there, legs braced and chest heaving, soaked with sweat, seawater and blood. Slowly he lowered his sword and glanced around, his energy was ebbing, but the exhilaration remained, flooding him with a sense of power and accomplishment. Examining himself, he found the blood splatter all over him was not his.

The shallows were full of floating bodies. Out on the shoal, Ivar and Harald were clambering toward the pirates' longship. Gunnar waded over to join them. They guided the ship in beside their own on the beach.

A cheer went up from the knarr; the rope ladder was tossed over the side and the ones on board swarmed over the rail to join the victors, slapping each other on the back. Two of the pirates had survived but were quickly beheaded. Gunnar joined the throng stripping the bodies of their clothing, weapons, and armour. He knew for sure he'd killed three but after that he'd lost count. The water in the bay was red, a crimson tide.

He waded out near the rocks to find his first victim, stripped the man of his clothes, knife, and pendant. He tied the belt and pouches around his waist. As much as they shared spoils, Gunnar had no intention of missing a good opportunity. He dragged the body over to the pirates' vessel to be put on board.

They separated their dead from the raiders, placing their own on the beach. Three of the longship crew had died and five of the knarr's. Eight bodies. Many more were injured. There on the beach, they buried each of them with their weapons, then sang prayers of honour to Odin and chanted for the journey of the dead to Valhalla. They stripped the twenty-eight pirate corpses naked.

The men had a quick discussion on whether to salvage the pirate ship or use it as a funeral pyre. Finn and Thorkell examined the vessel, finding it old and in dire need of repair.

"Finn, we don't have enough crew to man her, even though we might get some silver for her in the next port. Better we send these fighters to the gods," Thorkell said.

Quickly, all hands emptied the pirate longship of its sea chests, barrels of beef, and spare oars. Gunnar helped drag bodies to the boat where Thorkell, Ivar and Harald hauled them on board and stacked them in a heap. All of them pitched in to push the ship off the beach into deeper water. Thorkell and others stayed on board and set fires to piles of rags, stuffed under oars, then quickly lowered the sail, before jumping overboard to the safety of the water. Flickers of orange-red consumed the rags, and wisps of smoke grew. The sixty-foot longship bobbed into the waves, picking up speed as the current moved her out to sea.

From the shore, the crews watched as the wind sent curls of smoke into the air, the fire fed by the morbid cargo. Gradually, the flames ate away at her oiled planking, gaining ferocity with tar-coated caulking and tallowed sail. The sail caught fire, becoming a flaming banner that sent fiery shreds into the wind. Slowly, the ship settled deeper into the waves, then slid out of sight, leaving a vista of unbroken waves.

All the warriors rummaged through the sea chests. Every chest contained clothing, chain mail, spare swords, helmets, and pouches with silver coins. It was a rich haul and the longship crew got the bulk of it, since they were not paid like the knarr crew were.

Looking at the beach, Gunnar was surprised to see Fiona kneeling beside one of the wounded, holding a wad of blood-soaked cloth to the man's chest and belly. The seaman was dying, his skin pale, grey and damp, his eyes closed and breath shallow. She sang a mournful lament, her voice sweet and clear. Shouts dwindled to silence as every man stood quietly and listened. Even if they didn't understand her language, they understood the sentiment. The man died shortly after.

He watched as Fiona moved along the line of wounded, washing cuts and abrasions, applying herbs, ointments, and bandages. Some had lost ears, teeth, or fingers. Gunnar was amazed to see Ivar sit down on the sand, quietly offering his massive left arm to the diminutive girl; it was nearly as big as her waist. She gently cleansed the deep gash with moss, applied one of her ointments, then bandaged it firmly. Gunnar heard her say "two days" in Danish, pointing to the bandage. He smiled. *She was making the effort.*

Thorkell gathered everyone around. "The gods were with us. We need to move out of here. There isn't much wind this morning so we'll be rowing. Wicklow's the nearest port to pick up more crew. We've lost nine men altogether and seventeen are wounded. I don't know if the pirates were alone. If there's more of them, we're not in a good position to fight."

Finn stood up. "If we leave now, there's nothing but narrow beaches from here to Wicklow. The headlands are low. We'll be easy to spot, but so will they. Another thing: we're trapped in this bay. Wide open might be better. Can we hold off another attack? What say you?"

There was much discussion. It was put to the vote with a resounding "Ja" for Wicklow.

"Divvy up the chores as best you can. We'll take the worst of the wounded on the knarr," Thorkell said, directly a couple of knarr seamen to the longship.

Gunnar approached Fiona when she finished giving care. "Are you alright?" he asked, staring at her blood smeared hands.

"I am. That was savage—so many dead, so many hurt," she said numbed by the carnage around her.

"Wicklow's the next port, a day's sail from here. We'll be leaving shortly."

"I'm glad I could help a little. I couldn't stop that man from dying but I prayed for him. Does Wicklow have a market? I need more herbs and ointments."

"Ja, there is one."

"Can you find some old shirts for me? I need to make a lot more bandages," she said. He nodded. *That battle was not likely going to be the last.*

Looking up at him, Fiona said, "There's so much I don't know. That man's fingers are broken. I straightened them as best I could, but I've never done it before. I only saw my mother do it once. I've made a poultice of comfrey, which hardens as it dries to hold the bones in place. Could you explain to him to leave the poultice on? Broken bones take a long time to heal, at least a month," she said, with a frown on her face. "I don't know the words."

He went with her and translated as she spoke. She gently took the sailor's hand and showed Gunnar what she'd done. The man's fingers were swollen and bruised and he grimaced with the touch. "His fingers are warm. That's a good sign." She'd bandaged a piece of driftwood under his palm and wrist to hold everything in place.

"Thorkell can tell you more about Wicklow. I've brought another chest. You could use it for your medicines. You've used up a lot of the ointments already," he said helping her back up the ladder.

Everyone ate their beef and were very quiet. Gunnar scavenged four shirts that were torn but suitable for bandages. She thanked him and started slitting them with her knife into four-inch-wide strips.

The sun was high in the sky when they left the bay. Gunnar looked at his crew. They were seriously short of men on both ships. With Thorkell's top priority being the cargo, Finn spaced the crew apart to keep the ship balanced, but the gaps were very apparent.

CHAPTER 17

Wicklow, Irish east coast

After Gunnar went back to the longship, Fiona finished cutting up the shirts. She had plenty of bandages and slings now, although she was short of wooden splints. *I have no inkling of what might lie ahead. So many to look after.* It saddened her that she couldn't help the one who'd died, but with the massive injury to his gut, there was no way to stop the bleeding.

The crew were very quiet. Some of the more severely wounded were lying or sitting on the deck. A few more came over to Fiona for care of minor wounds. Slowly she began recognizing faces. These men were as old as her brothers. That thought took her back to the raid. The village was still a vivid memory. Today, her mother would have been proud of her for managing alone.

Fiona watched as Thorkell paced the deck, his eyes on the horizon. The helmsman was watching the coast.

The vista was changing to lightly rolling hills dense with forest, much lower cliffs and narrow open beaches that went for miles. Tiny villages were visible from time to time with two-man fishing boats, their nets and lines out. As soon as the longship came into view, they hauled in their nets and quickly headed ashore.

The sail was fully unfurled but the wind was intermittent. Periodically, the oars were used. The men were tired but everyone was edgy.

"Thorkell, the last time you were in Wicklow, was anyone selling herbs?" she asked.

"Yes, I've seen several stalls with people selling herbs," he said, his eyes never leaving the horizon.

She could see he was preoccupied and didn't ask any more questions.

That evening they camped on the beach but lit no fires. Fiona combed the shore for driftwood, finding several smooth useful pieces showing the wavy grain of the wood. Back among the trees, she found moss growing over the rocks around a trickling fresh-water stream. She hitched up her skirt and filled it with the short dark green plants.

Fiona noticed vines growing up the trunks of the birch, ash and alder. Aoifa's words came crystal clear, reminding her that each tree was a symbol. Vines represented trusting her intuition and instincts to guide her on a healer's path. The birch meant new beginnings,

SUSAN K. KEHOE

the alder was about making choices, while the ash was being locked into a chain of events. *All of those are true right now.*

Gunnar stood at the edge of the trees, watching the area intently, his hand on his sword. Men were filling small kegs with water from the stream to top up the big barrels on deck. Under his watchful eyes, Fiona washed the moss in the running water and carried it back to the knarr, laying it out to dry on the crates on the bench shelves.

A distant sail on the horizon had everyone watching until it moved out of sight. She sat on the deck with Gunnar and they ate their meal together. Having watched him during the battle, she'd found his strength and savagery frightening. He became a different person when he was fighting. Darkness surrounded him. Now Gunnar just looked tired. That night they went to bed early, they coupled briefly then slept. Fiona was getting used to it.

By the next afternoon, the town of Wicklow appeared on the starboard bow. The weather held. Fiona spent most of her time spinning or checking the wounded. She changed the dressing for the man who'd lost an ear. The wound looked awful, but it was clean and starting to scab over. A gentle wipe with fresh moss removed the clotted blood from his hair and she applied meadowsweet ointment, followed by a bandage around his head. He thanked her in Gaelic. *The men are so tough.* Thorkell paced the deck all day, constantly monitoring the horizon, expecting trouble.

Wicklow sat in a verdant flat plain with a small harbour protected by a rectangle of stone piers, allowing only one narrow channel for a ship to enter. Inland, there were distant hills and rugged terrain. The longship entered first then the knarr. Fiona counted five other vessels in the harbour as well as smaller fishing boats. None of them were shaped like Viking ships. She could see the stalls of the market place within the palisade.

Thorkell disembarked immediately and after speaking with the soldiers at the gate, went inside. He returned shortly with a group of men who gathered around the ships. Potential buyers came down to the beach to look at the armour and swords the crew had taken from the Norse raiders. There was a lot of interest and bargaining was lively.

After Gunnar had sold some armour, he asked a citizen about the herb dealer, then came to fetch Fiona. Together, they walked through the gates. The people spoke Gaelic, so Fiona got directions to the booth down the narrow and winding pathways. The vendor was a wizened, toothless old woman sitting on a dilapidated chair, assisted by two younger girls. Her booth was full of hanging bundles of dried and fresh plants, as well as jars of creams and ointments.

Fiona took bunches of meadowsweet, comfrey, yarrow, and nettle from the girls and even found some willow bark. *That's always been a good pain killer.*

"Gunnar, I need some money," Fiona said, knowing she only had a quarter piece of the hack silver.

He nodded, reaching into his pouch.

"Do you have any beeswax?" she asked and was shown a brick-sized piece, which she could make her own ointments. "How much for everything?"

"One dirham," the crone said. Then the bargaining started.

Fiona looked at her, emulating Erin's stance, then re-examined the herbs. From her pouch, she extracted the quarter piece and put it on the table.

The woman got to her feet, threw up her hands in despair, and started a rant that put Onkel Bersi's performance to shame. "Three quarters is the best I can do."

Fiona stood there politely listening, then shook her head. "I'm the best customer you're going to have all day. Make it half," she said, hands on her hips.

After much muttering, the woman looked at her, then at Gunnar who was looming and scowling behind her, wild haired and blood-stained. "Well then, half it is," she spluttered, tottering back to her chair.

Gunnar took out the other quarter and placed it on the table. The wide-eyed girls put the wax and the armload of greenery into a burlap bag, handing it to

Fiona. She thanked them in Gaelic and turned to walk beside him, back to the ship. For a moment, she could see Gunnar was barely containing his amusement, quite aware of the impact he was having on the vendor.

He gave her another silver quarter piece for her pouch. "Happy now?" he asked.

"Oh yes. Those herbs are good quality and have been properly dried. I think I got them for a good price because you were there and they were afraid of you. Her prices were about the same as the seller in Dublin. I don't think it will take me long to get used to bargaining."

"Well, let's see if I can sell some more armour and swords," he said with a grin as they returned to the ship.

CHAPTER 18

*Present-day archaeological
dig site, Hedeby*

The professor had spent the entire morning at the university, justifying his expenses to the chancellor. *Bureaucrats! Royal pain in the butt and a waste of my time.* He hurried back to the site, getting soaked by a sudden rain shower, which didn't improve his temper much.

The only good thing that had happened was a report on the sword. "Hey guys, listen to this. From the photos of the pieces we had and the odd curved shape, it's saying that it was likely deliberately damaged, possibly by heating. I've heard of that custom before. Don't know if I can recall the author of the paper, but it has been hypothesized that it was "killed" to prevent it from being stolen after the burial. I suppose that's a possibility. I certainly haven't seen another sword treated that way."

He stepped inside the shed, where the team were working on their projects. It was proving very difficult to get them to all work together. Helga's desire to work alone and her sharp tongue often annoyed the others. He didn't have time to referee so he divided the work accordingly. Their individual work was excellent.

Miles and Gena had found more shards of blue glass. "We've found a researcher who would be willing to do a computer reconstruction of the pieces from a photo. I thought you might be interested," Miles said, looking at the broken four-inch-tall bottle. Jon had already sent one small piece to the lab for chemical analysis of the glass.

"What would that cost?" Jon asked

"Here's his name and email address Probably better if you contact him about that," Miles replied. "Do you think it's Venetian?"

"It could be. The quality of the glass is excellent and the time periods fits. Once we have it analyzed, we'll know the percentages of silica sand, calcium oxide, potash, borax, and maybe a lead component, too."

"So that's how they identify the point of origin." Miles said. "Interesting. Very specific—comparing the glass to the soils in a certain area."

"It makes you wonder how a piece of glass this fragile could survive all the trade routes it would have taken to get here intact," Gena marvelled.

"Yeah, there would be shipments by Italians across the Mediterranean to one of the Muslim caliphates, either in Africa or Iberia, then possibly here but more likely to Dublin, then here," Lars added. "Incredible when you think of a crate of this stuff being loaded and unloaded from ship to ship in the Atlantic and bad weather for weeks on end."

"I didn't know you were into that sort of history," Helga said.

"Well, I'm full of surprises," Lars said sarcastically and moved back to screen more soil.

Jon was in the mood for getting grubby and climbed down into the trench, trowel in hand. It was the best cure for bureaucrats and argumentative young people that he could think of. *Personally, I don't care what they think of each other. I just want to get this project done and done well. I want to get home at a decent hour tonight. Elsa will be mad if I miss our anniversary. At the very least, I should take her out for dinner.*

CHAPTER 19

The calm before the storm

Gunnar hauled his sea chest over to the landing where other crew members were set up, then displayed the armour he wanted to sell. The locals as well as men from the other ships gathered around and the bartering began.

Watching the activity in the harbour, he could see Thorkell hiring several seamen. Four of the severely wounded had been removed from the ship and were sitting against the palisade, joining other one-legged or maimed unfortunates who were begging. Included in that group with the man with the broken hand. If the injured couldn't work they were left behind to fend for themselves.

Gunnar noticed Fiona on the beach. She'd built a small fire and was stirring something in her new cooking pot. It wasn't mealtime so it had to be something herbal.

He was pleased with her. She was trying to speak Danish, far more than he was learning Gaelic. The crew were helping her, too. She adapted quickly and was continuing to care for the injured. *They'd better not get too friendly with her or they'll have me to deal with.*

Clouds were coming in from the north and it looked like rain. They would only be in port that night so it was imperative to sell their goods and hire more men. The next leg of the journey was difficult, following the southbound current of the Celtic Sea as the Irish coast curved westward, yet the current was pushed eastward by the greater forces of the open Atlantic waters.

Last year, there'd been no landfall for three days until finally the ship had been driven by wind and waves into the narrowing channel separating Britain from mainland Normandy and Brittany. We gave up trying to go ashore on those wild British shores along the Devon and Cornish coasts. The massive chalk cliffs and fierce warrior tribes prevented any landing or raiding. We'll be lucky to replenish the water supply without a challenge, he mused.

By the end of the day, Gunnar sold two swords, a set of chain mail, and three shirts that were too small for him. That night he intended to count his silver and hide it in Fiona's sea chest. *I've done well, but I still don't trust Harald. He has ample opportunity to steal if I'm not on board.* Getting back to the longship, he removed the coin pouches from the chest, tucking them in his belt and pulling his cape over them. He noticed two new men on board. They were older fellows and were talking to Finn and Ivar.

Gunnar joined Fiona for the evening meal, noticing that Thorkell had an extra barrel of fish on the fore deck. *Good move; he's thinking ahead.* Gunnar then entered the shed to count his money and hide it. "Fiona, I'm going to stow my money here. I don't trust the men on the longship, especially Harald. Thorkell has juggled the crew around, but that still leaves us short-handed. You're doing a good job treating our men. Some of them should be able to work in a day or two," he said in Gaelic.

Going through his pouches, he counted the silver coins and was amazed to find he had more than two hundred. *That's enough to buy property and build a house!* He had booty from past voyages stored at his parents' home back in Hedeby.

"It's really important not to tell anyone about this, or your father's torque for that matter. I don't want to get robbed. If anyone asks, all you own is one piece of hack silver. Do you understand? It's our secret," he whispered, grasping her shoulders and looking at her intensely.

"So, I pretend we're just poor folk and my stingy husband won't give me anymore?" she queried with a look of total innocence, only marred by a slight twitch of her lips.

"Ja, very good," he said, chuckling quietly. "What were you doing on the beach?"

"I ground up some herbs and made an ointment using melted beeswax. The mortar and pestle worked really well, and the pot and spoons came in handy. I spent the rest of the day checking wounds on the crew. They're healing well. Ivar wouldn't let me re-bandage his arm. Why did Thorkell move the really sick ones ashore? Who will care for them?"

"If a man is too sick to work, we leave them behind," Gunnar replied.

"You mean he's leaving them here to die?" she said, her face contorted in horror.

"They have their own money, so they can buy their own help. Running these ships is a business. We can't afford to feed and look after anyone who's not pulling his fair share of the work."

He could see her seriously thinking about that. Obviously, it had never occurred to her. She frowned and stared at the deck, trying to work it out.

"Even you, his brother?"

"Probably. I'm the youngest, so I'm expendable. The only one who really counts in my family is Steinn, my oldest brother. I doubt even Thorkell would be given any special treatment if he wasn't fit. You're earning your keep by treating the men and spinning. Visitors and traders are Thorkell's responsibility and are treated differently than the hired men, but they are expected to work as well to protect their goods."

Darkness slowly descended over the harbour and the pair settled on the bench. She shyly undid Gunnar's braids and combed his hair. There were still knots and tangles with residue of dried blood from the raid. He didn't seem to care if he looked rough and smelly. Fiona got most of the mess out and left his hair unfettered, running her fingers across his broad shoulders. He turned and passed his fingers through her tresses, pulling her close to him.

He lay side by side with her, enjoying the fondling and coupling. Fiona was always aware others were listening. She surprised him sometimes. *She was tougher than she looked and was always curious, asking questions.*

CHAPTER 20

The storm

The next morning, Fiona watched Gunnar wade back to the longship. She was thankful he'd gone. His constant need to touch her, especially in view of the crew, and his crude comments were embarrassing.

The sky was leaden with ominous dark clouds racing across the sky in a bracing wind. Thorkell took one look at that and broke routine. Cook didn't bother with a fire and was handing out stale bread while opening up the meat and water barrels. Thorkell motioned her over.

"Fiona, take your meal now. We're in for rough weather. We may not be able to eat later," he said, as he started checking the ropes on crates and barrels.

She took a long drink of water, and grabbed some bread and a chunk of beef. Fiona saw the crew attaching extra ropes to the rails. Thorkell hopped down into the cargo hold, tied a long piece of rope to the upright post of the shed and secured it around her waist. "Can't have you washed away," he said as he disappeared up top.

In no time, they were out of the harbour, racing south under full sail. She could feel the turbulence in the air. The gulls had disappeared. By mid-morning the western horizon was totally obscured in black clouds, punctured with forks of lightning and peals of thunder, leaving just heaving seas. *Nothing now, just cascading water; the land has been swallowed.* The lowering clouds were dense, sheets of rain obliterating visibility. The sail was taken in.

The ship was rolling with the higher waves and deeper troughs, making it impossible for Fiona to stand upright. Cooler air forced her to slip on her cape. She moved her two sea chests onto the bench and wedged herself between them. *Would the cargo hold flood?*

The sky darkened even more until it felt like night. The rain came down in torrents. The passing hours were a nightmare. There was no light, constant motion, and noise—deafening claps of thunder, the howling of the wind like a devouring, demented beast and the creaking of the ship, as if was being torn apart and dying.

Fiona crouched on her bench as the knarr pitched and rolled, in a foaming crush of waves that swept over the deck. The screaming air sucked her breath away. She clung to the posts, apprehensive of the rising, sloshing water level in the hold.

Eventually, dark figures of the crew descended into the hold forming a bucket brigade. After what seemed like an eternity, their persistence paid off and the water level dropped at least a hand's breadth, despite the ongoing rain.

The nearby lightning zigzagged down from the blackened air mass, so close by that the hair on the back of Fiona's neck stood on end. Emerging from the shed into the pouring rain, she raised her hands to the sky and prayed hard. She sang, she begged, she pleaded to Christ and Gunnar's sea god Njord for protection. Then the crew went silent, their eyes fixated on the top of the mast which was now glowing with an intense green fire. It sparked and flared in brilliant green, lighting up the spars. Despite the pouring rain, Fiona stood, her hair plastered to her scalp, as fascinated as the crew. *What was it?* Slowly it faded and the world turned black again.

In wonderment, she went back into the shed and curled up between the sea chests, wedging her body in as much as she could. Chilled to the core, she pulled her cape around her and tucked it around her legs and feet. Sleep was impossible but occasionally Fiona eyes closed as she cowered in her cocoon.

Many hours later, the wind abated somewhat, still remaining strong and gusty. She heard shouts as the sail was lowered. While the waves were still enormous, the ship was keeping forward momentum. She wasn't prepared to untie her tether yet. *How did Thorkell know where to go?* There was no sun or land, just waves and wind.

Thunder was distant now and the cloud cover lifted slightly. Finally, she uncurled her stiff body and stood up, grasping the post to take a look outside. A small sail had been rigged to divert rainwater into one of the barrels. *I had wondered where they got their drinking water if they didn't go ashore.*

Both Thorkell and his helmsman were manning the rudder, their feet braced, watching the horizons. They looked exhausted. The seas were still massive and grey, grey, grey. *No sign of the longship.*

The crew spent some time bailing out the cargo hold again, their exhaustion showing, too. By late afternoon, the wind subsided enough that once again they were under full sail. As the sea became calmer, Thorkell opened up the barrels. Fiona untied the rope around her waist and waited her turn. She was more thirsty than hungry but took the bread anyway. *Who knew when they'd find land?*

Fiona approached Thorkell after he'd eaten his meal. "What was that green light on the mast?" she asked.

He stared at her for a few moments, a deep furrow on his brow, looking very tired and much older. "That green fire is a sign from the gods. Your prayers were answered. They listened to you and we survived. I've heard of it before but never seen it so close. There's no sign of the longship. Hopefully, we'll catch up with them in Bruges."

Fiona understood the implications and went back to the shed. He was worried. The longship was under-manned. *What if it had sunk? What if Gunnar was gone?* Part of her would be glad but it would leave her unpro-tected in strange territory. She sat quietly on her bench and prayed to her God and his pagan ones that all had survived. Again, she thought of Aoife and wished her mother was beside her. A warm sensation coursed around her when she thought of her. Concentrating hard, she failed to get a sense or feeling that Gunnar had survived. Nothing came of that, either.

Sleep did not come easily that night but finally exhaustion overcame the "what ifs" and she closed her eyes, dreaming of running, hiding and being pursued by something huge, dark and nameless.

Fiona awoke to low clouds with shafts of gold radiating outward as the sun breached the eastern horizon. The storm had washed the air clean. Quickly, she climbed to the main deck. There was land to the south extending as far as she could see. Several ships were visible—one had a broken mast—but no longship.

The sail above her was full and they were moving at speed, the troughs nearly back to normal, making walking easier. She looked at the haggard faces of the men. There was no cheerful banter that morning. They eyed her warily.

By midday, they spotted wreckage floating on the waves—barrels, pieces of planking, tangles of sails, and wooden spars. Thorkell passed close, carefully examining the debris, but shook his head. She sighed. *Not the longship then.*

Land was now visible on both sides of the channel with stony beaches and cliffs on the British side. One ship had run aground on a rocky shoal with tiny figures salvaging what they could. She hopefully stared at the prow but no dragon.

That evening at meal time, she sat beside Thorkell again. "What will happen to me if Gunnar doesn't come back?"

He looked down at her, his lips pursed. After a long pause, he sighed and put his hand on her shoulder. "You are my brother's wife. By our laws, you are entitled to all his possessions including what my parents have stored. You would not be considered a thrall. I would take you to Hedeby and try to get you settled with the healer, as Gunnar would have done. Don't give up yet. Finn and Ivar are excellent navigators. That ship is very seaworthy. They may have run into a problem, but we'll find out in Bruges.

"Tusind tak" she said, feeling very small and very lonely. After eating her meat and bread, she made rounds of the wounded. The man who'd lost an ear didn't really need to be bandaged anymore; she just applied ointment. Fiona bandaged it anyway, the padding protecting the tender newly scabbed skin. His face would be scarred forever. It was ugly but it was healing well and he could still hear. His hair would grow back. *He'll probably consider it a badge of honour.*

The rest of the evening was spent spinning and listening to the men talk. Some words were becoming familiar like the numbers and directions—*nord, syd, ost*, and *vest*. It was vital for her to learn their language quickly. She didn't know how his family would react to her. She'd have to clean herself up, change her dress and wear her cap. When the men were at sea, they didn't change their clothes or bathe. *They stunk.*

Since the episode with the green fire, the crew including Thorkell treated her differently. It was subtle and hard to put a finger on what it was. They seemed to think she'd caused it but that was impossible. Only the gods controlled the weather. All she'd done was ask the gods to spare the crew and they had.

Boat traffic was busy between Britain and the south shore; other ships were following the coastal currents both north and south, fully loaded for distant destinations. There were several longships but no sign of their dragon.

The next day brought weak sunshine. The ship was steering closer to the southern shoreline dotted with sandy deltas and rivers, low-lying villages, and woods. The port of Bruges appeared around midday. The harbour was full of ships, arriving, departing or docked. The ships were all shapes and sizes—Viking ships, three masters, two masters, whalers, large and small fishing boats. Many had storm damage. Sailors were up the rigging, replacing broken spars, and untangling the lines. Torn sails were being replaced. The nearby sand bars had piles of wreckage including bodies. There were not only screeching seabirds but the poor, eagerly scavenging through the litter. She looked in vain for the longship.

Some of the sailors went ashore, including Thorkell. She watched him speak to an official and pay him money. The two men spoke at length. Thorkell then went along the waterfront talking to other captains, then she lost sight of him.

Fiona removed her cape and folded it on her bench. Once again, she took up her spindle. It was a mindless activity that kept her hands busy, but nothing could stop her from thinking about Gunnar and the longship. Three weeks had seen her abducted from her village, almost sold then married. Now she was probably widowed. Her life had changed so dramatically and so quickly, it was overwhelming. She was working hard at fitting in with the people. She had her spinning and weaving skills as well as her herbal knowledge. She also had Thorkell's support, at least as far as Hedeby. *Beyond that, uncertainty.*

CHAPTER 21

The longship

Gunnar and the crew had been rowing for hours. They had survived the storm but the sail had torn along a seam, rendering it useless. The rowing was constant, mindless, and exhausting. No one spoke.

Cargo ships under full sail passed them. There was no sign of the knarr. It could have sunk or it could be waiting in the Bruges harbour. The mere thought of losing all that silver was a torment. Fiona would be a loss, too. If they'd survived, Thorkell would take care of her. The longship would have to catch up. Norse piracy was very high between Bruges and Hedeby. The Norsemen sometimes had huge convoys with hundreds of ships, manned by thousands of warriors, heading for Normandy. They pillaged ships and towns along the way.

As the storm abated, they collected rainwater to fill the barrels. The coastal villages were too well fortified to go ashore. Nightfall didn't provide much relief, either. They stopped rowing to grab a few hours' sleep, lying in the spaces between the sea chests, but the rudder still had to be manned by either Finn or Ivar and everyone else shared night watch. Gunnar looked at every item of wreckage they came upon. Nothing could be identified as the knarr's. The wind was still too strong to drop the sail and make repairs at sea.

Morning saw them in more familiar territory. "I recognize these beaches," Finn said as they passed shoals on the Brittany coast.

At least they were getting closer. With their shallow draft, they could safely steer closer to the shoreline out of the paths of other ships. The current was favourable and strong, pushing them east north east.

It wasn't until the fifth day they saw Bruges. Gunnar felt the tension ease just pulling into the harbour. As Finn beached her, Gunnar looked at every ship in the harbour, but no sign of the knarr. Anguish wrenched at him. *Either she'd sunk or they'd left already. I might have lost everything.*

Finn immediately hopped over the rail and headed for the harbour master, with Gunnar right behind him. The stocky, pompous official in his flamboyant shirt and jacket remembered Thorkell but stated that the knarr had left the previous morning with two other north-bound ships. Finn paid the man and went into town.

Gunnar returned to the ship and spread the news. The crew were already lowering and removing the huge sail. Ivar was showing Harald and several others how to repair the fifteen-foot tear. Having been taught that skill by Ottar years ago, Gunnar promptly joined them. Four of them used awls and the hemp thread Ivar had found in the repair chest, buried under axes, knives, hammers, saws, and rivets.

Slowly he inserted the awl, pulling the thread tight, made a stitch then took the thread over the tear, securing it on the opposite side. By looping the awl under the completed stitch and pulling the thread tight again, it formed a herringbone pattern, binding the two sides together with the smooth, clean face of the seam facing forward. When they were finished hours later, others sewed a supporting piece of canvas over the mend, reinforcing the fabric. Finally, they waterproofed the new patch with fish oil and rehung the sail.

In the meantime, Finn had restocked the meat supply, bringing in bags of fresh bread and as well as picking up two more sailors wanting to return to Hedeby. Gunnar was thankful to eat a proper meal. Having the extra manpower would certainly make rowing easier. Every part of his body ached. He had no problem falling asleep that night.

The following morning, they were the first ship out of the harbour and steered close to the shore to take advantage of the coastal current. Gunnar looked up at the billowing sail that was holding the wind. *The repair's working.* Sails lasted as long as fifty years if they were looked after properly.

The grey sea had flattened considerably, the longship carving through the waves like a knife, leaving a foaming wake behind them—no ship was faster. Many cargo ships veered out of their way, the mariners arming themselves, preparing for an attack that never came. The dragon ignored them, surging northward.

It was early afternoon two days later when Finn yelled and pointed to the horizon. There were three sails. It took them several hours to catch up. Gunnar could see the ships starting to take evasive action. Finn shouted orders to adjust the sail as the longship edged within hailing distance of the knarr. Finn shouted to Thorkell. There was a moment of recognition, then cheers and shouts from both crews.

Finn steered the longship in front of the others and once again took the lead. Gunnar couldn't believe the relief he felt. *The silver's safe.* As the sun dipped below the horizon, the sails were furled and the four ships settled into night routine. He briefly glimpsed Fiona standing beside Thorkell and waved to them. They returned the gesture.

He slept better that night but was awakened for his turn at watch. There were no further distractions. At daybreak, after a quick breakfast, the crew took their positions and dropped the sail; the convoy followed. The weather was fair with moderate cloud and wind. No sign of Norsemen. Just one more day and they'd be home.

The rest of the voyage was uneventful. Gunnar was now in Danish territory. He knew every cove and bay on this stretch of coast. Gulls were following them as they got closer to landfall. It felt good. They'd been away three months. Once ashore, they'd unload all the cargo, haul it into Hedeby, and in a couple of weeks' time, start another run to Ireland and do it all again.

CHAPTER 22

Landfall

Fiona had been in the shed spinning when all the crew began pointing to the south. Thorkell shouted orders and the crew vaulting down to grab their weapons and armour. His eyes were on their pursuer. She didn't understand one word of what they were saying but it had to be bad.

Fiona huddled where she was and watched. The men were at the rail staring into the direction they'd come. Then they began shouting, stamping their feet and pounding their shields with their swords and axes. Sailors and traders became warriors—fearsome and deadly. She caught a glimpse of Thorkell, looking more like Gunnar—the helmet, his sword cutting the air, bellowing like a maniac. *Norsemen?* She could hear similar challenges from their two companion ships.

Suddenly, it became quiet. Thorkell was at the rail, staring at the intruder. There was a pause and he lowered his sword, shouting something to the helmsman. The knarr began to slow as crew lowered their weapons and began hauling in the sail. A cheer erupted from the crew as the approaching ship came closer. Her heart skipped a beat. *Was it their dragon?*

Fiona heard Thorkell yelling at someone. The distant reply sounded like Finn. The crew piled their weapons back into the hold and went back on deck. She sprinted topside and paused for one heart-stopping moment to see but almost afraid to look. Out there in front of them, leading the way was the dragon, their dragon. She stood beside Thorkell and waved. An oarsman on the longship waved back at her. *Gunnar!*

Tears trickled down her cheeks as the heavy curtain of uncertainty lifted. *Gunnar was safe.* Her ambivalence about her husband lifted for a moment. The immediate future was more secure. Thorkell looked at her and nodded. For the first time since Bruges, Fiona saw a smile on his face and the etched frown lines disappeared. Never before had she realized how the knarr depended on the longship. Fiona lay on her bench that night, and realized how much she had to rely on Gunnar to keep her safe, at least for the time being, despite the raid and the killings. Without him, going into a foreign country she didn't know, where customs and language were different would have been impossible. *I need him, whether I like it or not.*

The next day, Fiona could see a small port ahead. All four ships were heading into the estuary. There wasn't much of a village, just a few buildings: fish huts, a smithy, and the inn. Once on shore, Thorkell sent a rider inland. She watched as horse and young rider moved off at a fast trot down the log road that wound its way through swamp.

As word got out, horses and carts began arriving. The knarrs began unloading cargo. It was chaotic. Gunnar immediately left the longship, vigorously scaling the ladder. The two brothers met with massive hugs and joyous greetings. Gunnar brought their attention to the patched sail. They spoke quickly, then he turned to her, crushing her to his chest. To her embarrassment and the amusement of the crew, he kissed her, deeply and sensuously. Fiona blushed, which amused them even more.

"Is this Hedeby?" she asked.

"Oh no. Hedeby is eight miles inland across the swamp. Thorkell has sent a rider to Ottar and Steinn. They'll send wagons to collect our goods."

They spent the evening sitting on the main deck, sharing their stories of weathering the storm. Ivar sat with them, regaling them with stories of his travels and battles. He was waiting for a ship to take him home to Norway.

"Ivar, if you ever want to come back here, I'd be more than happy to hire you for the longship. Experienced crew are always welcome," said Thor. "If you want, you can sleep on the knarr while you're waiting. Both ships will be overhauled while we're in Hedeby. We'll be leaving again in about two weeks."

Fiona looked at the big man. The wound on his left arm had healed beautifully and was now a tight grey line through his tattoos.

"How long will it take us to reach Hedeby?" she asked.

"Once we get the carts loaded, a couple of hours at a good trot. It depends on the swamp and the depth of the water. The road is made of logs. The horses can't go too fast if it's wet and slippery. Sometimes we move longships on rollers to cross the swamp to the Baltic Sea where Hedeby lies. It's hard work but it saves weeks of sailing time through all those pirate-ridden islands north of here," he said.

Fiona couldn't even imagine it. Push a ship overland? *Have I misunderstood?*

Gunnar went back to the longship one last time to retrieve his sea chest. With it stashed under the shed bench, he was more than ready to fulfill his husbandly duties. Fiona was surprised to find that somehow it was not quite as unpleasant. At least she knew what to expect. *Tante Frida had been right; perhaps they were getting used to each other.*

CHAPTER 23

*Present-day archaeological
dig site, Hedeby*

The top layer of soil above the skeleton had been removed and sieved. Now the skull and chest were visible right down to the bearskin cloak. Trenches had been dug all around it for easier access. The emerging bones told a story.

The man was about five foot ten. Lars was brushing dirt from the skull. The rounded cranium was robust and appeared intact under the rusted fragments of helmet. Strips of iron radiated from a central point on the top of the head, curving down to a broad head band. The iron between the strips had rotted into rusty flakes. A metal visor with two eye slits tapered down to cover the nose. *The nasal cavities are long and narrow, indicating European stock,* Jon thought.

Under Jon's direction, Gena had already sent a lock of the long, fair hair to the lab for DNA sequencing and stable isotope analysis. The exposed jaw bone was broad with most teeth present, and she extracted one molar for diet analysis.

Earlier that morning, he'd found a few fine gold links, possibly from a pendant. All signs pointed to a well-preserved young male. They had a table full of bagged specimens awaiting the conservators.

The humerus was thick and sturdy. Helga had very gently removed, bagged and labelled the upper arm bone as well one from the right hand to add to the pile.

Jon measured the length of the humerus using the accepted ratio formula to estimate the warrior's height. It matched what they were physically finding at five foot ten.

Helga had finished removing the remnants of the sword, which had lain across the lower radius and ulna arm bones. She had already exposed the right hip and head of the femur but hadn't yet exposed the complete hip joint.

Once Miles had finished making notes, mapping, measuring, and taking photos, he continued to work on the lower right leg and foot. There were traces of leather shoes, several partial stitched layers where the soles had been. Some of the toe bones—the distal and middle phalanges—were missing, but most of the metatarsal

SUSAN K. KEHOE

bones were intact. Despite the pressure of the peaty soil and time, the general shape of the arch was still present. They were pleased to see that the joint where the talus ankle bone met the tibia and fibula leg bones was intact, too.

Much had happened at the site. The professor was delighted with the progress. In sheer desperation, considering the scope of the find, he had gone to the university for help. Now they were involved, life was more complicated with constant university inspections and paperwork as well as ministry ones, but they had financed a wooden shed with a metal roof and lighting as well as a generator to power it. The team often worked in shifts, deciding between them, who would work with whom. *That solved a lot of problems.* Security around the site had been beefed up as well. He noticed Lars and Gena were getting close and personal. *I hope that won't affect their work.*

So far, they had found small metallic chain mail on the shoulder and chest, typical of early armour. Beneath them were remnants of a linen shirt. Above the armour was a scrap of gossamer fine material in a pale blue. The chest had collapsed long ago as the body had decomposed but revealed more of the gold links and a T-shaped lump of metal. A pendant? *It looks like an ancient Thor's hammer.*

"So far it looks like a healthy man who died young," Jon said. "No evidence of bone injury so far. I got the report back on the fur sample. You were right; it was a Eurasian brown bear. They've done all sorts of studies on mitochondrial DNA on those and may be able to pinpoint its place of origin, which could be anywhere from Spain to eastern Russia. Likely a trade item. The tiny piece of material you found earlier might be a piece of Chinese silk. The shiny threads could be gold. We need to give him a name. What do you think?"

"How about Thor? Miles suggested.

"How about Hedeby Man?" said Helga as she looked up, brush in hand. "The university would like that."

"I'll think about it," Jon said went back to work. Peering at the spinal vertebrae still intact in the peat, he wondered what had killed the young man. The ends of the long bones had not yet fused, indicating he was still in his teens. There were no obvious sword or axe cut marks.

"Have you heard back from any of the DNA labs yet?" Helga asked.

"No, not yet. I'm impatient to get results too, but it could be months."

"Only another three weeks and we'll be back in class. Will you shut down the dig then? The permit expires at the end of October, doesn't it?"

"I'm waiting for admin to make up their minds. I'm hoping they'll reduce my classes for the fall and let me keep working here until the end of October when the weather will shut us down. That might be wishful thinking. It's too good a find to rush, but even exposing this to air could damage what's left," he said. "Our first priority is the fabric; it's the most fragile."

Hedeby Man was taking shape on a table in a locked storage room at the university laboratory; each bone cleaned, identified and catalogued. He was going to be magnificent when they were finished—so much to learn from him. Jon really wanted to do a facial reconstruction but it would have to be out of his own pocket. Elsa was not going to be happy about that expense.

CHAPTER 24

New beginnings

Early next morning, Gunnar and Thorkell went ashore to organize moving the cargo to the wagons. Thorkell left the crates of silk, spices, and glass until last.

Gunnar came back several hours later to find Fiona looking quite proper in her clean dress, shoes, and cap, the tight, neat braid of her dark hair just visible on the nape of her neck. She'd taken the time to prepare herself for meeting his parents and seemed nervous.

"Gunnar, do I look all right? What if they don't like me?" she asked looking up at him.

"Father won't be a problem, but I don't know about my mother, Mor Signy. She rules the house. Our thralls do as they're told or else. We have several Irish girls, but a woman of your status doesn't usually talk to slaves."

"What happens if they don't obey?"

"She gives them a beating," he said casually.

"But I'm not a thrall, am I?"

"No, you're not. You're my wife."

By mid-morning, all the chests, crates and barrels of goods had been moved to the pebbled beach. One of the other ships was already reloading a new cargo of hides, beeswax, and sails. When the knarr was empty, Gunnar helped Fiona down the ladder for the last time. He listened to Thorkell give instructions to two local families to take care of the ships and do the mainte-nance, preparing for the next voyage.

He saw her wobble when she disembarked. *She'll have to get used to walking on land again.* The three of them clambered up on the first wagon and sat on their sea chests. The rest of the crew boarded the remaining wagons and with chirps and a flick of the drivers' whips, the horses moved forward on the log road. Fiona waved goodbye to Ivar who was standing on the dock.

Gunnar looked at her perched on her sea chest, watch-ing everything around them. *She is probably looking for plants. It's a good opportunity to talk to Thorkell.*

"Let's stick to Danish for a while," he said, flickering his eyes back towards Fiona. "Have you got Bersi's box?"

"I'm sitting on it."

"Good. I think we did well this trip. I might have enough silver to buy property."

"Problem is, there's nowhere left to build. Where are you going to live, now we're back?" Thorkell asked.

"Hopefully, we can stay with Far for tonight then I want to see Old Runa and see if she has room for us. If not, I'll have to find somewhere quickly. We'll be at sea again in two weeks. Onkel Bersi did say I could have a place with them in Dublin if I wanted to. I'd still rather be a warrior than a trader, but I must find somewhere for her to live."

Thorkell nodded. "I need to talk to you and this is the first time I've had the chance to discuss this," he said in hushed tones so even the driver couldn't hear them.

"Oh?"

"During the storm, when it was at its worst, there were times it took two of us just to handle the rudder. I've never been so unsure, so overwhelmed by the anger of the sea. I doubted we'd make it. Suddenly our mast shone with that ghostly green fire. It flickered along the spars and up the mast. I've heard other captains speak of it, but I'd never seen it myself. Fiona came out of the shed, where I'd tethered her beforehand. She clung there, singing and praying. I honestly don't know who she was praying to, her gods or ours; the wind took her words away. When she was finished, she just stood there in the pouring rain looking up to the sky, begging for help. Then the light faded and the anger of the storm eased. Gunnar, the gods listened to her," Thorkell said, looking at him then at the sixteen-year-old slip of a girl sitting on the sea chest behind them.

Gunnar was dumbfounded. "What does it mean, Thorkell?"

"It means you have a young woman who doesn't seem to be aware of her power. I don't think you have to worry about the crew bothering her. She's got their respect all right. I wanted to tell you before you heard rumours. She prayed a lot for your safety."

"First, she kills Snorri to avenge her father, then she prays to the gods and we both survive the storm." They both turned and looked at her—so quiet, so innocent.

"She's afraid of meeting our parents. Wants to make a good impression," Gunnar said.

"She might have good reason to be afraid of Mor. One can never tell. I can't wait to see Astra and the children. Ottar should be pleased with the goods we are bringing back. I'm not looking forward to being the bearer of bad news to our new widows when we arrive," Thorkell said. "Three of the four injured we left behind should have recovered enough that we can bring them home on our next trip."

They spent the rest of the journey catching up on news with their driver, who kept the team at a fast walk or a slow trot if the undulating log road permitted. The man spoke of people in town they knew, births, deaths, and politics. Gunnar looked at Fiona from time to time and smiled. He was baffled by what Thorkell had told him. *What was she capable of? Had her mother taught her the dark arts? Was she a witch?*

CHAPTER 25

Hedeby, Denmark, 905 CE

The horses walked or trotted and Fiona could feel the undulating road beneath her as the big wooden wheels of the cart rolled over it. The logs were green, slimy, and wet, lashed together with rope. She'd been raised in marshy swamps but the idea of a road through one was beyond her imagination.

The reed bed was dense and tall, over her head, but she recognized many familiar plants and somehow that was comforting. The marshy smell was damp and sweet in places. She could see coltsfoot, comfrey, and a large, ancient elderberry tree. No meadowsweet yet. The marshes here were huge, flooding miles of woods and lowland. *There's bound to be moss around.*

Eight or more wagons were spaced behind them. For more than two hours Fiona listened to the conversations that sometimes included the old man driving. The team of horses looked well fed. She looked at the condition of the cart and harness as well as the man's clothing. He looked prosperous, his clothes clean and well-made but not fancy. She understood a few words but not much. *These men are familiar with each other.*

Gunnar caught her eye periodically and smiled. Both Gunnar and Thorkell were still wearing their armour. *Did danger lurk here too?*

Finally, the town came into view. Within the semi-circular earthen wall topped with palisades that extended miles on either side, was a bustling harbour full of ships. The town looked bigger than Wicklow but smaller than Dublin. Hundreds of buildings crowded the inner core, ranging from thatched wooden-planked houses and storefronts lining the waterfront to larger individual homes behind, right near the back palisade walls. Log pathways kept people out of the mud. Several streams meandered through the town. She could see the river and fjord extending further east, past shoals of wooded islands to another vast expanse of water.

Crowds had gathered outside the wharf, mostly women and children. Fiona saw anxious faces as well as joyous ones. It was a varied gathering; a lot were like Gunnar, fair and blue-eyed. Others were dark-haired and shorter with wider, squarer faces, a mixture of peoples. The parade of carts came to a halt. Some families rushed forward to greet their husbands in noisy boisterous reunions, children hanging on to arms and legs, demanding their father's attention. The wife of the one-eared man was running her hand over her husband's scarred face. Others stood waiting, worry clearly written on their faces. They would be the families of men who hadn't come home—the dead and the injured.

"Stay on the cart, Fiona," Gunnar said.

Thorkell hopped down from the wagon and went over to them. He paid each crew man in silver. Fiona watched him speak to each of the women. There were tears and wailing as the bad news was received. *It's so sad.* Youngsters clung to their grieving mothers. Those women had to be strong. Their men had been away for months. They'd looked after everything and now the husband wasn't coming home. *How would they cope?* Her thoughts flew back to the man with the broken hand. She prayed it would heal well so he could return on the next trip or sooner if he found another ship to crew on. He might never be able to work again if her care had been faulty.

The wagons began unloading at various buildings. Their cart continued along the path, turning into a side street leading to the larger houses and small fenced enclosures. Two men came out to meet them. The family resemblance was striking, reminding her very much of Onkel Bersi in stature and dress. The older man, his hair and beard completely grey, was shorter than his sons, but authority radiated from him; he was definitely the family patriarch. Fiona noticed his aura was large but dark. He shouted at the driver to unload their cart at the smaller building behind the main house.

"That's my father and brother," Gunnar said hopping off, then lifting her down and removing their three sea chests. She followed him and watched. The greetings were amicable then Gunnar brought her forward, introducing her. Words were said. They looked her over critically and nodded to her.

"Fiona, this is my father, Far Ottar, and my brother, Brar Steinn," he said, slowly pronouncing the Danish words.

She nodded to Ottar and haltingly said in Danish "I am honoured to meet you, Far." She'd practiced that with Gunnar, determined to get it right. She watched Ottar's face, maintaining soft eye contact, but stepped back until Gunnar put his arm around her shoulder. Ottar's serious, critical visage changed slightly. The frown line softened.

Steinn was standing back, watching her. His face was inscrutable, only acknowledging her with a nod. A discussion took place between the three men. Gunnar knew he was a contrast to them. Although they were taller, he was far more muscular and wild with his unruly hair and weapons. Eventually, Ottar ushered them into the house, calling to his wife. Gunnar led Fiona inside. Thorkell went with Ottar.

The wagons moved to the house next door to unload the goods as Ottar supervised. Gunnar shifted the sea chests inside the doorway. Fiona could see an older woman and several younger ones around the fire pit as well as many children. The four younger women working the looms were thralls, being shorter, dark-haired, and poorly dressed. *So far, so good. Now to meet his mother.* Gunnar had told her that there was a Viking rule of hospitality. No one was turned away, not even your worst enemy, at least for the first night.

The woman approaching them showed greyish-blonde hair under her cap. She was tall, broad and hefty, with the air of a bossy matriarch, her mouth set in a pursed line. She was wearing a rich, green wool dress, adorned with a white pinafore and necklaces, and a spotless cap covering her head. Two of the elaborate gold chains bore heavy gem-studded pendants; the other beadwork was in amber. She had keys on her belt—the keeper of the locked chest, the real head of the household.

Gunnar greeted her. She smiled at him briefly, then pushed him away to arm's length to look him over, clucking at the smell and his filthy attire. As she brushed herself off, she ordered one of the girls at the loom to heat water for his bath.

SUSAN K. KEHOE

"Gunnar, who is this girl?" she asked, eyeing Fiona, who went forward, looked up at her face, then dropped her eyes.

"Mor Signy, this is Fiona, my wife. She's the daughter of a healer and helped us on the voyage by treating our wounded. She knows a lot about plants and remedies. I thought she might be useful to Old Runa," he said.

"So, she's Erse then," she humphed using the Gaelic word for Irish. "You can stay here tonight but you'll have to find somewhere else tomorrow. No room here for you," she said looking at the crowd of children and other young women in the house. The children ranged from babies to ten-year-olds.

Gunnar had explained to Fiona earlier that more than twenty people were living there. "Mor, I know. Thorkell doesn't have any room either, now that some of Astra's family are living with them. What's Runa's situation?"

"She might have room. As far as I know there's just her one married son and daughter and their children. Their house is small though," Mor Signy replied. A bowl of tepid water was provided for Fiona to refresh herself with. *His mother was blatantly telling Gunnar it was his problem.*

Fiona watched Mor Signy very closely as Gunnar spoke to her. The woman was not pleased to see her, if the scrutiny of those cold eyes was any indication. When Mor Signy had said "Erse" with such contempt,

Fiona realized her status was awkward; Irish, but not a thrall.

Fiona joined Gunnar at the bench beside the table. His expression was neutral but she could see the tension. His mother was a formidable woman and she was not pleased. Except for furtive glances, essentially, the adults ignored her. There were two older women who didn't appear to be slaves, maybe concubines.

Some of the older, more adventurous children were more open in their curiosity but none came close. She watched the thralls weaving and Mor Signy ordered another thrall to start baking bread. Several local women visited to chit-chat, their baskets full of produce. She listened to their conversation as Mor Signy spoke of Gunnar and Thorkell. The women looked at her when Mor Signy mentioned "Fiona" and the word *kone,* the Danish word for wife. After they left, Mor Signy sat down on the bench across from her.

Being idle made Fiona even more unsettled. She couldn't just sit there. Fiona caught Mor Signy's eye, pointed to herself and the one empty loom. "I weave," she said, using her hands in the motion of the shuttle.

The woman took her over to the loom, indicating she should sit beside the thralls. Settling herself on the bench, Fiona examined the pattern of the weave—double strands, two up, two under, in a herringbone pattern. She felt the texture of the wool, then she worked the shuttle, bringing the heddle bar up after each pass then tighten each strand in place. She repeated it for the return pass. She paused and looked up at Mor Signy who was standing behind her.

"Ja?" Fiona said. Mor Signy examined it and nodded, so Fiona continued working. She was very conscious of the intense malevolent presence behind her. Finally, Mor Signy moved along the line to look at the work of the other girls. Periodically, Fiona glanced at the thralls. She was about to speak, but the girl beside her paused momentarily, raising a finger to her lips and shook her head, a warning not to speak. Fiona noted bruising on the girl's wrist. The message was loud and clear.

She settled into weaving, feeling some of the tension leave her as she concentrated on maintaining the pattern. It was not a difficult one, but it did demand concentration. Most of the fine fabric produced by these thralls was destined for clothing.

A clean Gunnar emerged from the back room. He walked over to her. "Fiona, I'm going to the warehouse to see Ottar. I'll be back shortly," he said.

He looked a lot better now he'd changed his clothes, his similarity to his father was even more striking in those trousers and over shirt, but his sword and his long blonde mane, hanging in limp, damp strands over his shoulders, still marked him as a warrior, not a trader. Gunnar had braided the side portions to keep his hair from his face. His beard was thickening, making him look older. *He smells a lot better.*

One of the thralls heated water for Fiona, and took her to a small area to bathe. That was refreshing, much better than seawater.

The men returned several hours later, and as daylight faded, the older boys came back from wherever they'd been working. The other thralls left the looms and worked around the fire pit, preparing bread, slabs of fresh beef, and fish for the evening meal. Fiona stopped weaving, double-checking the pattern for errors, then turned around to watch everyone, trying to figure out who people were and which children belonged to them.

For the evening meal, Ottar sat on an ornate chair at the head of the table. Mor Signy sat closest to him on the left bench, with Steinn and his wife on the right. Gunnar sat beside his mother, with Fiona beside him. The other two women sat further down. Older children filled the remaining spaces and the younger ones sat on the floor. There were more boys than girls.

The thralls served meat on pewter platters, first to Ottar, then the food was passed down the table. Fiona was famished. She kept her eyes on Mor Signy and the woman across from her. Gunnar skewered a piece of meat with his dagger and took one for her, too. She grabbed several large chunks of bread and slabs of butter, while Gunnar filled her mug with beer, passing the jug along to the next woman. Many hands were grabbing food within reach.

"Who are these people?" she asked, after taking a bite of the beef and licking her fingers. *Oh, the meat was delicious! Much nicer than the salt beef on board the ship we'd been eating for the past month.* Of course, these people raised their own beef on their farm, wherever that was.

Gunnar was just about to answer when she felt a solid thump against her back. Fiona turned to find a small boy looking up at her with wide, startled eyes. An older boy had obviously shoved him against her and was waiting for a reaction. She quietly took a slice of beef dripping with gravy, placed it on a piece of bread, and gave it to the child. The little eyes got even bigger. Fiona winked, smiled, and turned back to the table to listen to Gunnar's explanation. From the corner of her eye, she caught a glimpse of a grinning, gravy-smeared face as the lad scampered back to his mother. His tormentor moved on.

"Mother, Father, and Steinn, you know already. The woman beside Steinn is his wife. The two women beside them are Far's other two wives. He's not married to them so they are lower status than Mor but they have borne him sons."

Fiona looked at him. "So, a man can have multiple wives. How does that work? Do their sons had the same status as you?"

"A man can have as many wives as he wants or can afford. As far as children are concerned, we are all his sons, so we are ranked by age. I'm number three. It does create problems for the very wealthy. Kings usually send their oldest son away to be raised secretly, so they don't get murdered by other family members."

Fiona just looked at him, shaking her head. With the initial scramble for food over, she glanced around. Wealth was evident everywhere. The chalices they were drinking from were gold and adorned with carvings of gods and beasts. Shields and swords of all kinds lavished the walls. While adults had pewter platters, the children had wooden trenchers. All the women wore gold pendants and bracelets, each a walking display of Ottar's status. Their clothing was exquisite.

Fiona didn't need to know the language to pick up attitudes and nuances; some of the children were pushing others aside, bullying them, not letting them eat. The little one earlier had been one of them. She also noted the few little girls scrounging to find tidbits, only getting leftovers unless their mothers shared. She could see the reactions of their mothers and the rivalry. *It was not a happy household.*

The men spent the evening listening to Gunnar tell his story of the voyage, the storm, sale of the cattle, and the success of the trading mission, while Ottar and Steinn spoke of happenings in Hedeby. She understood a few of the words. The women dealt with the children, preparing the younger ones for bed. From time to time, Fiona felt the eyes of the women on her. She watched them quite openly. She wasn't challenging them but didn't want to appear afraid, either.

Fiona watched Steinn talking to a lad, close to her own age, who resembled him; it was likely his son. He was taller than her and looked around the table with an air of superiority. Well-dressed in a deep red wool shirt, he bore a short sword on his left hip. *Arrogant?* To her surprise, she saw a shiny tentacled web of darkness emanating from him, an unexpected halo of evil. *Caution was needed with both of them, at least until I know them better.* After the meal, Mor Signy pulled Gunnar aside and spoke with him. Then he came back to her.

"She's set up a bed for us in the house next door. There's no room in here," Gunnar said, looking at all the benches overflowing with youngsters and adults. Hefting his sea chest over his shoulder, he led her next door. Fiona could see that part of the storage shed had been cleared to accommodate a sleeping bench. There were crates and chests of trading goods stacked from floor to ceiling.

While he was retrieving the other sea chests, she used one of the outhouses. There was another very small building in the yard, fenced to keep out the chickens. The thrall told her it a shrine to the Viking gods. Only the wealthy had them if their property was big enough, and small animal sacrifices were offered weekly. A small dead animal, possibly a squirrel was skewered on a rod.

The thralls did speak Irish but were very guarded. Fiona was grateful not to be in that house. There was nothing but dislike bordering on hatred. It was so different from her home. All the extra wives and sons— that was just asking for trouble in her mind, but the men seemed to feel it was their right. Daughters were expendable; they only counted as trade items between wealthy families.

Fiona was quite content to sleep in the warehouse. It was private and separate from the chaos of the main house. Gunnar was strangely quiet, seeming moody and preoccupied. He had his way with her then rolled over to sleep. The family didn't seem to care much about him. All their attention was on Steinn and his son.

The following morning, Gunnar awakened her early.

"Fiona, get up. Far Ottar will be in shortly to load goods for the booth. It will be a very busy day in the market. Everyone knows we've come home and we always bring the luxury items they're craving. All the wives will be vying for the best goods. Far specializes in expensive foreign goods and jewellery, all for status," he said, helping her braid her hair.

"You were very upset with your parents last night for sending us here to sleep," she said.

"I know I'm the youngest son and I don't expect much, but we don't even warrant staying in the main house," he said, realizing that even if she didn't understand the language, she didn't miss much.

She thought for a moment before answering. "Ottar could hardly trust the younger ones in here, could he? He trusted you not to damage or steal the trade goods. After all, you and Thorkell risked your lives to bring the goods back here. I'm thankful we were on our own. No one is happy," she said hoping he understood their garbled half-Danish, half-Gaelic conversation.

"Perhaps I shouldn't have brought you here. It might have been better to have stayed in Dublin. At least Onkel Bersi made us welcome, but I want so much to be a warrior," he said, pulling her close to him and holding her tightly.

"You'll be back to sea in a few weeks. You can think about that the next time you see Bersi. You might find a good place for us to live on your travels. Take me to see your healer and find us a place to live for now. I want to be safe while you're gone. I wouldn't be comfortable next door if you weren't here," she said looking up at him.

The jangle of harness, the rumbling creak of the wheels on the rutted path, and the call of the carter outside gave them due warning of a busy day, as Ottar flung open the door and came in. He gave strict instructions for which crates were to be loaded and the workers carried them out.

Fiona recognized the crates of fabrics and glassware among others. She paused in the doorway for a moment just as the sun broke the horizon and remembered one of her mother's rituals. Aoife would stand in the doorway of their house, barefoot and bare headed—her long hair hanging freely, her eyes closed. Then she would open her eyes; the first thing she saw was the omen of the day. It was an old custom called *deuchainn*—interpretation of the first moment.

Fiona wanted to be a *frithir*, a seer like her mother. She took a deep breath, closed her eyes, and stood perfectly still. The noises of the street faded away. It was just a few moments then she opened her eyes. She saw the sun, a smattering of clouds, a flock of pigeons sitting on the roof of the house across the way, cooing to each other, and the shiny chestnut coat of the carter's horse.

What did that mean? The sun was shining—that was good. The clouds were gathered on the horizon, flat on the bottom and grey, perhaps indicating rain later. The pigeons were peaceful—no hawk hunting them this morning. The horse looked old but healthy and it was the beginning of a new day and a whole new way of life for her. Fiona wished her mother had explained these things in more detail. She tried to remember all the little rituals and what they might have meant. Maybe the old woman, this Runa, could help her, too.

With the wagon loaded, Ottar locked the door to the warehouse, climbed up on the seat beside the carter, nodded briefly to them then signalled for him to move on. Moments later, they were gone.

The aroma of fresh bread wafting from the main house had Fiona salivating. Inside, Mor Signy said good morning and told them to sit at the table. The other women and all the children were milling around. It was chaos as usual. A huge cauldron of oatmeal was simmering over the fire. One of the thralls brought over two full bowls, setting them down before the pair.

"Help yourself to honey and cream," Gunnar said, grabbing enough slabs of bread for both of them.

Fiona watched the older boys, including Steinn's son, swilling down mugs of oatmeal while preparing to leave, tool bags slung over their shoulders. "Where are they going?"

"They're apprenticed to various tradesmen in town— carpenters, ship builders, and the blacksmith."

"What's the name of Steinn's son?" she asked, as the boys left the house.

"Bjorn," Gunnar said, wiping crumbs from his shirt, eyeing the boy who was shoving one of the younger children out of his way.

She quickly changed the subject. "Gunnar, I need another dress. Can we afford to buy one? The one I wore on the ship is beyond repair, and I want to save my wedding dress for formal occasions. This one is the only practical one I have."

"Once we find somewhere to live, we'll go to the market," he said, looking at his three nieces, empty baskets slung over their arms, heading out the door. A few of the female thralls were walking across the lane to another house where the open door exposed a dozen already weaving. Gunnar led Fiona back through the throng of children, into the main house, and found his mother busy chastising one of the slaves.

Fiona could hear a small child crying. She saw Ottar's third wife rocking a wailing, inconsolable infant on her lap. Its tiny arm was roughly bandaged.

Gunnar talked to the woman and was told the child had been scalded with hot water earlier.

"I have an ointment that might help," Fiona said. "Will she allow me to look at it?"

He relayed the question and got a "Ja" response.

Immediately, Fiona went over and the mother unravelled the bandage. The child's tiny arm was scarlet and blistered from the shoulder to the wrist. She very gently examined it. *Oh, it is a nasty burn.* Taking a piece of clean cloth from her pouch, she soaked it in cold water from the pail beside the fire and draped it over the child's arm.

"Gunnar, I need my sea chest for the ointment. Ottar locked the warehouse. Does your mother have a key?"

"Yes, she does. I'll get it," he said and returned shortly carrying the chest.

Meanwhile, Fiona changed the cooling cloth several times and sang the healing song to the little girl, who looked about two. Rummaging through the box, she found the jar of coltsfoot ointment and some moss. Aoife had used those herbs for burns with good results. With utmost care Fiona gently cleansed the skin with the moist moss, then dabbed on a thin film of ointment, leaving the moss to cover it, before bandaging the little arm. By then the child had changed from screaming to sniffling, pouting, and watching her with big solemn, teary eyes. Fiona smiled at her and the mother, then put her things away, locking the chest. The mother gave her a grateful tusind tak.

She managed to put together the words "I'll change it in two days," getting understanding nods from Gunnar and the mother.

Gunnar led her outside and together they walked the streets into the poorer section of town to find old Runa.

CHAPTER 26

Poor Town

The rutted streets in town were crowded with trades-men and women heading to market. The doors of the houses were open to the street, revealing cluttered hearths and grimy urchins in ragged clothes. Gunnar could smell the stench of sewage, rotting waste, and hear the strident cacophony of mothers shouting at their children. He recognized several faces, point-ing out to Fiona where a few of their crew lived. If it hadn't been for Ottar's success as a trader, his family would still have been on the farm raising cattle instead of trading luxury goods.

He found Old Runa's home at the very end of the lane, near the back gate of the palisade. There was an old man with a bandaged foot sitting on a bench outside the house. His handmade wooden crutch was propped against the wall.

"Is Runa home?" Gunnar asked.

"No, but she'll be back in a little while. She's visiting the sick right now. I'm waiting for her, too."

Gunnar stuck his head in the door but the house was empty. Herbs were hanging from every hook and rafter. Although small, the house was neat and tidy. The hearth had been cleaned and new logs stacked. A pail of water sat beside it. The floor had been swept and fresh reeds put down. He noted there were four sleeping benches. *How many lived there?*

Gunnar sat beside the man and drew Fiona down beside him. The neighbours were curious, sticking their heads out the doors, no doubt speculating what a well-dressed warrior and his woman were doing in their neighbourhood. He had a pleasant chat with the old man, a seaman relegated to home port after an injury at sea. The man's ravaged face lit up and he broke into smiles, listening to Gunnar's tale of the pirate attack and the storm. He told them how he now fished in the bay and mended fishing nets. "I don't venture on the open sea anymore."

About an hour later, Gunnar spotted Runa limping down the lane, a blackthorn cane in her right hand and a large basket in the other.

"That's her," he said to Fiona, watching her reaction. Both of them got to their feet as Runa got closer.

Gunnar turned to watch Fiona. When she met someone for the first time, she would get very quiet and had a strange blank look on her face, like she was seeing right through them. She'd done it yesterday when she met Ottar and Steinn. She was doing it to Runa right now. He looked at Runa and, oddly enough, she was doing the same thing to Fiona. *What were they seeing?*

"Good morning, to all of you," Runa said, addressing the old man then both of them. "Good morning, Olaf. I suppose you need another jar of meadowsweet," she said, ushering him into the house. Olaf grinned. Runa rummaged around in a wooden box, finding a small ceramic jar of cream and handed it to him. "There you are."

He opened the burlap bag laying at his feet and presented her with a large, fresh fish in exchange, placing it on her table.

"I was lucky this morning. I caught a couple."

She smiled, checked his foot, applied some cream, then bandaged it. He took his crutch and limped out the door.

"Now what can I do for you? You're Ottar's son, are you not?"

Her face was old and wrinkled; her hair under the cap was grey, but her eyes were a clear blue and missed nothing. Her clothes were simple and clean. Around her neck she wore two pendants, one a quartz crystal, the other an eight-legged horse and rider carved in amber and silver. These marked her as a seer, a person of importance.

Gunnar recognized the pendant as a shaman's charm—Odin on his horse, Sleipnir.

"You're right. I'm Gunnar, Ottar's son. This is Fiona, my wife. Fiona's mother was a healer and was training her. I know you lost your apprentice last winter, and I wondered if you still needed one.'"

"Has she any real experience with using the herbs and making the ointments?

"Yes, she has. I believe she knows her plants well. She treated some of the wounded on our return trip from Ireland. We are looking for a place to live. There's no room at Ottar's or Thorkell's. She's just learning to speak Danish, but doesn't know much yet," he said.

"Come, have a seat," she said. Going back to her box of ointments, she placed several on the table. "I want her to tell me the name of the plant and what it is used for," she said, keenly observing the girl.

Gunnar did a quick translation. Fiona immediately nodded. She opened the first jar, smelled it and said, "That's meadowsweet. It's used for arthritis and fevers, stomach troubles, and helps stop diarrhea," using her hands and body to convey her actions. It became obvious that Gunnar couldn't translate well enough, so Fiona went to the wall, removed a bunch of leaves, smelled them then began using her hands, body, and facial expressions to convey the illness symptoms as well as saying the Irish name for the plant.

She selected bugleweed, started coughing, then mimicked making tea. She pretended to cut her arm with her knife, then apply the cream to heal it.

Runa gave the Danish word, then nodded. "She is right about that one," she said to Gunnar.

Fiona continued selecting plants and acting out the symptoms for each, burped, feigned an aching head, clutched her stomach, pretended to retch.

At one point, Runa stopped and extracted a small pouch from her medicine chest. She handed it Fiona, who removed the leaves, examined them, smelled them, and rubbed them between her fingers, a puzzled expression on her face. Finally, she cupped them in her hands and stared at them. There was silence in the room. "Runa, I don't know this one at all. The light around them is tight and dark, so I wouldn't give them to anyone."

Runa nodded again with a tiny smile on her lips, then returned the plants to the pouch. "Those were wild lettuce. Never use it," she said, motioning her to continue.

Gunnar watched her role play as many of the symptoms as she could for each remaining plant, much to his and Runa's amusement.

Runa gave the Danish word for each plant, but pretty soon all three were laughing. Fiona's depiction of diarrhea and hemorrhoids had Gunnar doubled over with laughter.

"She's going to have to learn our language quickly," Runa said. "I think this could work out well. I need a younger person to run errands and gather plants. I need someone who is kind and gentle; a good sense of humour helps, too," she said.

Gunnar felt a huge sense of relief. "Runa, I will be going back to sea in less than two weeks and I will be away two months. Do you have enough room for us to live here?"

She undid a pouch from her belt, gently shook it, then reached in and removed an oval flat rune stone with a symbol carved on it. She placed it on the table. Carefully, she removed five more, each different, placing them in a straight line. Fiona's eyes were fixed on the table, fascinated.

"Gunnar, that's Futhark on those stones, isn't it? I saw Onkel Bersi writing like that. Mother's style was different. She wrote on tree bark in Ogham. Each piece represented a different tree and had meaning. She could tell the future. I know very little," she said. She looked sad for a few moments. It never occurred to him that she was thinking of the raid.

Runa looked at the symbols for quite some time as if weighing the possibilities. "There are difficult times ahead, but it will work out for the best. You can use the bench over in the corner. I cannot afford to pay her, but she can live here if she helps keep the house clean and helps me with the sick. I can't go to the swamp and pick plants these days. I will teach her what she needs to know. My son, his wife, and three children live with me as well as my widowed daughter and her two children. Atli is out fishing, and everyone else is at the market."

Gunnar explained that to Fiona, who smiled and thanked the old woman. The two women looked at each other and he could see they had reached some sort of understanding. "Runa, we're going to the market and will be picking up our belongings from Ottar's house. We'll be eating here. Do you need more fish or flour?"

"Yes, by all means bring more fish, some flour, and oats," she said.

"Are you not afraid of leaving your house wide open?" Gunnar asked.

Runa looked at him. "There is nothing here to steal, other than drying leaves. It wouldn't be wise to harm a healer. If someone stole, I would know it. If it is the starving who steal my food, then who am I to stop them? The gods will determine their fate."

A few more people were sitting on the outside bench, waiting to see Runa when Gunnar and Fiona left.

Gunnar was satisfied. Although this part of Hedeby was the poorest and the least desirable place to live, Runa was a formidable woman people respected. Fiona would be in good hands while he was away and that was a relief.

Hedeby's market along the waterfront was similar to Dublin's. There were artisans of every kind: fish stalls; wool shops; the blacksmith shop with goods ranging from horseshoes and tools to weapons; the butcher shop with its gutted carcasses on display; produce-laden carts from local farms filling the roadways; the brewery; the bakery; leather goods; honey and beeswax candles; furs from the north; tables with amber beads and jewellery from Sweden; tables loaded with wheels of cheese; carpenter booths; and the main attraction, the crowded booth where Ottar and Steinn were working.

Well-dressed men haggled and shoved, being urged on by their even better bedecked wives, vying to get close enough to the luxury goods to make their purchases. The booth had been open all morning and business was brisk—no sign of it slowing down.

Knowing Fiona wanted a working dress, Gunnar found his way to the tailor's house and led her in. Shirts and dresses of varying quality, colours, and patterns hung on poles or were in piles on the table.

"Is this what you're looking for?" he asked.

She sorted through them, finding a smaller dress in plain wool, dyed a soft brown. The weave was good.

With a nod to Gunnar, she asked the price and haggled for a while, eventually getting two dresses for a half piece of hack silver.

The next stop was the shoemaker's booth. Gunnar watched her select a very simple pair of leather shoes, similar to what the poor were wearing—just an oval of leather laced around the foot. *She is getting adept at bargaining.*

After, they visited the mill for flour and oats, which came in burlap bags. Gunnar threw them over his shoulder. Down by the docks were stalls with fresh fish. He quickly spotted King Olaf's soldiers, who routinely patrolled the area. Danish Hedeby was under Swedish rule at least for now. Battles and skirmishes happened periodically, but it had been quiet for several years.

The pair visited the fishermen at the docks. Fiona was looking at the different kinds of fish. "Is this one the same as the old man gave Runa?" she asked.

"Ja."

"What kind is it?"

"That's cod. Sprats are good and cheap, too," he said, pointing to a bin of tiny silver fish. "Take two cod. That should be enough to feed six adults and five children."

Their entry into Runa's house was different this time. Gunnar could see the house was full. Everyone stopped what they were doing as he set down the bags of flour and oats on the table and Fiona deposited the fish. The atmosphere was friendly.

Runa looked at the provisions and nodded, then introduced her son, daughter, daughter-in-law, and the children, who ranged in age from four to nine. There were three girls and two boys. The children stood with their mouths open, staring up at Gunnar, but the boys were fascinated with his sword. He smiled. Fiona greeted each one, saying her name and listening to theirs, bending down to their level to speak to them. After that she went to their bench and hung up her dresses on a hook.

"Fiona, I'm off to Ottar's to get our sea chests. I'll be back as soon as I can," he said and gave her a hug. *She'll have to learn on her own.* He needed to help Thorkell prepare for the next voyage. He hoped the women would teach her what she needed to know.

Walking out of the poor quarter, he immediately noticed the air was fresher. He didn't understand why outhouses hadn't been built in poor town. Throwing the slops in the street made them smell dreadful.

He searched for the carter, finally finding the man at the smithy. The carter was watching the muscular smith bending over, the horse's left foreleg between his knees as he trimmed its hoof with the nippers and a rasp. A skinny dog happily gnawed on scraps.

Gunnar got the carter's attention and told him there were four chests to be moved from his father's house to Runa's. "As soon as the smith is finished, I'll pick them up," the man said. They chatted for a while.

"Why are you moving there?" the curious man asked.

"Far's house is full, and there's no room for me and my wife. She's a healer, so it makes sense to have her work with Runa," he said.

"Rough part of town though," the man replied.

"Sometimes youngest sons don't have a choice. She'll be safe there," Gunnar said, thoughtfully rubbing the stubble on his chin.

It was an hour later when Gunnar jumped down from the cart in front of Ottar's house. He could hear Mor Signy yelling at someone. *Fiona was right. There was no laughter here.* His mother was arguing with wife number two, who was standing there with her hands on her hips, belligerently jutting out her chin, her lips pursed.

He walked up to his mother who turned to him. The yelling stopped.

"Mor, I need you to unlock the warehouse so I can get my sea chests. Fiona and I will be living at Runa's. She has room for us."

"I see. She's still in Poor Town?"

"Yes, her house is right by the back gate. She's willing to take Fiona as her apprentice and she'll teach her to speak Danish."

Together, they walked next door and she unlocked it. Gunnar loaded the three chests onto the cart.

"Where do you keep my old chest?" he asked.

Mor Signy went to the back to another locked door and opened it. Gunnar looked inside for the very first time. There were at least a dozen large chests. He surmised this was his father's treasure stash. Gunnar pulled out his small sea chest and hoisted in onto his shoulder. As he deposited it on the cart, his mother locked the doors behind her and looked at him.

"If Far wants me, I'll either be at Runa's or Thorkell's. I promised him I'd help get the knarr and longship ready for the next voyage," he said, already irritated by her attitude and general lack of interest, omitting his customary kiss on the cheek.

Mor Signy looked at him with a very solemn expression on her face. "I must go," she said as she turned towards the house.

Gunnar was silent for a moment, then climbed up on the wagon seat beside the carter as the old horse ambled off. Somehow, he felt he'd been dismissed like a thrall—and that rankled. Gunnar sat quietly all the way back to Runa's. He knew full well that the youngest had to leave but it still made him angry.

CHAPTER 27

*Present-day archaeological
dig site, Hedeby*

For Jon, it was the moment of truth. He was on his hands and knees in the dirt, positioned behind the skeleton's head, the students clustered around him. Very gently, he slipped his gloved fingers under the skull, following the curve of the bones, manipulating his way beneath the mat of long, fair hair. For a moment, nothing happened. Then the last remnants of peat fell away and he raised the skull. Helga slipped the padded box beneath it as Jon set the skull down. On the periphery, Lars was taking pictures.

Getting that skull and its accompanying mane of hair had been the main event of the whole week. The air of tension dissolved. Jon took the box over to the table where the lighting was better and they clustered around.

More formal shots were taken. The empty eye sockets looked up at them, the long hair snaking all over the cranium like a Medusa.

"Now to get this beauty to the lab for cleaning. This a good time to keep some specimens for Y-chromosome DNA analysis," he said. *That would give him male lineage back generations. What tribes would he find?* Very careful to avoid cross contamination, he plucked a lock of hair, a finger bone, and a molar, placing them in separate sterile containers, capping the bottles before removing his gloves.

Gena took the samples and began the labelling process. As the morning went on, they continued excavating. She found a few more pieces of the metal helmet, that had been under the skull. She also retrieved strands of hair that lay on the bearskin cape.

Miles had finished removing the last pieces of the knife scabbard, still finding tiny pieces of the blue fabric. Under the left hand lay a piece of wood and a pile of small stones carved with human or animals faces, with a few scraps of a leather pouch they'd only discovered the day before, possibly a gaming board and pieces.

The days were shorter now, and it was cooler outside. Jon was staying late some evenings and needed the heater on. His students would be back in class the next week. They'd only got the left hand and leg to finish— then they were done. More to do in the lab, though.

Much more. *What an experience!* It would take a year or two to get the skeleton properly cleaned.

Each of them was contemplating the papers they would individually write as well as the joint one. Helga had suggested they prepare an exhibit at the university museum, because the skeleton had been so complete and would keep the Viking theme alive for the general public. *That had been controversial.*

Lars had objected strongly, saying it should be returned to the grave as soon as it had been fully examined and that a reproduction would suffice.

Gena pointed out that she was intending to apply for a foreign assignment, probably in South America, as soon as school had finished and wouldn't be available to help with that. Even their joint paper was going to be an online proposition. Miles tended to agree. To finish the project at the site on time, all of them offered to work over the weekend.

Jon was exhausted from the work and hadn't seen his own family for days.

The bickering at the site was a constant, but the silence at home was worse. I often can't even get Elsa on her cellphone and she seemed to be visiting her mother a lot more often. Hopefully, it was her mother. The woman had been ill. Any other possibilities are too much to consider.

CHAPTER 28

The neighbourhood

Fiona went out with Runa. Gunnar had gone to work with Thorkell that morning. She was apprehensive about being on her own now, and her priority was to learn Danish quickly and memorize the plant names.

The previous evening had gone better than expected. The family made them feel welcome. The two younger women had accepted the strangers without comment and Fiona didn't feel any hint of disapproval. There was none of the bickering that went on at Ottar's. Even the children were getting more curious, coming out from behind their mothers' skirts.

Gunnar seemed to get along with Runa's son, Atli. He was short and sturdy, with dark hair, a total contrast to Gunnar in looks and behaviour. A very quiet man, if he didn't approve of the new additions to the household, he didn't show it. The two men had ended up playing the board game during the evening. She watched the boys edge closer to Gunnar to look at his sword as he was playing. Each man contemplated what to do, then moved one of the shaped ivory pieces onto another tile.

Fiona had been told by Onkel Bersi that each piece represented either a god, a king, or a warrior. Gunnar claimed a piece with great glee, snatching it from its square and then groaned when Atli made a better move. Gradually, the number of pieces on the board diminished so only a few key pieces remained. Eventually, the final move was made by Atli, claiming the king piece. Gunnar shook his head—beaten. By that time the fire was down to embers. The boys were hustled off to bed.

She'd had the impression earlier, when Gunnar had come in, that something had happened back at Ottar's house. He'd been very quiet and withdrawn in an "angry" way, the light around him dark and shadowy. It was hard to define what she was sensing. *Things were difficult for him, being the youngest son.* Right away, the atmosphere at Runa's was different. Although Runa's family were poor, they were genuinely pleasant to her and each other; she could tell from the bright colours and light around them.

After dark, when the door was closed and everyone had gone to bed, she and Gunnar curled up together on their bench. Gunnar whispered to her, "Don't tell anyone, not even Runa, that we have money in our sea chests. Don't tell them about your father's torque, either. This is a dangerous neighbourhood. I'll talk to you more when we have a chance to be alone." When he took her that night, he was as rough as he had been their wedding night. It seemed he'd taken his anger and frustration out on her.

The next day, Fiona followed Runa through the streets of Hedeby. She thought back to the previous evening and was pleased at the family's acceptance of both of them. She'd met Atli, who had played the game with Gunnar. Both men seemed to get on well. As she walked, she remembered Gunnar's anger and about not telling anyone about their money. *I certainly have no intention of telling anyone about the coins or my father's torque.* It bothered her that Gunnar had been rough with her. *There's nothing much I can do about that except distract him.*

Poverty was ever present along those crowded streets. Fiona was alert to every movement around them as Runa led her through narrowing paths with the ramshackle huts, and many more people, eventually reaching a house crowded with mostly women and children. She walked carefully, mindful of the slops, which had flung out to rot. The stench of waste water was appalling There were so many people, she couldn't even count them. All were thin and barefoot, wearing filthy rags.

Hair went uncombed. Many were missing teeth. It reminded her of the poor on the mud flats in Dublin.

Runa made her way to one of the benches. What Fiona first thought was a bundle of blankets turned out to be an old woman, or perhaps she only looked old. The life force around her was dim. Fiona helped Runa position her semi-upright, but the woman groaned with movement, opening her eyes, giving a tired smile when she recognized her healer. Extracting a small bottle from her basket, Runa uncorked it and administered a spoonful of the oily golden liquid over the thin, dry lips. Fiona held the woman steady, her arms cradling the bony shoulders.

She could smell the meadowsweet; it was a good pain killer. She said the Danish word for it and Runa nodded. Fiona looked at the failing woman and felt an upwelling of sorrow for her in those awful surroundings. Very quietly she started to chant the healing song, stroking her hand. *She won't care if it's in Gaelic.* When she finished singing, the woman looked more comfortable, fewer frown lines on her face.

Fiona watched as Runa sat quietly for a few minutes doing something with her hands, moving them just a few inches over the woman's body. She was concentrating hard, that far-away look on her face, like she was in a different place. *What was she feeling? It had to be some kind of healing.*

SUSAN K. KEHOE

She looked up at Runa and their eyes met. There was a silent connection and exploring as if gauging each other, without the need for words.

As she pulled the blanket back over the woman's thin frame, Fiona became aware that the room was very quiet. Everyone was staring at her. She shyly smiled back. Most avoided her eyes.

The rest of the morning was like that: malnourished households, sick and dying people, young girls barely older than herself with two or three children. Deep in her heart, she knew most of them would not live long. They'd survive by stealing or raiding the middens for food. The men would get what work they could and probably crew on ships. Life was harder in the poorer side of town.

"Why don't I see many little girls?" she asked.

"The boys get fed first; the girls get what's left—if there is any. They are often weaker and die early of diseases. Unwanted ones are killed at birth," Runa said.

As they walked home, she counted the male and female children in any group they saw—on average two girls to five boys. It seemed so brutal. Back at the house, with the afternoon sun still bright, there were customers awaiting Runa on the outside bench.

Under her direction, Fiona washed and cleaned wounds, applied ointments and bandages, gave cough syrups, and administered herbs for headaches and achy knees. She was starting to remember names of herbs. Some of the customers corrected her attempts at Danish. She didn't mind in the least, encouraging it with a smile. There were many who just needed a good meal which she couldn't provide.

She was learning a lot. She heard them pray to Eir, goddess of healing, wishing she understood who their gods were. It was similar to the pagan Irish gods in her village, but different, too. Each Irish village worshiped different woodland deities, but here, the gods were the same no matter where they went. The crew had often called on Thor or Odin, their warrior gods. Gunnar wore a Thor's hammer pendant for good luck. For pagans, those gods were as real as people. She hadn't met any Christians yet.

By the end of the day, Fiona was tired and hungry. They hadn't had time to eat. She wondered how Runa survived. The people were too poor to pay her anything for the care she gave. Someone, like the old man yesterday, at least gave her a fish, but that wouldn't be enough to pay for the plants, oils, and jars and making a living.

It was just starting to rain when Gunnar came home. He put two fish down on the table as well as two loaves of bread. The women immediately gutted the fish, chopped them in pieces, and tossed them into the cook pot simmering over the fire. Earlier, Atli had hung a line between two upright posts, threading tiny silver sprats to dry. The children were less cautious now, sitting beside them at the table.

After the evening meal, Fiona looked at Gunnar. He seemed in a better mood.

"I promised Ottar's wife I'd go back to change the baby's bandage. Could we go that now?" She was scared of walking alone at nightfall. She wasn't oriented to the streets well enough yet to know where she was going. Everyone was still a possible threat until proven otherwise.

Gunnar got up and looked outside. It had stopped raining. "We may as well go now and get it over with," he said.

She quickly gathered up a jar of ointment, moss, and a clean roll of bandage in her basket and they headed out, plodding over the muddy logs. People thronged the pathways. Open doors revealed families around their fire pits, smoke accumulating in the rafters. Children were everywhere. A pall of smoke hung over the town from the cooking fires.

"Now I can talk to you," Gunnar said, keeping his voice low. "There's a lot of silver in my sea chest, enough to build a house wherever we settle. I've got several gold chalices and three swords that I can sell if I need to. There's a good sturdy lock, and I'll give you the key when I leave. It's really important that you keep that secret. Don't open it when anyone is in the house, not even Runa. Never show anyone that torque or your father's sword. Always pretend you're poor."

It only took fifteen minutes to reach Ottar's house. She memorized the route. As before, they could hear Mor Signy yelling at someone, and it was the usual chaos when they walked inside.

"Did you forget something?" Mor Signy asked, hands on her hips.

"No, Mor. Fiona promised to change the baby's dressing," Gunnar said, gritting his teeth, then deliberately walked past her to talk to Ottar, who was finishing his evening meal and downing a mug of mead. His father beckoned Gunnar to sit beside him, the young ones moving out of the way.

Wife number two was sitting on the bench, the baby in her arms. She motioned Fiona to sit beside her. She immediately smiled and started to unwrap the bandage. The soiled material was quite wet. The child whimpered. As Fiona removed the last of the moss, she took a good look at the burn. It was still very red. Most of the blisters had broken. She lowered her nose to smell it, but couldn't detect any foul odour. *The moss was working.* She gently washed the fragile skin, patted it dry, then smeared ointment on with fresh moss, showing the mother everything she did. She re-bandaged the arm and left the pot of ointment. With hand gestures and words, she instructed her to change it in two days. Fiona wasn't sure if or when she would return if she was out with Runa every day.

Gunnar looked over at Fiona, and seeing she was finished, said goodbye to his father. He ignored his mother, and they left. As the sun set, shadows crept down the walls of the houses, darkening the narrow, muddy lanes. Somehow it was sinister. She was thankful he was with her.

Fiona told Gunnar all that she'd seen and done with Runa that day. He told her about his day working with Thorkell. As they walked and talked, she watched the dark shapes of men standing in their doorways, backlit from their hearth fires. At one point, three scruffy inebriated men deliberately blocked their way. Gunnar pushed her behind him and drew his sword, standing braced with his feet apart. He uttered a feral growl.

She slipped her knife out of the scabbard and glanced around her. No one was coming from behind, although people were looking out their doorways. For a moment, everyone held their breath, then one of the men laughed and pulled the others away. Gunnar watched them shamble off but continued to hold his stance. When he turned to look at Fiona, he saw the knife and smiled.

"Seems I've got a reputation. Good thing. They backed off. You'd fight for me, would you?"

"Yes. I'm your wife," she said, putting her knife away.

Amused, he led her down the alley, still vigilant, his eyes watching the paths and doorways. Finally, he sheathed his sword and continued his story as they walked side by side through the streets.

"We took one of the carts and went back to the coast to see the ships. They've put a new sail on the longship. Both ships are ready. They didn't need re-caulking. Thor's already putting out word for sailors and warriors."

"Will your cousins move to Britain?" she asked, dodging a couple of small children who darted out of a doorway.

"Oh yes. Both of them have decided to settle their families in Britain near York, instead of your old village. It's much closer, just across the North Sea, only a couple of days' sailing. Danes have been settling there for over a hundred years. There's plenty of land there."

"Would you consider going there too?" she asked, wondering if there was any possibility of getting closer to Ireland. Fiona walked quickly, trying to keep up with Gunnar as he strode along, glancing at her as he spoke.

"The lords have regular armies. They always need soldiers. My cousins are farmers though and are taking some of Ottar's bulls with them. Given the size of their families, there'll be at least thirty of them, so the knarr will be full. We'll drop them off in Tynemouth, then continue north on our usual route."

"Is there a different way to go?"

"Far and Steinn are seriously considering if it's worth staying on our present route. It's getting harder to find Irish slaves, and the Norse have settled in many places on both sides of the Irish sea and Scottish coast. They're the usual pirates we have to deal with. The shipment is just about ready to go for Onkel Bersi. We'll be leaving early next week."

"Gunnar, if you ever go back to my village, could you tell someone I'm still alive. My mother doesn't know and she'd always wonder."

"If we go there, I could do that," he said, slowing down a bit.

When they arrived at Runa's, the children were getting settled in bed. Very quietly, he pulled out his sea chest. She watched Gunnar offer two shirts he'd outgrown to Atli, who tried them on; they fit well. She watched Gunnar nonchalantly lock his chest and slide it under the bench to the back, placing her chests in front of it, so it was out of sight.

"Always be vigilant when you're out and about with Runa," Gunnar said. "If you'd been alone tonight, you'd have been in trouble. Children around here are expert thieves too. Trust no one. Use your knife if you have to," he said slipping his arms around her and nuzzling her neck. He was gentler this time.

Everyone was up early the next morning. Atli had already left to go fishing. Apparently, it was market day for Runa. Atli's wife, Lilja, was stirring a pot of oatmeal that had been simmering over the fire all night. Runa and her daughter Olrun were taking down dried herbs from the rafters, sorting herbs and ointments. They had a small wheeled hand cart. When they'd filled their chest, Olrun loaded it onto the cart.

"Since you'll be at the market, I'm heading to Thorkell's," Gunnar said, scooping up a cup of oatmeal and downing it quickly. Then he left. The children were clustered around getting their share, too, boys and girls equally. Soon the pot was empty, and Lilja wiped it clean. The oldest boy, Eric, brought in a pail of water from the community well.

Quickly, Fiona combed and braided her hair. She watched everything Runa and Olrun were doing. Breakfast finished, the women put on their caps, and Runa led the way. Olrun pushed the cart along the rutted street. Neighbours stuck their heads out their doorways and shouted greetings or waved as they passed.

Olrun paused at one particularly deep rut and Fiona stepped in to help her. Between the two of them, they slogged through the mud, pushing the cart ahead of them. Fiona was glad she'd decided to be barefoot and didn't want to mess up her new shoes. She looked down at her dress, which was now splattered with mud. *Never mind, it will dry.*

The children were having fun jumping in puddles, sending sheets of muddy water flying. Olrun cursed them roundly, causing them to giggle and scamper out of reach. Runa's booth consisted of four large barrels and planks that served as the counter, and a piece of ship's sail anchored on one edge to the palisade itself, with two poles to prop up the front. Under Runa's direction, the women raised the sail above them, ramming the poles into the ground to provide shelter from the sun or rain. Olrun opened the barrels, pulling out two smaller ones they used for seats. The big barrels formed the corners of the booth, the planks formed the counters on top. It was easy to erect and dismantle, with nothing worth stealing.

Olrun strung several pieces of twine across the front, then started to hang bunches of dried and fresh herbs. Runa unloaded jars of ointment, bottles of tonic, as well as hair shampoo. Soap bars were broken out of their wooden moulds.

As Fiona ground the fragrant leaves, she casually glanced up to watch the other vendors and customers on the street. It was interesting to see the full spectrum of buyers, ranging from the very rich to the very poor, including sailors from different nations, women in expensive clothing with their well-clad daughters and sons, fishermen, traders and hungry-looking poor and their emaciated children—shoeless by necessity not choice, as well as tradespeople and haulage carts.

A young man about eighteen with blue eyes, ash-blonde hair and a beard trimmed short approached the booth. He was about Gunnar's height but slim and wiry, wearing a simple long-sleeved shirt and trousers. He swung the bucket he was carrying onto the counter, greeting both Runa and Olrun by name. Both women smiled.

Runa removed the leather cover from the bucket, lifting out a strip of honeycomb dripping with wax and nectar. In turn, she gave him ointments and shampoo.

As he spoke with them, his blue eyes glanced Fiona's way, and a glimmer of a smile followed his perusal. The light around him was as golden as the honey in the bucket. *Who was he?*

After he left, she asked Olrun if they used beeswax to soak the mullein heads for torches, like they'd done on the longship.

"We do if we have enough of it, but we could always use more," she replied.

"Who was he?"

"Oh, that was Ragnar. His father has a large farm north of here, and he brings us linen and honey. He's been a customer for a long time.

Fiona concentrated on mixing dried burdock leaves in rendered animal fat to make the ointment for sores.

Runa showed her how to grate the burdock root she'd boiled the night before to make a tonic for digestive problems and sore throats. Yarrow was ready to be processed into an ointment to stop bleeding.

One interesting passerby was a monk. His tonsured head proclaimed his profession. He wore a cassock and carried a basket of fish. Around his neck was a simple cross on a gold chain. He gave the booth a wide birth, crossing himself and mumbling what sounded like a prayer, glaring at Runa.

Fiona thought he had to be Christian. The priests at home didn't like pagans, either, especially female healers. Her mother had always been very careful when the abbot visited. She told him that she didn't deal in magic, just simple medicines. He was always suspicious of her. It probably wasn't any different in Hedeby.

She watched a couple of scruffy boys. One kept the fishmonger busy while a smaller light-fingered lad stole a handful of sprats and slipped away. Later two little girls approached a maid carrying a basket of goods. One bumped the woman and the other girl approached from behind and took an apple from the basket. The maid walked on, none the wiser. *Gunnar was right.* Fiona had to be aware of the people around her.

Many people came to the booth for medicines or treatment from Runa. Those with money purchased the soaps, oils, and shampoos. To Fiona's surprise, she looked up and saw the one-eared sailor and his family. He waved to her and introduced his wife.

Fiona took a good look at his scarred face and smiled. "It has healed well," she said. Turning to Runa, she tried to explain how she had treated the wound.

Runa examined his face critically, and said something to him in Danish that Fiona interpreted as him needing to protect it from the sun and to wear a hat.

He listened intently and nodded. "I'm crewing with Thorkell again. We're leaving next week," he replied, in trader Gaelic.

"Take some moss with you and keep it clean," Fiona said.

He nodded then moved on, his family trailing behind.

Fiona was surprised by the amount of business done at their booth. Runa and Olrun seldom had a chance to sit down. Lunch was a bread roll and an apple each. She helped out where she could.

Several vendors were selling vegetables, and the stock was rapidly depleted by anxious buyers. *Hedeby must be like Dublin. No one grows their own food in town.*

When they were shutting down the booth and placing things back on the cart, she saw several of Ottar's grandsons, including Bjorn, going home from their apprentice jobs, their tools slung over their shoulders. She still didn't like the atmosphere around him.

As the day ended, she found it easier to remember the Danish names for plants. The cart was much lighter to push on the way back home, and the mud had dried out somewhat. All in all, it had been a good day.

CHAPTER 29

A day in the marsh

Gunnar spent most of the day with Thorkell, hiring locals to crew the ship. There was no sign of Ivar. *He must have found passage on a northbound ship.* Harald had signed back on for the voyage. Gunnar knew that although they were shipmates, they would never be friends. Snorri's sword was still a contentious issue. The one-eared seaman and most of the original crew were back. Cart loads of hides from the warehouse had been delivered, as well as crates of amber recently brought to Hedeby by a small Swedish fishing boat. Thorkell doubled the guard.

On their way back to town, they stopped at the butchers to order four barrels of salt beef to be delivered the next day. The crew on both ships had been instructed to scrub out the water barrels and fill them.

Gunnar was pleased with Fiona. She was getting along well with Runa's family and was making slow but consistent progress learning Danish. He planned on taking time the next day to stand guard over the women when they went out in the marshes to find plants, despite Runa's opinion that the marsh was safe. Until Fiona was familiar with Hedeby, he didn't like the idea of her being there.

While they were gathering plants, Gunnar intended to scout out the area and do some fishing. Atli had already offered to lend him a rod. With any luck, he might catch some trout.

When Gunnar arrived back at the house, Fiona was busy washing the mud stains from her dress and cap. She rinsed them in another pail of clean water, then hung them up to dry at the back of their bench. After washing her feet, she threw the water out onto the street and refilled the bucket from the community well.

After supper, the women spent the evening mending clothes, sorting herbs, and spinning. Olrun was weaving with flax. Fiona looked quite content, whorling fleece fibres. Gunnar found it reassuring that she was fitting in so well, easing his concerns of leaving her when he went to sea.

The morning dawned cloudy but no sign of rain yet. He watched Fiona stand in the doorway as she did every morning, looking for omens. Runa didn't go to the marshes anymore, so she and Lilja stayed behind minding the youngest girls while Fiona and Olrun took the older children with them. Atli had already left to fish in the fjord.

The girls went with the women and the two boys carried their fishing rods, tagging along with Gunnar. They passed through the open palisade gates, guarded by a couple of old fellows who'd probably been warriors in their day but were now King Olaf's men, guarding the town from Frankish raiders. On their belts they carried not only their swords but also cattle horns to trumpet a warning if needed. He stopped and talked to them, but kept it brief, keeping an eye on the women. Gunnar could hear their female voices singing and calling out to each other in the tall reeds.

It was pleasant in the shade of the low trees as he cast his line into the water. There was a constant hum of insects, the croaking of frogs, and bird calls. Gunnar looked at the boys. Eric, the oldest one, was Olrun's son. He was eight or nine years old, tall, and blonde. Six-year-old Sven was the son of Atli and Lilja, just as dark as his father. The two complete opposites were best friends.

Gunnar had been so intent on fishing that it suddenly occurred to him that it was quiet.

"Can you hear the women?" he asked, pulling in his line. The boys knew the marshes far better than he did.

Eric pointed to the east. "The last time I saw them, they were heading over there."

Gunnar sprinted up a small hill, giving him a broad view of the wet lands. He saw the stooping figures of many women but not Fiona or Olrun.

"I don't see them."

Sven shinnied up a tree and looked around. "There they are," he said, pointing.

Gunnar scooped him out of the tree. Heading east, he waded into the water and found them, totally obscured by the tall reeds until he got close. He heaved a sigh of relief. Both women had their skirts full of plants. The older girls had been gathering moss from tree trunks and stones, filling the burlap bags hung over their shoulders. They also collected fresh dandelion leaves for supper. They were almost hidden by the mass of greenery they had collected.

Gunnar escorted them onto the banks and as far as the palisade gates, then resumed fishing. The boys stayed with him. He quite enjoyed his afternoon but went back empty-handed, although each of his young helpers had caught small trout. They were bold enough now to tease him about his lack of fishing skills. He hoped Atli had done better, or there'd be little for supper.

At the house, Runa and Lilje had prepared a meal of pork, carrots, parsnips, and fresh bread. They graciously accepted the boys' fish, quickly gutting them and leaving them in a pot of salt water for next day's meal.

After the dinner, Gunnar decided it was a good time to introduce Fiona to Thorkell's family. It was important she get to know as was many people as possible before he left. Thorkell's wife Astra had been born in Hedeby. She was a strong, generous woman and knew everyone who mattered.

As they walked the paths to Thorkell's, Fiona asked. "Would you consider joining King Olaf's army and guard the gates?"

"I could but it wouldn't solve the problem of getting our own house, and they don't fight very often. It's been years since we've had a raid—before I was born. It's all right for old men, but not much challenge for me."

The closer they came to Thorkell's and Ottar's houses, the more affluent the neighbourhoods became, with bigger houses and fresher air. They had their own outhouses. Laughter could be heard from Thorkell's house with its open door, bright light streaming in from the street.

Gunnar walked in with Fiona right behind him. His brother was sitting at the head of the table, a mug of mead in one hand and his young son sitting on his lap. Conversation momentarily stopped. Astra put down her spinning and came over with her hands outstretched in welcome. Gunnar saw Fiona pause for a moment, as she often did, then broke into a smile, extending her hands to her hostess.

Astra was tall, and big-boned with ruddy cheeks, a substantial bosom and a firm but gentle presence, mother of the house. Chattering, curious children clustered around them.

Gunnar felt an instant wave of gratitude to his brother. The welcome was genuine, so different from his reception with his parents and Steinn. His sister Gyda, and her husband, as well as Astra's youngest brother, also lived there, and bid them welcome.

One of the older girls brought them mugs of mead. Everyone shuffled around to make room at the table, and they spent the next few hours in pleasant conversation. He explained to them that Fiona was living with Runa and would be her apprentice.

Astra asked many questions. Fiona stumbled her way through explanations, but was managing one- or two-word answers surprisingly well. He knew Astra would stand behind her, just as Thorkell did for him. He had a high opinion of Astra as a sensible, caring person. There were things he wanted to discuss with Thorkell but privately, and now wasn't the time. As Gunnar and Fiona took their leave, they walked back to Runa's house in the night-blackened alleys, pleased with their evening and the contacts she had made.

The next few days were hectic. Much of his time was spent with Thorkell, getting cargo on board both ships including enough hay for the bull, for the two- to three-day trip.

During a lull one afternoon, they sat side by side on the knarr. "Thorkell, if I don't survive this trip, will you and Astra look after Fiona for me? Runa's place is the safest place for her to live at the moment. Although she's doing well with the language and all, she's still at risk."

"Brother, we leave shortly. If you don't come home, we'll surely help her. Astra likes her. She's seen her at Runa's booth on market day. I'll speak with her tonight," Thorkell replied, grasping him by the shoulder.

Gunnar awoke the next day with no particular plans. His cousins would be arriving at the shipyard—all those people, their belongings and the bull. Runa's house would be empty. Atli was fishing; Runa and Fiona had gone to treat someone in Poor Town, while Lilja and Olrun had taken the children.

Gunnar was worried about leaving her with all the money and treasures. The house was often unattended. Anyone could walk in and steal things. He quickly dug a two-foot-deep hole in the dirt floor beside their bench. Fiona wouldn't need much silver, maybe a quarter dirham per week, so he buried the chalices, the remaining silver, and the torque. Even if the house burned down, his stash would be safe.

Quickly, he shovelled the dirt back in the hole and tamped it down until it looked like the rest of the floor. He finished by scattering dried reeds over top.

Gunnar went through his sea chest, choosing the bearskin cape, his helmet, a spare sword, a woven blanket, spare shirt and pants. His shoes and leg wrappings were in good shape. The ivory comb was in the pouch on his belt. *I'm ready.*

Gunnar quietly grasped his pendant and prayed to Mjolnir for a successful and profitable voyage. Once they docked in Tynemouth, he wanted to find out about joining the army there. He'd heard there was steady pay for a warrior and land available. Gunnar's cousins would be well established by then. The only other option was to become a mercenary in Normandy.

He went back to the marshes, fishing rod in hand, determined to hook a trout and outdo the boys. Sitting quietly, Gunnar's thoughts wandered. Atli had told him that fewer large ships were coming to the harbour because it was silting up in places, so only boats with a shallow draft could enter. He couldn't imagine Hedeby not being a trading centre. They'd have to dig it out somehow. In the afternoon, he managed to land a trout and triumphantly carried it home, getting a cheer from the young lads. At least he was contributing to the family meal.

That night, when he lay in bed with Fiona, he whispered in her ear about the treasure beneath the floor. She understood the need for secrecy. Gunnar had a restlessness night, anticipating the upcoming voyage. Once again, their coupling was fierce.

Fiona was up before him as usual, looking out the door, to see the day. After downing a mug of oatmeal, he quickly dressed, then gathered his belongings, and strapped on his sword and knife. He handed Fiona a pouch with a few silver coins inside and with a brief hug, kissed her. Heaving his sea chest on his shoulder, he headed for the causeway where carts would be waiting. It would be a couple of months before he saw Fiona again, providing all went well.

CHAPTER 30

The Christian monk

Fiona watched Gunnar striding away with that cocky sway to his shoulders and hips, eager to go to sea. *Another adventure for him.*

Most of the day was spent sorting and hanging the remaining piles of plants. Olrun was stripping the outer stringy stems of the nettles for cloth making. Runa had plenty of customers dropping by for treatments or just to say hello. Lilja did most of the cooking, and the children were constantly in and out. Most of Runa's income came from the shampoos and ointments, enough to carry the household, while Atli's fish fed them.

It wasn't until the sun started setting that she thought of Gunnar. He wasn't coming back tonight or for a long time. She could imagine him on the longship, keeping just ahead of the knarr, rowing steadily all day and, about now, chewing on a hunk of salt beef. *It was a relief to be free of him.*

She glanced at the floor beside the bench. He'd chosen a good hiding place for his stash. It certainly wasn't obvious. Yet, the bed felt cold and empty without him, so she invited the girls to share it with her. They were more than happy to make the move, freeing up space in the other crowded benches.

The following day was market day, just a repetition of all the others—loading the cart, pushing it to market, setting up the booth, and treating the sick. Runa made sure Fiona dealt with all the customers directly, bartering and bargaining. She was starting to recognize faces, but struggled with the names.

Astra and the children stopped by. Fiona introduced them to Runa. It seemed that Astra always bought her shampoo there. She discussed which cough syrup to buy and Olrun recommended coltsfoot. Ragnar appeared with another bucket of honey, making a point of staying longer, talking to her, and laughing in a good-natured way at her mispronounced words. *I like him,* she thought.

The monk appeared later in the afternoon but this time was agitated. He approached the booth, holding his cross before him, screaming, *"Volve! Volve!"* May God strike all of you witches down!" he shouted, pointing at them.

Runa held her ground, proud and upright, but said nothing as he stood there ranting.

Fiona wasn't sure what to do. *I'm not a witch. I'm a Christian, not a pagan.* All her care was natural, for healing. She stepped in front of him and knelt on the ground, her hands held in prayer and began saying the Lord's Prayer, just as the abbot at home had taught her. When she finished, she stood up and looked at him.

Quietly, she offered him a bar of soap and said, "Brother, although I am married to a Viking, I was raised a Christian. The Lord puts goodness in the plants. We make soap from the plants. There is no witchcraft or magic in making a person clean," she said.

"You and God cleanse their souls, while we clean and care for their bodies. That's all—no magic." She wasn't at all sure he understood her broken Danish.

There was total silence. He scrutinized her with a haughty look of disdain, tempered with confusion as he looked down at the soap in her outstretched hands. He was frowning so hard, his eyebrows met in the middle. He paused for a moment, then said a prayer and quickly turned away, his back very stiff and erect. Fiona could see the swirling clouds of darkness around him were broken with streaks of flickering grey. Her confrontation had disturbed him. The noise level quickly spiked as everyone in the street stopped staring and started to chatter.

Runa put her arm around her. "Fiona, it's an old battle between me and Father Matthew. It's not usually so vehement. Maybe his abbot is visiting. There is a small Christian congregation here. They are Frankish people, from the south and have been successful in converting many to Christianity, but it's a slow process. We like our old gods, and the warriors follow Thor and Odin. You surprised him. I didn't know you were Christian. I liked the way you told him we weren't witches," she said with a laugh. "These monks don't like female healers. They don't like that we have the power of the goddess. They want us helpless and under the thumb of men. Women in our society have power; we can own land, have our own money, and we can divorce our husbands if we wish. They don't like that one bit."

The days passed and never failed to be busy. With the changing season, fruit was ripening, there were berries and apples to be picked, as well as flax and nettle to be processed. In the late autumn sunshine, flower petals were floated in bowls of water outside the house, their essences seeping into the water to make gentle yet effective tonics.

Lilja showed her a dress made of linen fibre and it was incredibly fine. She told Fiona that Ragnar's family farm grew and harvested the flax, then soaked it in water for two weeks. After that, they stacked it to dry in the fields before bringing it to town. He brought it to them in bundles, which they later beat with a wooden paddle until the fibres were soft—a long and tedious process. When it was finally reduced to soft, pliable fibres, it was then linen and ready to spin.

Runa told her that nettle stems were used the same way. That was their winter project on those long, cold nights when they huddled together to stay warm. On their excursions to the marshes around Hedeby, they searched for elderberry for wine or tonic, burdock root for gout and arthritis, nettles for hair shampoo, wormwood for internal worms, yarrow for bleeding, as well as countless other plants.

"We should be gathering red clover, too. It's quite useful for coughs and colds, but is also supposed to ward off witches and black magic. Maybe you should give some to Father Matthew," Runa said with a grin on her face.

Fiona laughed. One day, they were visiting a sick woman in a different part of town and Runa pointed out a small wooden building with a simple wooden cross nailed to the front door.

"That's the Christian church. Father Matthew lives around the back."

"We didn't have a church in our village. The abbot and his man came several times a year for a couple of days. They stayed in our house, and we had the service outside where he married the couples and baptized the children. Can I just peek inside?" she asked.

Runa nodded and urged her to go ahead.

Hesitantly, Fiona walked up the path and pushed the wooden door open, stepping inside. It was a bare room, completely open to the beams and roof. Several benches graced the perimeter. On the far wall was an altar with a large black Bible and several candles. Centrally positioned on the wall above was a large carving of Christ on the cross, the crown of thorns around his head. She stared in horror at the nails through his hands and feet. To one side there was a smaller statue of Mary, adorned in a beautiful blue dress, her head covered with a white cloth, looking serene. On the other side was a white-winged angel with doves. Fiona stood there in awe, mouth agape, and dropped to her knees.

"The stories they told us were true," she said out loud. Quietly, she began to pray—for her mother, for her sister—likely now in someone's harem or slaving away as a thrall, for Gunnar's safety and for herself. A noise behind her broke her reverie. She turned to face Father Matthews.

"What are you doing in the house of the Lord?" he demanded.

She got to her feet to face him. "I was baptized and raised as a Christian, but I've never been in a church before. Our village didn't have one. The abbot only came a couple of times a year and we held our service outside. Father, I came to see the Lord's house. I've never seen anything like it. It brings all the Bible stories to life," she said gazing back at Mary. "I don't know if my Viking husband will allow me to come here. He's at sea right now. Will you let me worship here?" she asked.

There was a long silence, then he took a step toward her. "Our services are on Sunday mornings if you are able to attend," he said softly, though still perturbed.

She saw the colour around him changing from black to sparks of blues and greens. Fiona acknowledged him, quickly walking out to rejoin Runa. She had no idea if Gunnar would let her attend. They'd never discussed religion. *Even if he forbade it, I could still do it.* She might have to embrace both worlds to make it work.

Fiona enjoyed market days. It was hard work; she was speaking Danish all the time and becoming better at it, but would likely never lose her accent or the Gaelic cadence. The market was a good place to meet people. She was starting to not only remember names but sort out who was related to who. Occasionally, she saw Astra; rarely Mor Signy. The only acknowledgment she got from Gunnar's mother was a nod of her head. Sometimes the other two wives shopped. The one woman told her that the little girl's arm had healed well.

The booth had a decent view of the harbour, which was interesting in itself for the comings and goings of many ships from Baltic destinations to the north and east. Norse knarrs arrived carrying bearskins, seal skins, walrus ivory, and weapons. Many different fishing boats came in with full holds. Swedish ships arrived with lumber, amber and sometimes cattle. Often, the Swedish ships carried warrior soldiers to relieve the small garrison of men stationed at the gates of the Danevirke.

Everyone was stocking up on fish for the winter. Fiona was told that sometimes Schlie Fjord froze over with ice and snow so the smaller boats couldn't go out, and now they lay upside down on the beaches, awaiting the spring. Atli brought home extra fish for drying, hanging them from the rafters over the fire pit. Lilja was drying apples as soon as they were ripe.

One evening when the children had settled in bed and the adults were sitting around the fire, Alti came in with an armful of chopped wood, adding a couple of pieces to the pit. A shower of sparks blossomed. He remarked that the squirrels out in the forest were hoarding acorns early, so it would likely be a long, hard winter.

Runa broke the silence. "When you look at someone, Fiona, what do you see?"

She paused her spinning for a moment. "Most of the time, I don't see anything, but if I concentrate and go quiet, I can see lights around people. Sometimes it's colourful, other times it's dark. I remember my mother, Aoife, had a bright light around her most of the time.

It upset people if I spoke of it, so she told me not to tell, that it could get me in trouble, especially with the abbot. My father didn't see it. The light around the abbot was very dark, just like the light around Father Matthew. Ottar and the grandson Bjorn are dark, too. I stay away from the dark ones."

"How did she teach you the healer's way?"

"Most of the time, I just watched what she was doing and asked questions. She brought me with her every day when she was treating others, but she never took me to the sacred oak forest. I always hoped she would, so I could see the deities that lived there. She taught me all the songs and prayers." Fiona went to tell Runa all about Gunnar's raid, the voyage to Dublin and later, the wedding.

"Fiona, there are many things I need to teach you. In Hedeby, there are many good midwives, so I think we won't bother with birthings for now. You need to know how to make the medicines, and some of our rituals for making them use the phases of the moon, or the stars. There is a right time to do some things."

Runa rummaged through her medicine box. "This is wormwood syrup. Tell me what you see and feel."

Fiona held the jar and stared at it. "It gives off a darkness with pulses of green through it, like it's alive. There is a heat. What does that mean?"

"The life force of plants is just like the ones around each of us. It might mean that it is not the right remedy for the illness you are dealing with. It might even mean that the medicine is old and shouldn't be administered. You must feel that this is the right medicine to use."

"How do I tell the difference?"

"Use your ability to see the light. It's just the same as young people having more light than old ones. If it is stale, your sense of smell is helpful. Think of the smell of freshly made hawthorn ointment. It is less potent over time. Be mindful of what you are using and what you are using it for."

"I've seen you give away some of your ointments to the poor," Fiona stated.

"I often do that when the remedies have lost some of their potency but are still useful on the skin."

"Runa, I think each healer has a different set of skills. I see colours, but you are skilled with touch. I see you moving your hands over people, feeling something. What do your hands tell you?"

"My hands give me different sensations. Healthy parts feel different to sick parts, and that alerts me to what is wrong. I see by the way people move, where pain is. What symptoms are they showing? Watch their breathing or movement. That will tell you a lot. I always work with the Goddess Eir. I pray to her to send love and health to them. I can't stress enough that I am not the healer; she is. I am her servant. Explore your talents. Always use them for good, never for evil or to cause harm."

"Do you ever use the runes for healing?" Fiona asked, thinking about Aoife's Ogham-style divining.

"Sometimes I do. I'll show it to you next time I use it. I think much of what you are doing is intuitive."

"You're right about that. Sometimes my hands just go to where the problem is, and I somehow 'know' what to do, but I don't understand where the knowing comes from."

"When you explore your talents, you may discover you have other abilities."

Fiona went to bed happy that night. Runa hadn't treated her like a weird creature—like it was normal. She was tired from her busy day and fell into a deep, untroubled sleep.

The next morning, skies presented with a bank of dark grey low-lying clouds and a strong, gusty cold wind. No sun was visible. There were no pigeons on the roof, and the streets were empty. The few people out and about were bundled up and scurrying. Atli wasn't going fishing. A storm was coming in fast. Fiona could feel it in the air and wondered if Gunnar had reached Tynemouth. If they were still crossing the North Sea, it could be a wicked storm like the one they'd survived in the channel.

It rained so hard they didn't go to the market and like everyone else, stayed inside. The rain was torrential, falling in wind-driven sheets for what seemed like hours. The puddles in the streets changed into ponds, collecting in low areas, seeping under the doorways of homes on lower ground.

Fiona took out her mortar and pestle and sat at the table grinding dried leaves. She looked at them, held them in her hands, and smelled them, trying to sense their meaning. She filled leather pouches and strung some up, ready for making tonics when the time was right.

Olrun commented on the quality of her mortar and pestle, and Fiona explained it had been a wedding present from Gunnar's cousin in Dublin.

By late afternoon, the force of the wind abated, although the rain was still steady. The house was strong and well built—no leaks in the thatch, but even it had shuddered with the gusts. Inside, it was warm and cheery with the fire going.

She spent time learning to use Olrun's smaller loom that rested on the table. It was two feet wide but only four feet long. Olrun had spun some flax stems into long panels of linen. When sewn together, they were easily made into shirts, trousers, and dresses.

Dawn was cloudy with a clearing horizon and a hint of sunshine. A few of the pigeons were back on the roof. Quickly, the women headed to the market to set up the booth, skirts kilted up to avoid the mud. Fiona could see the devastation caused by the storm. Boats had sunk in the harbour, and some had been driven ashore around the docks, lying in shattered pieces on the banks. Several houses lay in tangled piles of beams and thatch. A steady stream of injured presented themselves for broken bones, lacerations, and bruising.

Rumours were flying about deaths from the collapsed homes and missing sailors. Mid-morning, a Swedish trading ship limped into harbour, the mast broken in half. Chaos erupted on the dock as the crew beached her. Several Viking warriors quickly disembarked, talked to the locals and were directed to the booth.

The two warriors were very different. The tall red-headed man wore a chain mail shirt, helmet, and carried a sword. What caught Fiona's attention was the second warrior who was much shorter and slimmer in build. As they came closer, the features of the smaller one leading the way, made it obvious it was a woman. She had her arm in a sling. *A woman warrior?* Fiona had never met one before.

The line of injured melted away as the two approached the booth. Unperturbed, Runa stood up and beckoned them to come and sit. The male warrior was a step behind, closely observing everything around them, for any threat.

The woman was young, maybe twenty, with massive bruising on her face and shoulder. "I am Helga of Birka, a trader. We don't usually come this far west, but we needed amber. Our usual route is east on the Baltic to the land of the Rus. We took shelter on an island when the storm started, but were attacked by pirates. Many of my crew are injured. We survived but the storm shattered the mast and it fell on me. My arm is broken. They told me you are a healer. Can you help me?" she asked in trader Gaelic.

"Helga, I am Runa. Let me see your arm," she said.

Fiona stood close, watching as Runa extended the tear in the sleeve, cradling the obvious deformity midshaft on the left forearm. Immediately, she went to Runa's basket and retrieved moss for cleaning, comfrey for the poultice, bandages, and splints.

Runa looked over the supplies and nodded. "Fiona, get the black jar in the other chest. We'll need that, too."

"Helga, straightening the broken bones will be very painful. I have a syrup made from poppy juice, which I got from Arab traders. It is a potent pain killer. Do you want to use some?"

There was a growl from the scowling warrior, standing there with his hand on the hilt of his sword.

Runa looked up at him. "No harm will be done to her. It will ease the pain and make her sleepy."

Helga raised her right hand to him. "Balder, I will try it."

Runa carefully poured a spoonful of the dark liquid and gave it to her, then recapped the jar. Then they waited in silence. Fiona had a feeling that if anything went wrong, Balder would have no qualms whatsoever in killing them both.

They didn't have long to wait. Helga's eyelids began to droop, her body gently slumping against Balder. Runa shifted to the side, while maintaining the tension and support on the left arm. "Fiona, I'm going to hold her hand straight. I want you to feel the bones and ease them back in place."

Fiona stared at the arm. *Oh, lord; Runa wants me to do it!* She took a deep breath to steady herself. A picture flitted through her mind of the carcasses hanging in the butcher shop. Human bones weren't much different. She cleansed the whole arm with damp moss, removing the dirt, and feeling the shape of the bones with her finger tips. Kneeling beside Helga, she prayed to Eir, the goddess, to guide her, for the bones to move into place and heal.

The sharp, jagged edges formed ridges beneath the skin. Slowly, she pushed the pieces back in place, aligning them carefully so the joins were smooth. Helga softly moaned but remained asleep. Finally, Fiona was satisfied with the way it felt. Despite the swelling and bruising, now it was straight. The light around it was good. Fiona sat back on her heels to assess her handiwork. Helga's fingers were pink.

"Hold her hand. Just let me check," Runa said running, her gnarled fingers over the arm. "Good work, Fiona. Put the poultice on and splint it."

Water mixed with the powdered comfrey leaves quickly turned into a sticky, green gelatinous mess, which Fiona spread over the arm. She swathed the arm in bandage, then took three smooth sticks, positioning them around the arm and bandaged them in place. Bending Helga's arm at the elbow, Runa made a sling, tying it around Helga's neck.

"Balder, put her on the blanket and let her sleep it off. The comfrey dries quickly," said Runa. "It won't take long for her to wake up. What does your crew need?"

He gently lowered Helga to the ground, watching her closely. "One man has a broken leg, several have stab wounds, many have cuts and bruises. We lost one overboard," he said.

"Fiona, when she's ready, go back to their ship and take care of the wounded. I'll stay and look after the ones here," Runa said, looking at the curious who had come out of hiding and gathered to watch.

By the time Fiona had collected the supplies, Helga had roused enough to be sit upright on the small barrel with Balder's help. Gently, she applied comfrey ointment to the bruises on Helga's face, neck, and shoulder.

Helga refused further help and stood, Balder right beside her and Fiona followed them back to the ship where carpenters from town were dealing with the broken mast.

Fiona spent the day tending to the crew. Fortunately for the man with the broken leg, it was a lower leg injury, much easier for Fiona to deal with than an upper leg fracture. He staunchly refused anything herbal for pain, but one of his shipmates had brought him several jars of mead, and he was well into it before she was pulling on his leg. With help from the other seamen to keep him still, she pulled the bones in place, using the same ritual to Eir, as she had done with Helga. Again, her fingers felt their way until the edges slipped into place, and the light guided her like a little voice in her head. *I'm going to run out comfrey at this rate.*

Oblivious to the noise and turmoil going on around her, she treated all the wounded. Finally, the cleaning, stitching and bandaging was finished. After repacking her basket with empty jars, Fiona stood up and stretched, looking about her at the work being done. A team of horses had dragged another massive mast into position beside the ship. The tangle of cordage and spars had been removed and the splintered mast was being hacked apart and removed in stages, leaving a gaping space in the deck.

There were many small tears in the sail and already, small knots of men were patching and stitching the holes. Crates of goods had been removed from the ship to make room for crew to put the new mast in place.

Fiona could see Balder's broad back as he moved among the others. He was definitely second in command. Helga was sitting on a sea chest with her left arm in the sling but still very much the captain, occasionally shouting orders to the workers. She beckoned for her to come over.

"You're not Danish," Helga said.

"No, I'm Irish. I was a slave, but a Danish warrior married me. He's at sea right now."

"You and Runa have been of great service to me and my crew. What do I owe you?"

Fiona paused, sensing an open channel to the powerful young woman. There was a band of yellow around her—good light. "I have no idea. You'll be here for a few days yet. I will talk to Runa and find out."

She finally gave way to curiosity and asked, "Have you always been a warrior?"

Helga looked at her with sharp blue eyes and burst out laughing at the small girl standing before her. "It is not unusual for women to be warriors. I became one when my father was murdered by a competitor on our eastern trading route. Norse and Swedish women are often part of raiding parties."

"I was taken in a raid on my village by the man who is now my husband. During the raid, I killed the man who murdered my father, using my knife."

"The gods must have been on your side to kill one of theirs and not be executed," she said.

"I was angry," Fiona replied, with a shrug. "While you are here, could you teach me to use a sword? I have my father's. Hedeby can be a dangerous place for a lone woman. My husband is at sea quite often.

That amused Helga even more. She called out to Balder to come. He left the work on the mast and approached. "Balder taught me to fight with a sword, so I could continue my father's business. Balder, we'll teach Fiona to use a sword. Come here tomorrow, and we'll give you lessons while we are here," she said.

Balder huffed, not looking pleased, standing with his hands on his hips, but reluctantly nodded.

"Thank you. I'll come tomorrow," Fiona said to both of them, then picked up her basket to trudge back to the booth. She felt vulnerable by herself, especially in Poor Town. Knowing how to protect herself, Runa, Olan, Lilja, and the children was not only useful but a necessity with Gunnar away. Atli was often out fishing. Runa was protected by her reputation; Fiona wasn't.

Back at the booth, she told Runa that Helga wanted to know the cost of the treatments and about her upcoming sword training. Runa looked at her as if she was crazy.

"I think two dirhams would cover it. We've used up a lot of ointments. Why would you want sword training?" the old healer said, looking perplexed.

"I have my father's sword in my sea chest. He was a good man. I have a feeling that I may need that skill in the future, but I can't explain it."

Runa looked at her again through narrowed eyes as if seeing beyond her.

First thing in the morning, Fiona went to the docks. Carpenters were busy erecting a framework to raise the mast. Balder and Helga had found a small cove where they could practice. He examined Carraig's sword, and although it was old, declared it a good one. It was two inches longer than Helga's and slightly heavier, more unwieldy for Fiona to use.

Helga showed her how to hold it. Shield work would come later. They did slow motion fighting to show her the moves, then Balder challenged her, constantly giving instructions.

Fiona listened to her speak of many things like keeping out of reach of a stronger and bigger opponent, looking for weaknesses and vulnerable target points on his body, angles of attack, right or left-handed opponents, and when to turn and run. Because she was smaller and weaker, speed and agility were her advantages. Even with her arm in a sling, Helga was still able to demonstrate sword strokes with her right arm. Helga paid her the two dirhams to give to Runa.

A quick glance at the ship revealed the man with the broken leg sitting on a sea chest mending a sail panel, his casted leg stretched into the aisle. A cursory glance at the rest of the crew showed most of them working.

On returning home, Fiona gave Runa the coins and spent the rest of the day making ointments. Lilja was tearing old shirts into strips for bandages. Olrun was out with the girls, scrounging for weeds and seeds in the marsh. Atli's boat had survived the storm, so he continued local fishing whenever he could.

Another week went by before the Swedish ship was fully repaired. Fiona thanked Helga and Balder for their efforts.

"If we had more time, we might have made a warrior out of you," Balder said, with an unexpected grin. "You're quick on your feet, you watched how I was moving, and you're beginning to anticipate my moves. You're moving your shield well to counteract me."

Their last fight was a round with Helga and she managed quite well but realized that Helga was being lenient. Even with her shield arm in a sling, she was formidable. Fiona probably wouldn't stand a chance in a real fight. She watched as their ship left the harbour under full sail, rapidly diminishing to a dot as it moved on its eastern course back to Birka. It had been an interesting interlude, and she had learned a lot.

The autumn harvests were progressing well. The children told her all about the equinox celebrations in September and preparation for Samhain's new year's festival the last night in October. It was the end of their year with the male sun's descent in the heavens and the rise of the female winter moon. Runa made several tonics, showing her when to prepare them in relation to the phase of the moon.

Gunnar should be home before then. He'd been gone over a month. She'd missed the harvest fire festivals where her parents had celebrated the harvest and the god Lugh. She'd missed her birthday, too. She was seventeen now, no longer a child.

Fiona thought back to the abbot's visits to her village. Christians had a different calendar based on Christ's birthday. She intended to say a prayer for Gunnar in the little church.

A week later, when she awoke, she felt nauseated. She thought no more about it, and continued her work, accompanying Runa to the market every week and making syrups and ointments when the stars or the moon suggested it was the right time. Any spare time was spent weaving. Father Matthew continued his tirades from time to time, but for the most part just grumbled at them.

Ragnar spent more time with her on each visit, when he brought honey or flax to the booth. Fiona thoroughly enjoyed his company. Olrun told her that he was the oldest surviving son of a farming family who owned a large farm north of the town and his first wife had died in childbirth. It was a large extended family, including his married sisters and many cousins. He seemed a very pleasant, hardworking and capable young man. The light around him was consistently mellow. She found herself looking forward to seeing him on market days.

The children were getting adept at making candles, melting the beeswax then dipping the wicks repeatedly until the dripping layers formed tapers. Atli had even started a barrel of mead, combining water and honey, then floating slices of bread on the surface to provide the yeast. The barrel sat in the back corner, aromatically brewing.

Fiona and Olrun spent the day in the marsh gathering moss. By late afternoon, the moss had been washed and she had strung bunches up on the wall to dry. Olrun was in the middle of making a yarrow ointment. Fiona inhaled the aroma from the pot and felt a sudden wave of nausea. She sat down.

"You're pale. Are you alright?" Olrun asked. Both Lilja and Runa stopped what they were doing and looked at her.

Oh, my lord! What's going on? "I'm not feeling well. The smell of the yarrow is making me feel sick. Maybe I'm pregnant! I never even thought of that! I don't remember when I had my last bleeding time. It was just before Gunnar left, I think. Oh, what am I going to do now?" she said, quite distressed. *That's the last thing I need.*

"Gunnar will be pleased when he gets home," Runa said.

"Only if it's a son. That's all he ever talks about. Having his own house, and having a son. I don't care if it's a son or a daughter as long as it's healthy," she said picking up her basket again. It would be easy to end the pregnancy. *There's enough pennyroyal around here to do it, but should I or could I?* The more she thought about it, the more she knew she couldn't do it. That would fly in the face of every teaching from Aoife and Runa, not to do no any intentional harm. It would be a Christian sin, too.

"Where does he intend to build a house for you and the child? There's no room around here," Olrun asked.

"Oh, sorry. I was thinking about the baby. Good question. His cousins just moved to Britain near York. He's mentioned maybe joining the king's army there since it's steady pay and land is available. His Onkel Bersi offered him a merchant's job in Dublin, but Gunnar wants to remain a warrior."

Runa was straightforward as usual. "You can bear your child here and be part of our family, just as you are now. One more child in this household won't make any difference. You'll be more sympathetic to a pregnant woman if you've been through it yourself," Runa said with a kindly smile. Fiona had the feeling that somehow Runa already knew.

That brought tears to Fiona's eyes and they hugged each other

"Mint tea is good for morning sickness," Runa said, promptly making her a cup. After slow sips of the aromatic tea, the nausea eased and Fiona managed to nibble on a crust of bread, which stayed down.

At one point over the next few weeks, Fiona accompanied Olrun to the funeral of a family friend. It gave her the chance to see the graveyard and the burial ceremony. There were several cemeteries in town and a couple more outside the Danevirke. The burial took place up near the old chamber tombs of the well-to-do. Since the man had died of recent war injuries, he was entitled to full honours: placed in a dug grave dressed in his armour with weapons, food and wine. After the grave was filled in, a flat slab of stone was erected with his name carved in Futhark writing.

Olrun showed Fiona each letter on the stone, which looked like twigs on a tree, giving their names and sounds. It was the same script she had seen Onkel Bersi writing, and was identical to the symbols on the runes at Runa's house.

Observing a misshapen sword beside the body, Fiona asked, "Why was his sword twisted like that?"

"Many warriors believe that if they kill a man in battle and take his sword, then in the afterlife the man will come back to claim his sword. The blade is no use if it's damaged. It's an old custom and many don't follow it any more. If he'd been a rider, they would have buried his horse with him."

"They speak of Valhalla and fighting the anti-gods. What is Ragnarök?"

"That is the final battle between the gods and the anti-gods and will be the end of everything on earth, our world, Midgard."

"Do we know when?" Fiona asked. *It seemed so final.*

"No one knows," Olrun replied, thoughtfully.

There was much drinking and raucous laughter from the men present, who toasted the deceased, and sang songs of his exploits to send him on his way.

A Christian burial taking place at the same time further up the hill was in stark contrast a very quiet and solemn affair. Everyone was dressed in dark clothes and were quiet, other than muffled sobs from some of the women. Father Matthew stood at the head of a wooden casket, reading passages from his Bible for the family.

"They bury their dead differently in the wooden box, but there are no grave goods. I've seen some Christians burn their dead and bury the ashes, too," Olrun commented.

The golden leaves were falling, colouring the hills and woodland valleys in a carpet of yellows, browns, and oranges. The sun was setting earlier and evenings were much cooler. Autumn had definitely arrived. Other than occasional bouts of nausea, which the mint tea took care of, Fiona was feeling well.

Atli was spending more time ashore now with the seasonal change in available fish, working instead to replace the wooden seat in the boat and honing the boys' fighting skills. As she watched them using the staves, it occurred to her that the movements were very similar to those for sword practice.

One night when the boys and Atli were whacking away at each other, Fiona grabbed Lilja's broom by the handle and joined in. Everyone was laughing at the total chaos with the four of them fighting in the small space, dodging around the table, and over benches.

Ten minutes of that tired her out. Eric was quick and gave her a good thump on her thigh with an overhand blow that stung. Atli cautioned him about hitting too hard. At the beginning, he'd been reluctant for her to join them, but in the end agreed and now was laughing as hard as the rest of them. Using the stave was good for both strength and agility.

Fiona was careful to avoid getting hit in the belly. She couldn't risk damage to the baby. Atli had warned the boys about that. The fights were risky, but she had the feeling she needed to keep up her sword skills. Carraig's sword was in her sea chest out of sight, but all of them were aware she had it. *Something was looming.*

The days were going by and she thought of Gunnar more often, trying so picture his face. His beard would be at least an inch longer now. This time she would be one of the women waiting at the dock for her husband, or waiting for Thorkell to give her bad news.

Runa and Fiona were late getting back to the house one evening after tending to an old couple with severe arthritis in Poor Town. Suddenly, a knot of brawling men tumbled out of the tavern. Fighting bodies were all around them, punching and flailing. Fiona's last view of Runa was seeing her being shoved and falling to the ground.

She saw the flash of a boot as one man kicked Runa out of the way, in his effort to reach his opponent. She grabbed a broom from someone's front step and entered the fray, striking at the men, trying to clear a space around the fallen woman. Fiona dodged, thrust with all her strength, catching someone in the face, another in the gut, dancing out of reach. Meanwhile, neighbours joined in, using their staves to protect the two women. The Swedish guards suddenly came running down the path, their swords drawn. The fighters scattered with the guards at their heels.

When she turned around, other women were helping Runa to her feet. Tossing the broom aside, she rushed over, clasping Runa tightly.

"I'm alright, Fiona," Runa said, looking at her, pain etched on her haggard, old face.

"Are you able to walk the rest of the way?"

Runa nodded.

It was slow going, with Runa limping worse than usual. Alerted by a neighbour, Atli came running down the path and met them. He was furious when he saw his mother bruised and dirty. He offered to carry her, but she shook her head. So, supported on either side, the old woman carefully walked home.

Runa changed her clothes and cleaned herself up, refusing help from anyone. Fiona watched the light around her, looking for signs. Bruising, yes. Broken bones, no. Injured pride, yes. Anger, smouldering. Holding her hands over Runa's head and shoulders,

Fiona prayed hard to Eir to heal this feisty, elderly woman and was thankful she'd put her stave training to good use. *Too bad I didn't have my sword.*

The next day was market day but Runa stayed home, too stiff to move. All the vendors were talking about the fight. Fiona heard a lot of false stories of her warrior skills, but decided rumours like that might protect her and Runa in the long run. She was hoping to see Astra and Ragnar again before the bad weather arrived, when there would be fewer market days. The last time she'd seen him, he'd given her some candles and his hand had lingered on hers. She had shyly allowed that for a brief moment, then withdrawn it, and thanked him, wishing she wasn't a married woman.

Astra came to the booth with the girls. "Thorkell's still not back. We haven't had any word. It's such a worry. They may have run into bad weather or Norsemen. I pray Ottar will change the sea route and we won't have to go through this every time."

Fiona worried, too. She vaguely sensed Gunnar's presence but it was dark and distant.

CHAPTER 31

Changes

Gunnar heaved a sigh of relief. *Finally, I'm home.* He eased up on his oar as the longship nosed her way onto the beach. He sat there for a moment, just thankful to be still. The pain in his left shoulder was unrelenting. The crew took in the sail. Meanwhile, villagers were coming out of their cottages to see who'd arrived. He looked over at the knarr, where Thorkell had dropped anchor.

Thank the gods they'd survived the Norse, bad weather, and injuries. His left arm was a mess. *I'm lucky it wasn't my sword arm; it's bad enough I can't use my shield properly.*

Gunnar didn't want to do this anymore. Working ashore would be more rewarding. Tynemouth was a better prospect. He could settle there with Fiona, join the army for regular pay, and build a house. All the men around him were tired, disgruntled, and dishevelled. They'd lost four good warriors in the Norse raids and had scant booty to show for it.

As soon as Thorkell landed on the beach, a rider was dispatched to Ottar for the carts. It was too late in the day to travel through the marsh. The local pub served up bread and a hearty fish stew, plus jugs of beer, plenty for every crew man. He was sick of salt beef and didn't intend to eat it for a very long time. Gunnar sat beside Thorkell on the deck and they ate their meal together.

Thorkell looked at him. "I have to say, that's the worst trip we've ever had. The Norse are firmly entrenched all around the Scottish coast. It really limits our chances for slaves and plunder. They're settling in the islands and coastal communities. Your arm's still giving you problems, isn't it?"

"It's a good thing Fiona gave me a lot of moss. I'd be dead by now or missing an arm if I hadn't kept it clean. I can tell you plainly that the next time I'm on this ship it will be a one-way trip to Tynemouth and I won't be coming back here."

Gunnar slept fitfully that night, waking several times with the pain, but it was a blessing to be on something that wasn't moving, even if it was only the rough shingle beach.

The bearskin cape kept out the damp and chilly morning air. With difficulty, he removed his sea chest from the longship and placed in the sand. The crew began unloading the goods from the knarr. The aroma of fresh bread wafted from the pub, and there was a cauldron of fresh oatmeal simmering. The tavern keeper rang the copper bell when it was ready. Gunnar joined the lineup and scooped a mugful of oatmeal when it was his turn. The cook had sweetened it with honey. It was good. Freshly baked bread was a treat, too. He felt better after that.

Helping move the cargo was out of the question. Gunnar sat on his sea chest, his head bowed, and impatiently waited for the carts to arrive. Finally, they appeared and loading started. He ignored some of the dirty looks from the crew but the arm was agony. Thorkell helped him put his sea chest on the cart and they climbed on board. His thoughts were on Fiona as they moved through the marsh to Hedeby.

Several hours later, the town came into view. His eyes searched through the hordes of women and children. There she was, standing beside Astra and the children.

He'd forgotten how beautiful she was, especially the look on her face when she saw him and started worming her way through the crowd to reach him. He slid off the wagon, pulling her close. The smile on her face faded when she saw the healing scar on his cheek and the dirty old blood-soaked bandage around his left shoulder.

"Oh, Gunnar, what happened?" she cried, running her finger gently over his face and filthy beard.

"A broken sword," he said. "I was lucky. I could have lost an eye. The shoulder's giving me grief." He pulled her close with his good arm and kissed her hard.

Thorkell shouted behind him and lowered the sea chest down for him to take. He then unloaded his own chest and walked over to Astra before continuing on to the line of apprehensive women whose husbands hadn't come home.

Gunnar hired one of Thorkell's older boys to shoulder the sea chest back to Runa's as they wound their way along the back streets, away from the port. He wasn't prepared for the warm welcome as they entered Runa's house. There were smiles from everyone, even the children. Runa took one look at him and ordered him to bathe. Eric and Sven ran to the well for more water, and Atli put more logs on the fire to heat the cauldron. Gunnar submitted out of pure exhaustion.

An hour later, Fiona had scrubbed him clean and towelled him dry, being very careful around the wound. It felt very strange to be tending to her husband, much more personal. *She felt his pain. She opened her heart and the pain washed over her. More than that, she felt his anguish of somehow being reduced as a man no longer able to fight, not in control. Fear.*

Fiona got a good look at his wound. *Nasty.* She went through his chest under the bed and found clean clothes. He sat at the table bare-chested as both Runa examined his arm.

"Gunnar, when did you get this injury?" Runa asked.

"Over a week ago when we were in Bruges. Norsemen attacked us. I was fighting with a warrior, and his blade shattered when he struck mine. One piece hit me in the face, then he slashed at me with the broken hilt. I killed him. The cheek's fine but the shoulder's different. I cleaned it with the moss like Fiona told me to, but it's not healing. It's draining all the time and it hurts to move," he said, wincing as Runa poked and prodded the red, swollen and weeping tissue.

Fiona watched every move Runa made.

"Bring my poppy juice, Fiona," she said.

Gunnar interrupted. "No, Runa. I don't need anything. Do what you must," he said, looking grim.

"All right then, but I need you to stay still. I suspect there's a piece of metal in there. Get up on the table and lay flat. Olrun, more candles. Atli, be prepared to hold him down," she said, her own injuries forgotten.

He stretched out on the hard planks of the table, looking up at the flickering lights all around him and the ring of concerned faces. He closed his eyes and listened as Runa and Fiona chanted prayers to the goddess. Runa moved his arm out straight then upward

and immediately the pain jabbed. He flinched and grimaced. Her fingers probed the edges of the four-inch
cut, searching and sensing.

Opening his eyes briefly, he watched her bone needle
pierce the wound. The deeper she probed, the worse
the pain became—red hot, burning. He gritted his
teeth and tried to stay still, but groans escaped his lips.
Atli's strong hands pushed down hard on his shoulders,
the women held his legs, and the boys were hanging
onto his right arm. Runa moved her small knife so it
followed the path of the needle and slit down into the
tissue. Gunnar screamed. Darkness swallowed him.

He awoke a short time later to find himself still on
the table. Runa was just tying the bandage in place.

"Ah, you're back with us. Just lie still for a few
moments, then we'll get you sitting up," she said, rinsing
her bloody hands.

Fiona looked down at him and stroked his right arm.
"Runa got the metal out."

"All right Gunnar, let's get you up."

He raised himself to a sitting position, dizzy for a
few moments, but it quickly dissipated. He sat still,
aware of the family around him. Fiona slipped his clean
shirt over his shoulders, then stayed beside him as he
stumbled to the chair.

Runa handed him a bent triangular fragment of metal
about half an inch long. He took it and examined it.

"It's hard to believe that something so small took me down," he said, his brows furrowed.

"That wound is going to take a long time to heal," Fiona said. "It's been open for so long that it's too late to stitch it. It will have to heal from the inside out, so I'll wash it with moss every day and put on a new bandage. You'll have to be patient with it. No sword play, using an axe, or carrying anything heavy."

Looking around the room at the smiling faces, for the first time in a long time Gunnar felt truly welcomed. He sat there all afternoon, watching the women prepare the evening meal, the boys practising their stave fights, and Atli mending his nets. He felt tired and heavy, yet strangely at peace. It occurred to him that every word Fiona had spoken had been in Danish. *That's good.*

Fiona put a mug of mead in front of him. "You're finally home. We were all worried when you gone so long," she said. When she sat down on his right side, he put his arm around her. He felt her acceptance as she shifted closer.

That evening, when they were sitting around the table finishing their fish stew, young Sven asked, "Fiona, did you tell him about the baby?" Everyone stopped eating and there was dead silence.

"What baby?" Gunnar asked.

"Your baby," said Sven with a grin.

Gunnar set down his mug and looked at her, eyeing her flat stomach. She blushed and looked back at him.

"Our baby?"

"Yes, our baby," she said.

He was speechless. He'd been gone more than two months. She wasn't showing yet. *A son— no, my son,* he thought, running his hand over her belly. Everyone was laughing. He needed to find work over the winter and somehow earn a living, even with his bad shoulder. The money he had was for a house, not for daily necessities.

Atli spoke. "Gunnar, I run a trap line in the woods during the winter months. Catch mostly rabbits. The boat needs caulking. I could use some help when you feel up to it."

Thor must have heard me, he thought. "That will suit me fine, outdoor work."

Before bedtime, he wobbled over to the bed bench, opened his sea chest and offered Fiona a small flat package. "I saw these in Dublin and thought you'd like them."

She smiled and opened it. He saw the look of wonder on her face as she unfolded a three-yard piece of shiny, pale blue material that fell in soft, gentle folds. There was also a small glass jug of the same colour. It was so delicate she gasped and ran over to the others to show off her new treasures. They were enthralled, noting the delicate weave of the material and the tiny embedded gold threads along one edge. Olrun held the jug up to the light and was fascinated that she could see through it.

"The silk is from the Iberian merchants in Dublin. They tell me it is made from the caterpillar threads from China, over a year's journey by land and sea. The glass is from Venice in Italy, somewhere in the Mediterranean. I don't even know where those places are."

That night, he lay in bed, too tired to do more than hold her, his hand resting on her belly. It was the best sleep he'd had in days, and he thanked the goddess for Runa's skill.

First thing in the morning, after a porridge breakfast, Fiona tended to his arm, replacing the wet, pink-stained bandage. She insisted he wear a sling.

"I'm a warrior. I'm not wearing that," he said, looking down at her frowning face.

"Be gentle with it then. I've got to help with the booth," she said, shaking her head as she helped the women load the hand cart. "Are you going to your parents?"

"No. They made it quite clear I'm not welcome. I'm going to help Atli as much as I can on boat repairs. I worked on my father's knarr when I was a boy. Don't worry. I'm not going to do anything stupid using this arm," he said, giving her a one-armed hug.

"Gunnar, did you have a chance to go back to my village?" she asked.

"No. The Norse now have a village set up just above the mud flats. Too much risk of losing the knarr."

She nodded, disappointment on her face. She felt sad, still not knowing for sure if her mother was alive. Lately, she hadn't felt any contact. She joined Runa and Olrun pushing the cart to the market while the men and boys went to the port, leaving Lilja and the girls at home.

CHAPTER 32

The runes

It was much cooler in the mornings now. Earlier, Fiona had stood at the doorway looking out as she usually did. Although cloudy, there was no sign of rain, the pigeons were content on the roof, and the street was busy already. *Good omens*

Part of her was glad Gunnar was home. Fiona missed him and was glad of his presence when they went out. He protected her. The gift of the blue silk and the glass jug had been a total surprise. She tried to imagine making an overdress of it to complement her wedding dress, but when would she ever use it? She'd placed the jug in her sea chest.

Being a wife on the other hand, was different. She resented him always being in charge. Her opinion didn't seem to count.

She helped Olrun push the cart to their booth, setting up the barrels and planks as they usually did. Runa was organizing the herbs, creams, tonics, and shampoos, seemingly back to normal, except for bruising that was fading to yellow. Already, there were a few customers requiring care. Fiona immediately attended to them, recognizing them, and knowing what their ailments needed.

Astra and her children stopped by to pick up soap and shampoo, her basket full of pork pieces. Fiona thought that she appeared much more jovial and content, now Thorkell was back for the winter. "How's Gunnar's arm?" she asked.

"Runa managed to remove a piece of metal, so it's going to take a while to heal. I doubt he'll be a good patient. Stubborn as a donkey. He promised to be careful, but right now he's helping Atli with boat repairs. He shouldn't be doing any lifting, either. I'll just have to wait and see."

Later that morning, Fiona saw a couple shopping and recognized the man. "Runa, that's the man with the broken hand I told you about," she said as she called him over. He introduced his wife.

"May I look at your hand?" Fiona asked.

He held it out to her. Examining the scarred and callused skin, she found the thumb and next two fingers flexed well, but the fourth and fifth were stiff with

SUSAN K. KEHOE

limited movement. Runa inspected them as well, asking Fiona to bring the broom over. He couldn't close the hand around it properly.

"I can still row and use an axe, so I'm lucky that way, but them little fingers aren't much good. At least I can work," he said.

"I'm sorry. I wish I'd known how to do it better," Fiona said.

"At least you fixed the others. You did your best," he replied.

"Make sure you keep working them, or they'll tighten up even more," Runa told him as the couple took their leave and moved on.

On the whole, Fiona was pleased with the progress she was making on all fronts. She now spoke some form of Danish with more words strung together. Most of the time, she was coping with Runa's regular customers but still hadn't conquered all the recipes for tonics and oint-ments, or all of the plant names. She thought about the Gaelic festivals, which she missed terribly, seeing friends and relatives, rejoicing in the seasonal changes. The Danes followed the seasons, but it was not the same.

Fiona liked Hedeby, barring drunken sailors. She knew her way around town now and was very careful to finish tending people by mid-afternoon. It would always be dangerous after dark unless she had Gunnar with her. She still missed open country.

Sometimes she saw Ottar and Steinn at their booth, bartering with their wealthy patrons, but they barely acknowledged her. Darkness still swirled around both of them and she wondered what they were really like.

She ate a piece of dried bread for breakfast, and saved the apple for later. She was thankful that the nausea didn't last long in the mornings. Later that day, when she was changing the dressing on an old woman's arm, she caught a glimpse of Ragnar who was homeward bound, minus the yearling bull she'd seen him bring to town that morning. He chatted briefly with Runa. He always had a ready smile for Fiona, though, with a twinkle in his eyes, and was never slow to tease her about her Danish and the growing bulge of her belly. *Too bad the baby wasn't his.* That thought stunned her. *What was she thinking?*

The fjord stayed navigable most of the winter. A few Swedish ships came in, holds full of deep-sea fish. Several bigger ships came in carrying soldiers to relieve the ones protecting the town and Danevirke, more than usual—a reminder that the King of Sweden still ruled them. That was a bone of contention for the townsfolk.

By late afternoon, the throngs thinned out. Fiona was starting to pack the goods back into the hand cart when she happened to glance at Runa, who was sitting on a barrel, lost in thought. The light cast deep shadows on her wrinkled face, catching a solemn and thoughtful expression. The usually bright aura around her, had dimmed. *Was Runa ill? Was this a lingering effect of her fall following the pub fight?*

Fiona kept an eye on Runa for the rest of the day, watching how she moved, nothing obvious but something wasn't right. When they reached home, Fiona unpacked the cart and put the jars away, setting aside those that needed to be refilled. Runa was very, very old. The strands of hair escaping her cap were snow white. Now she wondered if Runa would live long enough to see her child born.

She sat there for a few minutes, knowing she needed every available moment to gather all those gems of wisdom her mentor had given her. Often, they had no need to speak; a look was often enough. Her heart filled with a deep sense of caring for this woman who had taken her in, whom she'd grown to love. Quietly, she hummed and sang one of her mother's cradle songs, sending the goodness to Runa on behalf of the goddess Eir.

The sun was setting earlier, and Atli, Gunnar and the boys returned home before dark. She listened to the men talking during their meal. Gunnar had been teaching the boys how to remove the old caulking from the boat and make new caulking. That evening, around the fire, the women sat around spinning wool. Gunnar seemed content and was being careful with his arm. Later, he got out his board game and challenged Atli to a match, which Atli won, much to Gunnar's chagrin. Once, he pounded the table with his fists, and instantly regretted the pain it generated.

Fiona spent part of the evening sitting with Runa, learning about the runes.

"Their history is ancient from generations lost in time and represent two things; first they are letters of the very ancient Futhark language but are also used as symbols or omens," Runa said, emptying the pouch of polished stones marked with enigmatic symbols on the table.

Under her direction, Fiona spent time spelling simple words, just like the writing Onkel Bersi had used.

Runa picked out one with an inscription that looked like a tree trunk with two branches slanted upward on the right-hand side. "This one is called *Feoh.* If it lands right side up, it means good fortune, fertility, and success. If it is right side up but reversed, that means infertility or bad luck. If it lands face down and upright, then there are secret forces you must take into account. You will have to coax the creative powers to come forth. If it is upside down and reversed, good forces are at work but secretly. Obstacles must be resolved to achieve success."

"I didn't realize it was so complicated. Why do you lay out six?"

"That's the way I learned it from my mother. Say, for example, someone is not responding well to a treatment. I try to find out why. I randomly select six runes, then I look at each one to see what it means. It could be that there is something else happening in the marriage, the family, or with their health that I'm not aware of and is affecting the healing. These might give me an idea of what is wrong and I can then change my treatments," Runa said.

"Do you ever just get a feeling that one ointment or tonic is the right one to use?"

"Not often, but I know you do. I've seen you pick up two tonics, then pause before selecting one.

"Yes, but I can't even describe it; maybe it's a feeling in one hand and not the other, that one is better for that treatment."

Later when everyone went to bed, she asked Gunnar about his arm.

"Most of the time, I'm careful with it but sometimes I just forget," he said, distracting her by kissing her.

She gave him a kiss on the cheek and changed the subject. "Did you see the troop ships come in?

"I did. Word is that the Swedes are bringing more soldiers here. There's something brewing south of the border with the Franks and Slavs. The fighting might be coming north."

"Will Hedeby be safe?"

"I don't know. We haven't had an attack since before I was born. That's why we have the Danevirke. You'll likely see more patrols out on the walls."

A sore arm didn't stop his love making, and he fell asleep with his hand on her belly.

Lately he'd been gentle. Pending parenthood seems to have mellowed him a bit, and for that I am thankful.

CHAPTER 33

*Present-day archaeological
dig site, Hedeby*

Pulling up his collar against the sharp wind chill, Professor Jorgenssen looked at the dig site and felt a sense of relief. They'd managed to extract all the specimens from the grave just as the weather turned and their permit expired. Together, they had filled in the trenches, so now there was simply an earth mound, hidden by a light snowfall, indistinguishable from the surrounding graves. The shed and fencing had been removed. Gena had made a small sign reading "Hedeby Man—early 10th century" in Futhark lettering, a temporary substitute until the grave stone was fully restored.

All four were back in class, working on their final year papers. Jon rarely saw them together now, each going their separate ways. Helga was the only one who intended to stay in Europe. Her goal was to become a museum curator, while the other three were looking for fieldwork. Each had been very good in their own area of expertise, but as a group they had never gelled. They were working hard on their doctorates, and had applied for next summer's work all over the world.

Jon was teaching full time but was still involved with the lab, as the conservators cleaned the warrior's bones and artifacts. He had a stack of paperwork to finish. Plans were underway for an exhibit at the museum, though that was probably several years off. He intended to work on the grave stone over the winter, assembling the hundred shattered pieces.

Despite his ongoing workload, it was nice to spend time with his wife in the evenings and finally get some time together. *Nine to five like normal people. Eating together, talking together, going to a concert, making love on a Friday night, and sleeping in on a Saturday morning.* Jon was enjoying it and she seemed to as well. His sons were teenagers and rarely home, but he'd swear they'd grown an inch taller already.

Helga had suggested a diorama for the museum exhibit. That appealed to Miles and Gena, too. Lars was comfortable with making duplicates, rather than exhibiting the genuine items, which he still contended should be left in the grave. They had lots of suggestions ranging from a battle scene showing off the weapons, armour and helmet to a domestic scene in a Viking house, one that would display all the finds. The most intricate job was reconstructing the tiny delicate pieces of blue material.

Lab results were slow coming so there were large, important gaps in their knowledge base they needed to fill in order to complete their reports. The main one was Hedeby man's genetics. Was he of Danish origin or more Eastern European, like many others in that cemetery, possibly Obodrites from Mecklemberg? The incomplete epiphyseal growth plates on his bones confirmed he was in his late teens. The stable isotope analysis of the diet wasn't available yet, either. It would be interesting to see if his diet was land or sea based and if he had been well nourished throughout his lifetime, indicating higher societal status in his community, backing up the quality of his armour and grave goods.

His bone structure was sturdy, and for the most part indicated a rigorous physical life, very apparent in the upper body, likely due to rowing and weapons use.

The latest reports Jon had received had been on the warrior's woollen clothing. The species of sheep hadn't been identified yet. His linen shirt did match specimens from other local graves in Hedeby's cemetery. Flax was known to have been grown on farms to the north.

Attempts to classify the Eurasian brown bearskin cape could not be defined any closer than being either Norse or Swedish. The Damascus sword was of Eurasian manufacture with a Frankish hilt. The eagle on the scab-bard was typical of Frankish design. There was no word yet on the game board and its hand-carved ivory pieces or on the gold pendant of Thor's hammer. The writing on the silver dirhams from his belt pouch indicated they dated back to the caliphate of the seventh century. Those had created quite a stir, since the time frame and genealogy of the caliphates were well-documented. Overall, his analysis was of a young Viking warrior with seagoing trading or raiding background.

The cause of death was not obvious. No nicks or damage to bones. It must have been a fatal soft-tissue wound, such as a belly thrust or throat slash. He wouldn't have been buried with his "killed" sword and armour unless he'd died in battle. Pinning down the date was difficult as there had been frequent Saxon raids on the peninsula. The sword was too rusted to date.

The last item they uncovered from the collapsed rib cage was a lock of dark-auburn hair and a bundle of dried plant stems wrapped in a piece of the fine blue material, the stems inserted in the remains of a small shattered glass jug. Was it Venetian? That would raise questions of Mediterranean trade and possibly dating. *It will be interesting to see the DNA results on the hair. A wife's offering? If he was a raider or trader, what national-ity was she?*

CHAPTER 34

Before the darkness

Rain mixed with sleet had fallen daily for the past few weeks, ending any work on the boat. The door was closed to keep the heat in, making the house dark, lit only by the fire and reed torches. All of them had added extra layers of clothing. Gunnar sat quietly while Fiona removed the old dressing from his arm and cleansed it again. Although it continued to ooze, the fluid was clear, and the tissue was less inflamed. Slowly, it was healing over and was only a couple of inches long. He was getting more use out of that arm, but pain was a reminder to follow his wife's advice.

He watched Fiona as she wrapped his arm, noting with pride the small but growing bump in her belly. They smiled at each other when he ran his hand over it. Lilja and Olrun were working at their looms. Atli was coaching the boys with small carving projects. Gunnar enjoyed working with them, too. He watched them, hoping in the future, it would be his son on his knee.

He had overheard the Swedish guards discussing rumours of mysterious strangers from the south. *Spies?* A few seamen told of fighting between the Slavs and Franks again, which wasn't unusual. What was concerning was that the warfare was continuing despite the winter weather. Winter campaigns were unheard of. Thoughtfully, he rubbed his arm. *If a battle is imminent, I'm not sure my arm has healed enough to wield a shield.*

Gunnar looked at his old one, with the cracked and splintered wood and decided he needed a replacement. Maybe it was just an excuse to leave the confines of domestic chaos and take a trip to the blacksmith's shop. Leaving the warmth of the household, he moved quickly down the lane, the sleet stinging his face and dripping from his beard. Smoke rising from the forge's chimney told him the smith was working, and he opened the door to the roar of the fire and steady hammering. The smith stopped and lay down the massive hammer.

"Good to see you, Gunnar. Miserable out there, isn't it? What can I do for you?" the brawny man asked. In the back, the man's son stopped working the bellows and the orange-red flames over the coals dimmed to dull red.

Gunnar recognized the other boy working as Bjorn, and acknowledged him with a nod. "Jorgen, I'm looking for a new shield. Do you have any?"

"That I do. Bjorn, go up in the loft and bring down a couple for Gunnar to look at. Gunnar, do you think we're in for trouble?"

The two men watched as Bjorn clambered up into the loft and sorted through the shields.

"The Swedes were talking about fighting south of here, but there are rumours of spies. I'm not taking any chances."

"How's your arm"

"Getting better. Annoying, to say the least."

Bjorn brought down two shields, which he handed to Gunnar. Both shields were bigger and heavier than his old one but were of much the same design with a circle of wooden slats held in place with a shaped steel rim welded to hold them in place. Three radiating spokes met at the pointed central hub. On one shield that work was plain; on the other it had been intricately worked into a motif of Sleipner, the eight-legged horse of Odin on the spokes, and a more ornate hub.

Holding it with the leather hand drip, Gunnar turned it over and ran his fingers over the horse. It would look good with his sword and pendant. *I'll have both Thor and Odin on my side.*

The two men bartered for a while and Gunnar traded one of his other swords for the shield. Despite the lack of slaves and pitfalls on the last voyage, he'd still managed to bring home some money and goods from the Norse he'd killed.

When he got back to the house, he was just in time to participate in the afternoon stave training for the boys. He showed off his new shield which everyone admired. Atli took on Eric, while Gunnar took on Sven. The women simply got out of the way. Gunnar had just paused when he was struck from behind. He spun around, ready to kill, and was confronted with his wife who proceeded to attack him with her broom handle. At first, he was amused, then realized very quickly that she had far more skill than he could credit in a woman.

Fiona was quick, matching his moves, striking like lightning, whacking him on the thigh or knee. She dodged his blows, keeping just out of reach. He finally cornered her, picked her up, tossed her over his shoulder, and dropped her on their bed. Once he had her down, she was no match for his strength, and lay there laughing.

"Where did you learn that?" he demanded, not the least bit amused. Although not strong or experienced enough, her skill confounded him. *If she could do that with broom handle, what would she do with her father's sword?*

Atli cut in, "Hilda of Birka, a Swedish trader, taught her that while her ship was being repaired. Fiona set her broken arm and in return, Helga taught her to use Carraig's sword."

"You knew and didn't tell me," Gunnar snapped at the man.

"It wasn't my place to tell you," Atli retorted.

Fiona got up from the bed, smoothed out her dress, and stepped between them, facing her husband with a smile on her face.

"I wanted to surprise you," she said. "There may come a time when you and Atli aren't here and I might need to protect everyone, including this baby. It was the sensible thing to do, Gunnar," she said suddenly becoming serious.

He was silent for a few moments, amazed at her courage and abilities but also troubled. Fiona saw things and didn't always tell him. In her own way, she was confirming that war was coming.

"It seems I now have a Valkyrie for a wife. Odin give me strength," he said, putting his stave away and sitting at the table, where Atli was setting up the board game again. The noise level rose once again as the two boys continued their workout. Old Runa sat there, quietly taking it all in but saying very little, consulting her runes.

Another week passed, and the streets were no longer bustling with people. Smoke rose from the roofs and everyone stayed inside, clustered around the fire pits to keep warm. Sometimes people came to the house to buy ointments. Runa rarely went out any more. Fiona did the bulk of the actual care, under her direction. Market days were infrequent and weather dependent.

Gunnar sometimes went to visit Thorkell or followed Atli out to the woodland trap line, bringing home the occasional rabbit or bird. Atli was teaching him about setting the traps for different animals and how to identify the tracks of rabbits, hares, foxes, and bears.

Hallows' eve had long gone. It was a new year now according to the pagan calendar, and he was looking forward to moving to Britain and the birth of his son in the spring. Fiona had told him the baby would be born in late May or early June. He wanted to be home for that. He found confinement in the house difficult in the winter. He wasn't one to sit around and do nothing. Going beyond the gates to hunt gave him an opportunity to talk to the guards and keep up on the latest news.

Gunnar spent many evenings participating in the stave training, which Fiona insisted she continue to do, "until the bump gets in the way." She was adamant about him helping her with Carraig's sword. What she didn't have in strength, she had in cunning and agility. The neighbours often teased him that if he ever bedded another woman and she found out, he'd be risking his manhood.

Gunnar awoke to Fiona's scream of "Get dressed!" and the blowing of horns from the palisade walls. Leaping to his feet, he pulled on his clothes and dragged out his sea chest for his armour, while Atli was doing the same and shouting instructions to the boys and Lilja.

Gunnar grabbed Fiona and kissed her, then sprinted out the door, following Atli to the din of battle.

CHAPTER 35

The Frankish invasion

Fiona had woken abruptly with an overwhelming sense of urgency. She slipped out of the warm bed to peer outside into the morning gloom, leaving Gunnar still sleep. She spied a hawk on the roof, tearing the flesh and feathers from a dead pigeon clutched in its talons. Sensing an even deadlier, darker force nearby, Fiona screamed "Get dressed!" Moments later, many horns blared warnings from the palisades.

"The Franks!" Atli shouted as he and Gunnar scrambled into their clothes. Fiona, Olrun and Lilja helped them with their armour and helmets; the boys brought the shields and weapons.

Turning to the boys, Atli yelled. "Fill the pails. There'll be fires. You're in charge of the house. Protect the women. Lilja, retreat to the boat if you need to," he said, striding out the door, axe in hand.

Gunnar grabbed Fiona, kissing her hard, transforming into the warrior again. With one last look, he ran after Atli.

Outside, other men raced towards the noise of battle, most armed with staves or axes. Women in their night clothes jostled their way outside, babes in arms, older children clinging to them, crying. The echoing clash of weapons, shouts, and screams intensified. Runa took charge. The boys grabbed buckets and ran to the community well. Lilja gathered up bread and a pot of oatmeal, then put out the hearth fire. Fiona quickly dressed, then filled her medicine chest with extra bandages and ointments as well as her money pouch in case they had to flee. She hung Carraig's sword on a handy hook and buckled her knife on her belt.

Soon, the boys returned with sloshing pails, taking up their positions at the door, trying to look grown up with their staves in hand. Eric shouted, pointing to a billowing cloud of dark smoke and sparks flaring above the rooftops from several streets over. The battle was close, within the town walls, and loud. The Danevirke had been breached. Soon, the injured were being brought back, carried by others. It was pandemonium. Each told their own tale of carnage and loss as Runa and Fiona set up benches to treat them. Olrun was ripping up more old clothes for bandages.

"It's the Franks all right, a couple of hundred warriors," one man told them, as Fiona cleaned and stitched the sword cut on his arm. "I never thought I'd be saying this, but we're lucky the Swedes brought in troops on that ship last week. At least we've got a chance. They were expecting trouble." Rumour had it the fire had started in a house but now the whole tightly-packed block had gone up in flames so quickly that one family had not escaped. Fiona knew them from her visits. *God help them! What a way to die!*

News came that Steinn's son Bjorn had been killed. There would be mourning at her in-laws' home for their heir and grandson. She wouldn't grieve his loss. Within an hour, the sounds of battle became more distant as the action moved south along the Danevirke, interspersed with periodic cheers. The boys disappeared to scavenge the corpses of the Franks. Sven came running back, breathlessly telling Runa, "Atli's wounded. He can't walk. They're bringing him back on a cart." Now Lilja looked really worried.

"Have you seen Gunnar?" Fiona called to him, as she finished setting a broken arm on a young woman, who'd fallen during the confusion.

"No! Not yet! They're finishing off the last of the Franks. I'm going back to see what else I can scrounge," Sven said, quickly disappearing down the lane.

CHAPTER 36

Gunnar

Atli and Gunnar ran, joining the mixed mob of townsmen and warriors streaming out of the lanes towards the palisades. Atli headed towards the tower, but Gunnar saw a group of Swedish soldiers heavily engaged and lunged in their direction. He caught sight of Thorkell fighting hard. Moments later, Gunnar was swinging his sword and carving his way into the fray. The townsmen didn't stand a chance against the experienced Franks but still courageously fought with their axes. Men went down. He glimpsed a split-second view of his one-eared shipmate gutting a warrior before he disappeared in the melee.

After taking down several enemies, Gunnar spun facing the back of a Frank who had just put a sword through a townsman. He launched himself at the man who fought back but lost under the onslaught of Gunnar's anger.

He faced a new opponent, an experienced dark-haired fighter, and the battle was on. Both of them swung at each other, counteracting blows with their shields, looking for weakness, looking for a chance. Thrusting and parrying was difficult while being knocked off balance by the battling men around them.

Odin give me strength, Gunnar prayed as he concentrated on his enemy. He was tiring, and his left shoulder hurt. The new shield was heavier. He stared hard at the man and went for him, again deflecting the blow but the shield arm was slower to move, not responding as quickly as he wanted. Gunnar stumbled over a corpse and found himself falling backwards. He hesitated for a moment then saw the glint of the descending sword and raised his shield as he rolled out of the way, slashing at his enemy's legs.

Both men were down. Gunnar dropped his sword and shield, grabbed his knife, then struggled with his opponent on the bloody ground. Every muscle in his body drove the knife tip deeper into the man's chest until blood poured from the wound and the Frank beneath him lay still.

Gunnar rolled over, placing his hand on his sword and tried to stand up, but sensed someone close by. There was just a glimpse of savage eyes and gleaming metal slicing across his neck. With a last gasp of breath escaping, darkness engulfed Gunnar as he collapsed, his sword slipping away.

CHAPTER 37

Widowed

Momentarily, Fiona closed her eyes and tried to sense Gunnar, but couldn't feel his presence. Runa briefly shook her head. *That didn't bode well.* Many injured were now lining up along the path, waiting for care.

The pale sun was high before cheers were heard. The smoke hanging over Poor Town had dissipated to filaments of grey, carrying dark flakes of ash. The wounded were limping home, supported by family and neighbours. Wails of grief echoed down the lanes as the dead were brought home. Some women headed out to the battlefield to search.

A cart appeared on the path. Fiona saw Thorkell sitting up front with the driver. His shirt was torn and blood-splattered and he looked exhausted. Sven and Eric were in the back with a pile of booty. When the carter pulled the horse to a halt outside the door, the women crowded around. Atli was conscious and sitting with his legs stretched out, a large stained bandage on his left thigh.

Gunnar's body lay beside him. Fiona stood motion-less for a moment then gently touched his inert and cooling face, a gaping wound to his neck. His shirt and trousers were blood-soaked. She gasped for breath and her mind numbed. *It was too much to bear! First Carraig, now Gunnar. She still loved her father. But Gunnar had been her only protector. She had become accustomed to depending on him, and she did care for the man he was when he wasn't being a warrior. He had been dependable working hard, helping Atli and bringing home food. He had wanted the child in her belly.*

Meanwhile Thorkell, Olrun and Lilja helped Atli into the house and the boys began unloading the spoils. Thorkell emerged a few minutes later and put his arms around her. Silent tears were trickled down her cheeks. *In spite of the raid, Gunnar had been good to her.* Now there was a void.

"He fought like a demon. Even though his arm hadn't healed, many a Frank fell to his sword today. Gunnar died a warrior's death as he would have wanted. He's in Valhalla now," Thorkell said, gently moving away from Fiona, his own eyes glassy. "We'll bury him tomorrow, if

I can arrange it. Let Runa help you prepare his body. I'll take his sword and have the blacksmith 'kill' it."

She vaguely remembered when they'd been at the funeral that Olrun had explained that the smith would heat and warp the blade.

Thorkell grasped Gunnar's body and swung it over his shoulder, wobbling under the weight and carried him into the house, depositing him on the floor just inside the front door. He gave her another hug, then climbed back onto the wagon, looking haggard and depleted, Gunnar's sword on his lap. The carter urged the horse away to take Thorkell to the smithy, then home before heading back to the field for another casualty.

Runa was busy working on Atli's leg and the long line of injured were waiting. Not knowing what else to do, Fiona sat down and went back to work, cleansing cuts, applying ointments and bandages to burns and injuries. She lost track of the people—old, young, regulars, and strangers—and just kept going. Occasionally, someone patted her hand, expressed their condolences, or said a prayer with her. It sustained her through the afternoon although the numb feeling persisted. Olrun periodically replenished the ointments and bandages. It was nightfall before the last customer left.

Atli was lying on the bed, propped up on pillows, looking drowsy but comfortable. *Runa likely gave him poppy juice.* The bandage on his leg was clean. She sat on the edge of the bed and he smiled at her.

"Atli, are you alright?" she asked, looking at the abrasions on his feet and legs.

He put his hand on hers. "Runa worked her magic. The axe took a chunk out of me, but she's cleaned it all out and packed it with moss. I'll be fine in time. I'm sorry about Gunnar. Don't worry, we'll take care of you and the baby," he said, perceptive and practical as usual.

Runa called to her. "Get something to eat, Fiona. You haven't had anything all day. That's not good for the baby," she said, leading her over to the table where Lilja had set up bowls of honeyed oatmeal and mugs of mead. Everyone was hungry. The temperature outside had dropped. She shivered, glad for the fire and her woollen cape.

"I must get Gunnar ready for burial. It might be tomorrow if Thorkell can arrange it. What do I do?" she wailed, feeling lost, and alone in a totally different way. Gunnar was never coming home. The vacant space at the table haunted her. Even his spare cloak hanging on a hook forced her to realize he'd never wear it again. There would be no one to challenge Atli in the board game. No warm body in her bed every morning. *It seems I cared for him more than I thought I did.*

Runa interrupted Fiona's wandering thoughts. "When you've finished your meal, we'll wash him and dress him in clean clothes and his armour. We'll comb his hair. The Valkyries have taken his spirit in their golden chariot to Valhalla. He'll be feasting in the great hall, drinking beer with the warriors and playing his board game, no doubt swapping stories with the others. You're still part of our family. That doesn't change."

"I can't expect you to feed and clothe us," Fiona said, feeling a rising panic.

"Oh, Fiona," Runa said, putting her arms around her. "Now is not the time to worry about that. He has two sea chests of booty under your bed."

"Sorry, Runa. With all this, I'd forgotten all about that. Stupid of me. You're right. There will be enough to sustain us for a long while yet. Just tell me what to do so I can get through the funeral."

"Change has come, and life in Hedeby will be different from now on—for all of us," Runa replied.

When supper was over, they cleared the table. All of them pitched in to lift Gunnar's cold, blue-grey body onto the table. By the flickering light of the torches, they stripped him of his armour and clothing then washed him with their scented soap. The wound on his shield arm was a deep purple now, never to heal, and his throat wound reminded her of Snorri, the man she'd killed in Ireland.

Sven and Eric cleaned the dried blood from Gunnar's armour and knife. Fiona searched through his sea chest and found a clean linen shirt and trousers for him. Olrun sang hauntingly beautiful songs and prayers, but they were not familiar to her so she sang her old Gaelic ones. Bowing her head, she prayed that Christ would save his pagan soul.

Dressing a dead man was awkward, but they managed it. Gently, she combed his hair. His beard was too short to braid. As she fingered Thor's Mjolnir chain, she thought it hadn't protected him after all. Finally, they lowered him onto the floor on the bearskin cape.

She glanced outside. It was bitterly cold. The street was empty—not a sound, not even a dog. She quickly closed the door, wondering where the homeless were sheltering that night.

The girls snuggled close to her under the bed covers, and she felt their warmth enveloping her, slowly pushing the dark feelings away. Throughout the night, she woke several times, hearing Atli's groans and Runa's whispered words: more poppy juice. Gunnar was only ten feet away and yet he wasn't. He was an empty shell. She slept.

CHAPTER 38

Gunnar's burial

Fiona spent the early hours next morning sorting Gunnar's belongings in preparation for his burial. She decided to use the board game and pieces, his ivory comb, and a pouch with a few silver dirhams as his grave goods. Thoughtfully, she clipped a lock of her hair, tied it with a bow of silk, tucking different kinds of herbs into the glass jug—everything he would need on Valhalla's battle fields.

Thorkell didn't arrive until afternoon when the sun pierced the bank of snow clouds to the north, which did little to warm the chill breeze from the sea. She watched him climb out of the cart. He looked weary and solemn.

"Are you ready?" he asked, holding her at arm's length, looking her over.

"I am." Fiona was wearing the blue dress she'd been married in, with her heavy woollen cape, and gloves.

The rest of the family were in their best, albeit, plain clothes. "Atli's coming too. The boys found crutches for him."

"Atli can sit up front. We'll put Gunnar in the back and the rest of us can walk behind. I hired men to dig the grave this morning. There was only room for Bjorn's burial in the family plot near the old chamber graves, so Gunnar's will be further down the hill. Astra's taken the children up there already."

Sven and Eric helped him move the cloaked corpse onto the wagon bed. Runa decided to sit on the tail-gate, her arthritic knees bothering her in the cold. Atli managed to manoeuvre himself with his crutches so Thorkell could give him a leg up onto the wagon seat, but even minimal weight on his damaged leg made Atli grimace.

Fiona looked at the sword. Its blade was twisted and deformed almost into a knot. Sven found Gunnar's shield in their scavenged pile, so the armour was complete.

It was a solemn walk to the cemetery as the family followed the cart through the lanes. Faint tendrils of smoke were still rising from the burned houses, now reduced to low piles of blackened timbers and thatch, the stench lingering.

People along the street opened their doors and waved to them as they passed. Soon there was a procession of carts. More families, more dead. From their slight elevation, Fiona could see the battlefield speckled with figures moving from corpse to corpse, stripping them of valuables. The Swedish soldiers were hauling naked bodies to the burning pile in the middle of the field. Some of the poor were taking their dead, too. A huge flock of crows had gathered and were feeding, squawking, and flapping in aggressive competition. *How many people from Hedeby died?*

Their route took them closer to the marsh, but she could see Ottar, Steinn, and the family gathered up the hill. Astra and the children left the group, walking down to join them.

The carter reined the horse to a stop beside the freshly dug pile of dark, moist, peaty soil. The open grave was eight feet long and four feet wide and deep. Thorkell removed the bearskin cape, jumped into the hole, and placed it on the ground. With help from the neighbours, Gunnar's body was lowered and he arranged it on the cape.

"Thorkell, help me down," Fiona said, poised on the edge of the pit, with the bag of grave goods clutched in her hand. He carefully lifted her, setting her down into the grave. She placed the helmet on Gunner's head, framed by his long hair. Then she straightened Mjolnir. Eric handed her the Damascus sword, which she placed under the cold, flaccid right hand. She tied the money pouch to his belt, along with his knife, then set the game board and sack of ivory pieces by his left side, along with his ivory comb. Taking one last look at him, she said a Gaelic prayer, then took the jug with her lock of hair nestled in its silk ribbon and herbs and set it on his chest. Thorkell helped her out of the pit.

By that time, not only had Astra and the children joined them, but so had Far Ottar, Mor Signy, Steinn, and the rest of the clan as the hole was filled in. Fiona and Astra hugged each other and spoke with Runa. Unlike the funeral ceremony she'd witnessed months ago, there was no singing or drinking. Atli stayed on the cart. Ottar was visibly upset, yet Mor Signy didn't speak a word to anyone.

Why hadn't Gunnar been buried up the hill with Bjorn below? Because Gunnar didn't count! Bjorn was Steinn's eldest, and he would have wanted his son in the sacred tract near the ancestral graves. Ottar had complied.

Ottar did talk to her briefly, announcing he would have a headstone made in Gunnar's honour. "It will read: Gunnar, warrior son of Ottar," he said. Steinn could barely look at her, his face a mask of grief, his eyes glancing back towards the hill where his son was buried.

But Ottar must have cared somehow. At least he was giving the grave marker. There was little more to say. The two groups went their separate ways. A chill wind gusted in from the sea and it started to cloud over.

"Runa, I'll be in touch later this week," Thorkell said, helping her back on the tailgate. "Will Fiona be staying with you, or should I be looking for another place for her?"

"She's part of our family now, Thorkell, just like when he was at sea," Runa replied, putting her arm around the girl. "The baby's due in early June. She'll need us then."

He nodded and walked away with his family as Fiona and the others followed the cart back to Poor Town. A few wounded were waiting outside the house, shivering in the cold. Runa invited them inside as Fiona quickly changed her dress, prepared to give care. One man quietly gave her a piece of hack silver when she finished stitching his arm. She thanked him and gave the coin to Runa.

By then Atli was in severe pain, his face ashen, barely able to propel himself on the crutches to his bed. A large dose of Runa's poppy juice started to take effect as she changed his blood-soaked bandage. Later, an exhausted Fiona quickly fell asleep.

The next day, she awoke feeling lighter as if a cloud had lifted. When she looked outside, the only sign of life on the snow-covered street was the flock of cooing pigeons on the roof ridge. No hawk.

Lilja got out of bed, careful not to disturb Atli.

"How was his night?" Fiona whispered, adding wood to the fire. Everyone else was still snuggled in their beds under heavy covers.

"The poppy juice holds him for a couple of hours. I'm afraid for him, Fiona. He's not doing well. He's not used to being helpless or in that much pain. The hole in his leg is horrible, the size of my fist," she said, cupping her hand. "Runa only stitched part of it so it would drain properly. The moss and bandage were changed last night."

"I remember Runa telling me that poppy seed was a really good pain killer, but it can't be given for more than a week or they'll never stop craving it. We'll have to find something else to give him then, maybe willow or arnica. What can I do to help you? Do you need anything done for breakfast?"

"Could you grind the oats?" Lilja replied.

So Fiona sat at the table and filled the bowl with scoops of oats, grinding them down with the stone.

Meantime, Lilja looked around the room. "I really need to clean this place. It's a mess," she said, seeing the buckets of soiled bandages, the piles of armour and clothing the boys had brought in, as well as Gunnar's pile. "They'll have to do Atli's work now. He won't like that," she said, looking at the tousle-headed pair, still angelically curled up, deep in sleep.

By midweek, Hedeby started to come back to life; more people were on the street, shops were open, and fewer people were coming for treatment, mostly burn victims. Fiona found two other healers who had poppy juice. She bartered chain mail for it. That would be the limit for Atli.

The pungent stench of burning flesh hung over the town, permeating every nook and cranny. Fiona smelled it in her hair and clothes. She wondered how long it would take to burn all the bodies. Even lavender tucked in her bodice didn't keep the odour away.

Gossip was rampant about the dead and missing. The Catholic church was the only building on one block to survive the fires. Father Matthew proclaimed it as an act of God. Members of his congregation helped with the neighbourhood cleanup. She never got used to him speaking Latin. News arrived that farms south of town had been torched and farm families killed by the retreating Franks. They'd not been able to reach the areas north of town. The death toll in Hedeby was more than a hundred. Out of nowhere a thought surfaced. *Most likely Ragnar is safe; at least I sincerely hope he is.*

Gunnar was often in her thoughts, even when she saw a warrior on the street, or she caught sight of his pile of plunder; the boys practising with their staves could trigger it. Most of the time she was too busy to think about much of anything with the volume of continuing care.

It became apparent over the next few weeks that Atli's crutches might become a permanent feature. All Runa's care for her son and healings had prevented infection and saved his leg from amputation, but didn't resolve the numbness and inability to hold his weight. Fiona found him becoming sullen and short-tempered, frustrated with not being able to do his chores. The boys had taken them over. Eric was chopping wood.

"I can't even go trapping," Atli complained, looking at the dried fish hanging in the rafters. "This isn't enough to last 'til spring."

One evening when a storm was howling, driving and sculpting the deep snow in the narrow streets, they sat around the fire. Fiona was accustomed now to being a widow. No waiting for the ship to come home. No demands on her as a woman. She thought a lot about that. She had sixty pieces of silver coin plus the money buried beside the bed. Gunnar's stack of booty, separate from the boys' pile in the back corner, could be sold or bartered. Her growing belly was a constant reminder that there would another mouth to feed.

"Atli, I know you're worried about our food supply. If you can't walk by the spring, can you take the boys fishing? You still have a lot of upper body strength," she said.

"I'd need help getting the boat in the water, but maybe the neighbours could help. These two lads might be able to raise the sail and manage the nets with some help from me. I can manage the rudder sitting down," he replied, looking at them.

"What about your trapping? Could Sven apprentice with one of the other trappers, until your leg has healed?"

"I hadn't thought of that," he grudgingly admitted. "I don't want to be a cripple, pitied and despised because I can't provide for my family."

"Atli," Runa said with a sharp edge to her voice. "I doubt that very much. Healing a wound like that is slow. It will be months before it is well and truly healed. You won't be doing stave practice any time soon. Patience, son; it takes time."

"And I'm well known for that!" he said sarcastically.

Fiona looked around the room. "You have the advantage of knowing everybody in town, Atli. We have all this armour to sell, and there's no one better than you to trade them. In the spring, you could use the booth. Olrun and Lilja weave, and so do I. We're making our own clothes now. With the two looms, any extras could be sold. We can teach Dagny, Eydis, and Mildrun as well. They comb and sort the wool anyway," she said, casting her eyes over the fire-lit faces of the girls sitting on benches close by, looking angelic with their braided blonde hair.

Lilja was the first to speak. "Good ideas, Fiona. We all need to think about we can do. In a few months, you'll have your own child and you won't be able to go out so much."

"I can still make ointments and do treatments here, but you're right."

Runa looked at her. "Have you given any thought to marrying again?"

Fiona looked up sharply. "So soon? No. Why?"

"I've had two inquiries: one from a soldier, who spoke with me the other day when I went out, and the other a local."

"Oh? Who was interested?"

"Gorm, the butcher is looking for a second wife, and Turgeis, one of the Swedish soldiers, wants to stay in Hedeby. He's young and has soldiered for the Swedes for four years. There's actually a third party. Our honey man, Ragnar Sturlsson sent a message to Thorkell. His family was aware of the attack but just found out Gunnar had died."

"Do you want to get rid of me that quickly?" Fiona asked, joking yet defensive.

"No, my girl, don't take offence," Runa said, looking her squarely in the face. "Bringing up a child alone is difficult and dangerous for a young woman."

"I imagine it would be, but will these men be willing to take a woman pregnant with another man's child?"

"I believe all of them are aware of that," Runa said. "Sleep on it. I, for one, am ready for bed. We've all got a lot to think about. Enough for now," she said, shuffling off to her bed.

That night, Fiona lay awake. Second wife to Gorm, the middle-aged beer-swilling butcher with the whining wife was off-putting to say the least, relegating her to the same situation as Ottar's household. Turgeis was an unknown, but she'd had enough of warriors, always away, always fighting. She liked Ragnar. That was a union she could consider. He was a hard-working country man, not a townsman. Every time he'd come to the booth, he'd paid attention to her, joking and laughing. The light around him was mellow. He'd lost his first wife during her labour. *Would his father even consider her and be prepared to risk it again with her pregnancy?*

CHAPTER 39

*Present-day archaeological
dig site, Hedeby*

The fall semester was over. Professor Jorgenssen was sitting at his desk, working on the lecture series for winter classes. Finally, the lab results on Hedeby Man's genetics had come in. Looking at the results and statistics, it was clearly established the young man was indeed Danish, with Frankish and Eastern European ancestors.

A knock on the door interrupted his thoughts. Lars stuck his head in. "Can I talk to you for a few minutes?"

"Sure," he replied, moving the papers aside.

"I applied for a summer position in Belize on one of the Maya sites. They want a reference about my work. I know we aren't finished with Hedeby Man yet, but would you provide one?"

"Lars, you did a good job on the site. You're patient and methodical with both your excavation work and your specimen preparation. I certainly can give you a reference, providing of course that you intend to complete your year. There's only five months left. How's your thesis coming?"

"Of course, I'll complete it. I've got a start on our paper. Haven't talked to the others lately. I've got the basic premise set out, but it's far from complete. Have any other lab results come in?"

"The breed of sheep is still vague, but seems similar to the Old Norwegian Spaelsau. The isotope analysis of our warrior's diet had also come back, showing the mix of land and ocean-based diets, consistent with the mixed farming and local fishing. I haven't got back the results on the bundle of hair in that glass bottle."

"One detail at a time. Thanks. Have you heard from the others?" Lars asked.

"Not so far this week. Helga's in Germany, checking into a curator's assistant position. I think Gena's got a potential lead on a Peruvian dig. Don't know much about it yet, and I haven't heard from Miles at all."

"Don't work too hard," Lars said as he slipped back out and shut the door.

With that, Jon went back to his paperwork until his watch alarm went off at 6 p.m. He put all his papers away and locked up the office, determined to be home in time to take Elsa out for dinner.

CHAPTER 40

Springtime

It was the end of April, with the weather warming enough for Fiona to swap her heavy cape for a lighter one. The tree tops in the surrounding forests wore a soft pale-green haze of emerging buds. Most of the snow had gone, leaving wet, dead leaves punctured with spears of bright-green grass and weeds. Pairs of ducks were back in the swamp, quacking and splashing in their annual mating dance among the reeds.

Atli, with the help of his fellow fishermen, launched his boat that morning and took the boys on their first fishing expedition. She prayed he'd be successful. He was so hard on himself, so independent and stubborn. Although his leg was stronger, he still needed the crutches.

Hedeby slowly came back to life, literally rising from the ashes. The market had opened the previous week, and Fiona had thoroughly enjoyed working the booth and seeing everyone again. Even Father Matthew was in a good mood and hadn't cursed them when he walked by. On occasions when she had been near the church, she had slipped inside and quickly said her prayers in the empty building, leaving a loaf of bread for him.

Their new linen goods sold well, along with the soaps, shampoos, and tonics. It was so nice to be outdoors, instead of huddling in the house, around the fire. *Daylight and sunshine make me feel good.* Olrun sold two pieces of armour and a sword to a Finnish sailor. Once again, they collected hawthorn blossoms for the tonic water they made. Water bowls full of blossoms sat outside the house, soaking up the sunshine, the goodness of hawthorn seeping into the water, making gentle tonics.

Fiona decided it was time to sell some of Gunnar's plundered goods the next market day. She was tiring more easily, no longer quick and graceful. Much of her time was spent taking care of regular customers with old injuries, aches, and pains. By now she was much more adept in speaking Danish.

Astra came out of the crowd with her gaggle of little girls. The women hugged. "I'm so glad you're here. It's been weeks since we've seen each other. Not much longer, I see," she said looking at Fiona's bulging belly.

"Has Thorkell heard from Ragnar or Torfi?" Runa asked.

"They'll be coming to market soon and will want to meet you and Fiona," Astra replied.

"Do you think he's seriously interested?" Fiona asked. "Sometimes I just thought he was being nice. I must admit he's a good-looking man, and I enjoyed speaking to him whenever he came to the booth. I did wonder what things would have been like if I hadn't been married to Gunnar," she confessed with a smile.

"Did you now? If things go well, you might just find out," said Astra. "Thorkell told me Torfi has several choices for a new wife for Ragnar. One is the daughter of a wealthy sail-maker in Ribe, but Ragnar seems determined to bring him here to meet you. Don't be surprised if you get a visit," she added, rummaging through their stock of linen shirts.

"I'll take one of these shirts for Thorkell. He's off to Tynemouth next week. Ottar's changed the route; he decided it wasn't worth it to go all around Scotland and Ireland to get to Dublin. Too many Norse and not enough slaves. He's got a load of cattle and trade goods to go over but should be back within a week. It could be Bruges next time. Might not even need the longship. It'll depend on the Norse."

Runa broke into the conversation. "My late husband was Torfi's cousin. I knew him well when we were younger. I haven't seen him for many years. When Torfi comes, I'll bring Fiona to your house, Astra; it will better there than in Poor Town. Just let me know when he's coming." Astra nodded and herded her brood away.

Fiona knew full well that parents choose their child's marriage partner. Ragnar was no exception. If Torfi had to choose between the sail-maker's daughter in Ribe and her, what chance did she have? There had been a few moments when Ragnar had held her hand in the market as they had exchanged wares. Had he been signalling his interest even then? His aura was always colourful and energetic. *What do she have to offer as a prospective bride?* Mor Signy's attitude to her being Irish was fairly typical. Pregnant and Erse was not a good combination. Irish folk, thrall or not, were very low in the town's hierarchy.

The rest of the day went well, their cart much lighter to push on the way home. Local people were buying, and there were foreign boats in the harbour, so trading was lively. Arriving back home, all three women were delighted to see Atli and the boys sitting on the outside benches, cleaning fish, surrounded by scavenging neighbourhood cats and ragamuffin children scrambling for offal. Lilja was standing in the doorway smiling. Fiona hadn't seen that smile for a long time.

"Looks like you managed alright," Runa said, looking from Atli to the pile of fish.

"We struggled getting the sail up. I can't balance properly yet and the boys aren't quite strong enough but the three of us did it. Rocked the boat so much, I thought we'd tip over. Eric's fairly good at setting the net. Sven hasn't got the size and strength to do it yet, but we brought in half a barrel's worth. We'll be alright inshore in good weather, but not out to sea. We're not ready for that yet," he said, smiling at the younger boy and tousling the lad's hair. "I can manage the rudder if I'm sitting. Adjusting the sail's tricky too."

Lilja had been stringing the fish up to dry. The cooking pot over the fire was simmering with the aroma of fish, onions, and turnip.

After the meal, Runa gave Atli some willow for pain and changed the dressing. The crater in his thigh was gradually filling in with scar tissue but was still draining. She replaced the moss and bandaged it again, then resumed her seat at the table. Olrun was refilling the ointment jars. Soon, the boys and Atli were asleep, exhausted from their day on the water.

Fiona decided it was good a time as any to get her questions answered again. "Runa, all of a sudden everybody's interested in marrying me off, whether it's to the butcher, the soldier, or Ragnar."

Runa's head snapped around and she looked at her sharply. "By the gods girl—it's not that we don't want you! It's for your safety! You've seen firsthand what happens to young widows in Poor Town, if they don't have a man in the family to protect them. Think of the ones you've treated for rape or getting beaten by drunk sailors. Atli can't defend you yet, and the baby will be here soon enough. We survive because of Atli and my reputation. I won't be around forever!"

That caught Fiona off guard. She stared at the light around Runa and saw it wasn't as vibrant as it had been even a few weeks ago, immediately regretting that she hadn't been paying attention.

"Runa, I don't want to marry the butcher or the soldier. If I married the butcher, it would be like Ottar's house. His wife is just like Mor Signy. I really don't want another soldier or sailor always away from home."

"I think Ragnar would be a good match for you. I can't think of a better offer quite frankly," Runa said

"I like Ragnar. You know my background. I'd like to live on a farm again. That's what I'm used to. He seems a really decent man. But how am I going to compete with the sail-maker's daughter in Ribe when I'm carrying Gunnar's child?"

"You're walking proof you are fertile. A male child is another worker; a daughter another trading connection by marriage. If Torfi chooses you, ask him to take your child as his ward. It will give the child some security and guarantee a better marriage later.

Marriages take place near the summer solstice. Ragnar's been widowed for a year. Torfi will want him remarried by midsummer. There must be heirs for the estate. It's to your benefit that Torfi and I are related. He can access Ottar's trading empire through Thorkell more easily with a marriage connection, even if it's a distant one."

"I hadn't thought of that."

"You're not giving yourself any credit for your skills. You're a capable healer with all the experience you've had. I don't think their farming community has one. Your weaving is excellent, and that is a significant skill in the Sturlsson household. You're a country girl, not a town girl, and Ragnar likes you. I'm not blind. I've seen the way he looks at you and touches you . . . and the way you respond to him," Runa said with a sly smile on her face.

They looked at each other for a moment. "I don't think I can hide anything from you, can I?" Fiona said.

Runa edged sideways on the bench and touched her hand. "We are not trying to get rid of you."

"I'm not rich like the other girl," she replied.

"Shall we dig up Gunnar's hoard and find out what you do have?"

Surprised, Fiona stared at her. "You know?"

Runa nodded. "No secrets in this house, my dear. Gunnar kept looking over there. Torfi will pay Thorkell your bride price. We'll dig it up some day. You still have his pile of armour to sell at the market."

And so it went for the next few weeks. Fiona watched her surroundings. The pigeons on the neighbouring roof were content, the weather was warming, farmers from the north country were driving small herds of cattle, horses, and sheep into town on market days. Atli went out fishing with the boys at least twice a week depending on the weather, catching enough to feed them and selling any surplus dockside. His mood was improving, although he still needed the crutch.

The women took turns at the loom between other chores and the boys were systematically cleaning the armour in their hoard. Every week they sold a few items at the booth.

One day when Runa and Fiona were alone in the house, the older woman closed the door. "Now's a good time to dig up Gunnar's stash," she said, handing her the spade. Luckily, the soil was not too hard. Fiona felt awkward with her huge belly, but managed to remove the dirt. Two large leather pouches came into view. Bending over with difficulty, she brushed off the soil and handed them to Runa.

Runa felt the weight of the pouch, which gave a metallic jingle as she undid the drawstring, emptying the contents on the table. A mass of silver coins tumbled out onto the wooden planks. Fiona was speechless.

Runa patiently counted them out in piles of ten. "That's three hundred and five dirhams."

"This one feels different," the old woman said, opening the second pouch, withdrawing four individually wrapped items packed in wool. Her gnarly fingers unwrapped the first, revealing a sparkling gold chalice, beautifully sculpted, embedded with colourful gemstones, and intricate circles of gold filigree. A companion piece emerged from the second package. The third item was a Christian gold cross, the horizontal arm about six inches long and the vertical shaft over a foot long, supporting the Christ figure. The last piece was Carraig's silver torque. Fiona picked it up, stifling her tears.

"This was my father's. I took it from his body after the raid. This and his sword are all I have of them."

Runa sat for a moment, contemplating the chalices. "Only a king could afford these. By the gods, you could buy a kingdom with them. Don't show them to anyone. Not Thorkell, Ragnar, or Torfi. Men would kill for those. Put them back in the dirt right now, but keep the torque out," she said, handing Fiona the pouches.

Fiona did as she was told, packing down the soil again. She locked the sword and torque in the chest and slid it under the bench, scattering the reeds over the disturbed dirt.

"You're a wealthy woman, but it wouldn't be wise to tell anyone. Don't behave any different than usual. You are in a good bargaining position now, with Torfi. Bride price is roughly the value of a cow."

"So, he'll give about five dirhams then," Fiona replied, thinking back to her marriage to Gunnar in Dublin.

"Close enough," Runa said, opening the door again.

"I'll do some weaving," Fiona said, staring down at her swollen ankles that she could barely see, with the bulge of her belly. "I'm tired all the time. Is it always that way when you're having a baby?"

"Towards the end, yes."

The rest of the morning was quiet as Fiona did her weaving, while Runa ministered to several townsfolk needing care and Helga, an old acquaintance came in to chat with her friend. The women had known each other for years and reminisced of days long gone by.

By the time the sun was high, Olrun, Lilja and the girls returned carrying bags of flour, onions, and salt beef. The noise level ratcheted back to normal with their constant chatter and laughing. Atli and the boys returned later, bringing home a small catch.

Later in the afternoon, Thorkell's oldest boy arrived to relay a message. "Torfi sent a messenger. He will be coming to our house tomorrow with Ragnar. Could you and Fiona be there by mid-morning?"

"Thank you for bringing the message. Tell your father we'll be there," Runa said, and the boy quickly headed home. Looking at Fiona, she said, "Perfect timing," with a thoughtful smile.

Fiona was restless through the night, awoken several times with cramps in her belly. In their previous discussions of pregnancy and her vague recollections of Aoife's midwife experiences, she knew cramps would come. Right now, they were not regular. The fear began to swirl inside her that she could die. Even women with big hips sometimes didn't survive. *It's too early to be the real thing.* Her breasts were getting larger but no milk yet. Fiona could feel the baby moving. Finally, it settled and she fell into a fitful sleep, dreaming of dark places and Ragnar.

CHAPTER 41

Torfi's decision

Fiona was awake early, nervous of meeting Torfi. Her first view of the street was an empty path and a pale sun sending rays of light through the dark clouds to the east, tinging it pink and gold. Half the doves were still sleeping, soft grey mounds of feathers, their legs tight beneath them and their eyes closed. The sentinel on the chimney was cooing quietly. No hawk in sight. *That was reassuring.*

She took a deep breath and inhaled their calm. Today would change the course of her life forever, one way or another. It seemed that her whole life was like a chain, one link, then another, moving on. Behind her she could hear the rustle of Lilja and Olrun, waking and starting their chores.

Runa walked over to her, speaking low. "Good morning. Looks like a bright, dry day. Bathe and wash your hair. Wear your good dress. It'll be a bit tight, but it will do. I want you to make a good impression. A lot depends on it. Bring your torque, but don't wear it until we get there. It's too dangerous to wear it on the streets. Let me speak on your behalf. Keep quiet unless he asks you a direct question."

"I'll get ready then. Runa, I had cramps through the night and the baby moved a lot. I've seen girls die. Ragnar's wife did. It makes me afraid," she said, looking beyond the wrinkle face into those wise, grey eyes.

"I know you are. If he chooses you, I would expect Torfi to wait until the child is born before the marriage takes place. Then he knows what he's got. If it goes badly, then he can marry Ragnar to the other girl. There's only a few more weeks to go. The torque helps, being a high-status item. Fiona, you need to calm down," Runa said putting her hands on Fiona's shoulders. "Close your eyes, take a deep breath and imagine you are walking in a green meadow with grazing sheep, the woodland spirits all around you."

Fiona sighed, imagining the scene before her. The muscles in her shoulders relaxed under Runa's fingers. She could hear the baas of the lambs and chirp of the birds high in the canopy of leaves. Somewhere above, a squirrel scampered and called. There was a faint tinkle of water as it trickled over a rocky stream bed some-where in the forest.

"That's better. Keep your eyes closed. Feel the goodness of goddess flow through you, from your head to your toes. She's wrapping you and your baby in comfort and warmth."

It seemed like an eternity. Then Runa said, "Open your eyes, girl," removing her hands.

"Thank you, Runa. You have such wonderful hands. I was there, just like you said" and gave her a big hug.

"We'd better get ready while they've got the bread rising. I think Lilja's making oat cakes and scones too. My favourites."

The pot of water was already on the boil. Atli carried in an armload of wood, still limping but not using the crutch. Fiona filled a basin with water and washed her long hair with Olrun's lilac-scented shampoo. Leaning out over the front doorstep, she bent over, letting the boys take turns enthusiastically slopping pails of water over her head to remove the soap, managing to soak the rest of her and themselves, of course. Olrun braided Fiona's hair into two thick plaits, twining them around the back of her head in a knot, and fixing it in place with long brass pins.

Next, she washed herself, patted her skin dry and put on the blue dress and a clean overdress. It was a tight fit now with the baby bump. *For the first time in my life, I have cleavage.* The hem was definitely higher at the front than the back. Olrun kindly put her good shoes on for her as she couldn't even reach them herself. She tied her money pouch to her belt and loosely put it around her waist, then fitted her cap. Taking a deep breath, she was ready.

Runa had put on her best dress, too, a fine linen garment in a rich, rust colour. After a quick meal of oatcakes, it was time to go. The two women departed, slowly walking along the pathways, keeping clear of the wet spots. Although it was not far to Thorkell's house, they had to stop several times for Runa to rest, her weight on her cane and breath raspy at times.

Two horses were tied outside Thorkell's, so Ragnar was already there. Runa stopped in the doorway as Astra greeted them. The men were sitting at the table talking about shipping cattle and sail cloth to Tynemouth, but immediately arose to greet them. Much to Fiona's surprise, Ottar was there. too. That she hadn't expected. *Why would he care if I marry Ragnar? The trade connection, of course!*

Ragnar was looking regal in his fine linen shirt, his blonde hair and beard trimmed short, quite different from the market day farmer she was used to. The older man had to be Torfi. The similarity was striking. The air of authority was unmistakable in his posture and demeanour. Even Ottar was being deferential.

Introductions were made around the table and all sat down. Astra continued filling mugs of mead and the girls brought more oatcakes from the grill. The rest of the children were shooed outside.

Runa and Fiona sat on one side of the table, facing Torfi, Ragnar, and Thorkell. Torfi addressed Runa. "It's good to see you. I don't think we've seen each other since my cousin died, although Ragnar brings us the local gossip on market days."

"It's good to see you, too, Torfi. You are looking fit and well."

"As you know, I must choose a wife for Ragnar. He has expressed an interest in Fiona. There is much at stake. We have farmed our property for nearly two hundred years. It is imperative that I have a line of succession well established. If anything happens to me, Ragnar is my heir. Are you speaking on Fiona's behalf?"

"Yes, Torfi. I consider her as family in this matter."

"What does Fiona have to offer? What advantage would I have if I chose her over other women?" he queried.

Runa was not intimidated by Torfi, and took a moment to consider his question. "Fiona was raised in an Irish farming community. Like you, they raised sheep, cattle, and horses as well as planting oats and hay. She would fit in well. Ottar's longship crew raided her village. In that raid, Gunnar took her as a thrall, but married her instead of selling her. You are aware of the important trade contact Ottar provides, with his brother Bersi firmly entrenched in Dublin. Fiona is a skilled weaver and is also a gifted healer, like her mother before her. She has worked with me for more than a year, tending the sick and wounded in Hedeby. We've been very busy since the raid. Any local you ask will attest to that. She gathers the herbs and makes the ointments, tonics, and balms with my daughter. She is a hard worker and an honest woman."

Torfi paused, then looked at Fiona. "How well to do you speak Danish?" he asked.

"Well enough to answer simple questions and make myself understood at the market," Fiona replied, looking at him directly. "All our customers help me speak your language and correct me if I get it wrong. I still have much to learn."

He smiled.

Runa directed the question to him, "What bride price do you offer?"

"Five dirhams," he replied, scrutinizing both women.

"Gunnar was very successful with the plunder he amassed, so she is not without resources," she said. "Five is acceptable."

Torfi's eye brows went up then he squinted, deep in thought. He seemed hesitant. He took a sip of mead, considering the issue. "Do you have any of your weaving with you?"

Fiona paused, then quietly said "I didn't bring any but Astra bought one of my shirts a few weeks ago and Thorkell's wearing it."

Thorkell promptly got up from the bench and let Torfi examine it, placing the torch closer for better light. Torfi eyed the weave carefully and felt the texture of the sleeves and front piece. "Comfortable?"

"Yes, it is. Not itchy at all," Thorkell replied, sitting back down.

"It shouldn't be," Runa chimed in, laughing. "We bought the flax from Ragnar." Chuckles went around the table. It seemed to lighten the tension in the room.

Ottar interrupted at that point. "Where's your silver torque, Fiona?"

Fiona glanced at Runa, saw the tiny nod and extricated it from her pouch. "It belonged to my father. It was given to him by his grandfather on his father's side, and it's very old," she said, presenting it to him. She concentrated on Torfi, not daring to look at Ragnar or Ottar.

Torfi examined it carefully, then handed it back to her.

"I have his sword as well."

"I presume you can make bread, cook, and sew as any farm wife would, as well as farm chores looking after the livestock," he asked, maintaining eye contact.

"I'm from farming stock, Torfi. I have worked with the animals, birthed the lambs and calves, ridden and driven the horses. I've seeded the vegetable garden. I can make beeswax tapers. I haven't done much cooking, as Lilja usually does that, but I could do all the things any farm wife would do."

"Thorkell told me of your journey here. You have a reputation of being a healer, a mystic, and a fighter."

Fiona paused, thinking how best to word the answer. "When I do healing work, I pray to the gods for guidance to help that person. I used to pray to my mother's Celtic deities, but since I've been here, Runa and her family as well as Gunnar have taught me to honour the Viking gods. I will ask for help from any source, like which ointment to use so it heals a wound or lessens their suffering. If the patient is a Christian, I pray to the Christian god as well. I learned to use a stave or a sword to protect myself when Gunnar was at sea, but I've had to give that up," she said rubbing her belly. "Poor Town's not a safe place for women young or old, so I learned to defend myself."

"Do you use magic?" His eyes never left hers.

"I do not. I don't deal with dark things, nor would I know how."

There was a long silence. Finally, it was Torfi who broke eye contact, as Astra refilled his mug of mead. Ragnar was intently watching his father.

"I think Fiona would be a good match for my son; however, the marriage will not take place until after the child is born and I know both are safe. Runa, send me a message and let me know. We'll take things from there."

Fiona felt a palpable wave of relief. She smiled at Ragnar, who now had a big grin on his face.

Torfi slapped him on the shoulder. "Happy now?"

Ragnar nodded and smiled at her again.

"Do you want your bride price now? We came prepared," he said.

"No, we'll deal with it later," she replied. "Come Fiona, time for us to go home. Put the torque away."

Fiona slipped it in her pouch, and together they arose from their seat and hugged Astra. They were preparing to leave when Ragnar quickly joined them. He took Fiona's hand and held it firmly, looking happy, yet concerned. "Take care," he said looking at her belly.

Was he afraid for her, having lost his first wife in childbirth? "I'll survive it, Ragnar. I have Runa," she said squeezing his hands, feeling the warm sensation of feelings flooding between them. She looked into his eyes, seeing the want and the need, then gently let go as she followed Runa out the door. She glanced back at Ragnar as he stood in the doorway, bewildered by her own rising emotions.

CHAPTER 42

Motherhood

Two weeks later, Fiona was awakened by cramping that was persistent and low down. She sat up, rubbing her belly, and waited. Around her were the rumbling night sounds, snores from the adults, and snorts and snuffles from the children. She lay down and waited. Soon enough, it started again, stronger and more demanding. It gripped her, so she gritted her teeth and tried to bear it. It retreated, only to return a short time later. Sweat was beading on her forehead now as the pain ebbed and flowed.

It was Olrun who awakened first and came over to the bench. "Is it time?" she asked quietly, holding her hand.

Fiona nodded, engulfed in another spasm.

Olrun awoke Runa, then rekindled the fire, putting on a pot of water, and gathering the linens they would need. Runa dressed quickly and brought her stool beside Fiona's bed. After placing an old blanket beneath Fiona, she sat beside her, wiping the sweat away and raising her nightgown to expose her belly. The girls were awake now and quickly dressed. Lilja hurried them out of the way.

Atli took one look at the women and decided it would be a good day to take the boys fishing. They promptly dressed and were gone.

By mid-morning Fiona was exhausted. The pains were coming one after another with little pause. Runa continued to sit quietly beside her. Finally, there was a gush of wetness and Fiona felt the urge to push.

"Push now," Runa said."

Pause.

Pain—push.

Pause.

Pain—push.

Pain. More pain. No pause.

"Push, girl, push!"

Fiona pushed with all her strength, then something moved and slithered—*release!* She lay exhausted, feeling Runa's hands between her legs. There were hushed words and movement, then a cry, a loud lusty cry! She opened her eyes. A smiling Runa was standing there, drying and rubbing the tiny, pink squawking infant proclaiming its arrival.

Olrun offered a small, clean blanket and wrapped the baby in it. As Fiona sat up, exhaustion forgotten, Olrun put the baby in her arms, and Runa cut the cord, tying it off with a piece of fine thread.

"You have a lovely daughter," she said. "You are not done yet. The sac must be born as well."

"I've never seen a whole birthing," Fiona said, totally engrossed with the strange small person who was hers. Although the baby had blonde fuzz on its head, it was hard to imagine the tiny, delicate girl was Gunnar's. *He would have been disappointed.*

Runa checked the child over. "She's moving her arms and legs well. She's pinking up nicely. Nothing wrong with her breathing," she said, smiling at the next lusty squawk. "We wait now for the sac. If you were a midwife, you check the baby first, then the sac when it comes out. Have you picked a name for her yet?"

"I'm calling her Aoife, after my mother, and her second name will be Runa, after you," she said, gazing at the little face, the flawless skin, and rosebud lips, looking back at her. The baby clasped her fingers with its tiny hand. *Overwhelming.*

"Let her suckle. Here, hold your nipple so she can get it in her mouth," Runa said guiding her hand. After some rooting and nuzzling, Aoife latched on.

"That feels so strange," Fiona said as the milk dripped from the little lips and ran down her belly. Pains started again. Olrun took the child and wrapped her in the blanket. Finally, after more pushing, the large sac slithered out of Fiona and into Runa's waiting hands.

"Never pull it out. Let it come out on its own. See how smooth and shiny it is. Make sure it's whole. If a piece is missing, that's a very bad sign, as the bleeding may not stop or it will stay inside and rot. Either way, it is a death sentence. There is nothing you can do except keep them comfortable."

"Now what do you do with it?" Fiona asked.

"Burn it or give it to a dog. I should have sent you with the midwives for training but we never had time," Runa said.

That evening brought a celebration. Fiona had safely delivered. Atli and the boys had spent the day on a larger fishing boat, helping a neighbour who was short-handed for crew. They'd gone further out to sea, a new experience for the boys who were rewarded for their efforts with a large cod. Lilja baked it on the open grill. All the boys talked about was the size of the waves, losing sight of land and the wind.

"You're turning them into fisherman," Fiona remarked.

"That's not a bad thing," Atli answered, assessing the boys. "They're learning and will earn their keep."

Fiona watched him move. Although his limp forced him to hobble from side to side, he was managing much better and seldom needed anything for pain. No need for the cane or crutch now. He was back to his normal cheery self. Lilja was only changing the bandages once a day now. The wound had almost healed.

Neighbours stopped in, admiring the new arrival, raising their mead-filled mugs to the goddess Eir, and partaking of Lilja's honeyed oatcakes. Fiona was tired but happy.

Runa showed her how to knot her shawl, so she could wear it like a sling and tuck the baby inside, keeping her snug and warm while leaving her own arms free to get on with her work. The girls fussed over the baby almost as much as Fiona did.

That first night, Aoife woke her several times to nurse. Fiona was still awkward in handling her, trying to keep her quiet and not disturb everyone. Changing the messy pads was nauseating, but she'd get used to it. She already had a pail full of soiled cloths to wash in the morning.

At first light, Runa sent Eric to Thorkell's house to announce the birth and for him to send a message to Torfi.

The baby kept Fiona busy with its lusty demands to be fed. No one seemed to mind the change in the household routines. When the child was sleeping, the boys were a bit more subdued, trying to keep the noise level down a bit.

When Fiona got dressed, she burst out laughing.

"What's so funny?" Lilja asked.

"I can see my feet. My belly's shrunk."

The first real challenge was market day. Runa, Olrun, and Fiona loaded up the hand cart and set out for the booth. The day was sunny, warm, and bright. A lot of the trading ships were coming into port, bring the northern goods. It triggered memories of Gunnar, the longship, and the knarr. It made her remember her journey and how far she had come.

That day, she sold several pieces of chain mail and a sword, gradually diminishing Gunnar's stash, while continuing to care for the usual lineup of wounded and ailing. Runa just sat, directing the work but doing little, looking frail. Aoife sparked a lot of interest with the womenfolk, who swamped her with sometimes contradictory advice but meant well.

Astra appeared later in the day, her basket full of fish and fruit. "Oh, let me see her," she said. Fiona scooped the sleepy baby out of the shawl and placed the child in Astra's arms. "She's got Gunnar's colouring. You're looking good, too."

"I feel well. Tired. There's so much to learn about a baby—feeding her, watching her. It's hard to believe she's mine."

Astra turned to Runa. "A messenger came from Torfi last evening. They will come next market day to take Fiona with them. Thorkell's at sea right now. I'm hoping he'll be back in time. He'd want to see her. Ottar told Thorkell they'd found an overland route west of Tynemouth to the Irish sea near Carlisle. He might be able to access that route to reach Bersi in Dublin." She gently handed Aoife back to Fiona, gathered up her own brood, and waved goodbye.

Every day with Runa was precious, and Fiona took full advantage of it, asking questions about plants and baby care. Her bleeding had slowed now. She settled into a daily routine of feeding Aoife, washing the cloths, and hanging them to dry over her bench. She tired more easily and sometimes dozed when Aoife did.

Atli had the boys fishing at least three times a week, supplying enough to feed them all. Any surplus was dried or sold. Most often they took his boat but sometimes they sailed with their neighbour.

Olrun spend most of her time weaving and making the shampoos and soaps. Fiona occasionally went with the girls to gather marsh flower blossoms and moss. She had always loved to stand there, up to her knees in water, listening to the splash of fish, the fluid bird calls, and plops as frogs hopped out of her way. She missed the camaraderie of the town's women all there gathering plants in the shade-dappled marsh, just as she'd done at home.

Afternoons were often spent at the loom, when Aoife was having her afternoon nap and the house was fairly quiet. Looking at Runa, she saw how much the light was around her had dimmed. The old woman was shrinking into herself and fading. *She's dying.*

Runa raised her eyes and nodded as if reading her mind.

Fiona wrapped her arms around her and held her close. "Tusind tak," she whispered. "I will always remember you and all you have done for me."

Runa held her face in her hands, just staring, right into her soul. "You have been a very good apprentice and are like another daughter. Remember your lessons. Take care of yourself and Aoife," she said. Gently, she took the drowsy child into her arms. Old healer and new baby stared intently at each other. "She may have her father's hair and eyes, but she is an old soul. Even now, just a week old, I can tell you she is much like her namesake, even though I never met your mother. You will need to nurture and protect her," she said, handing the baby back to her.

"You mean she's already got my mother's abilities?" Fiona asked, totally unprepared for that revelation.

"Yes, indeed she has," Runa replied as she gave the baby back to Fiona, and shuffled to her bench.

CHAPTER 43

Beyond the Danevirke

Knowing it was her last day there, Fiona looked outside, taking in every detail as she flung a pail of dirty water out the door. It was dry and slightly overcast. The pigeons were preening, the male birds strutting and cooing, flashing their iridescent green and purple chest feathers to impress the females. *Favourable, yet there was an air of caution.*

There's so much to do. She fed Aoife and set her down for another nap, then dressed in her good blue dress and leather shoes, setting her cape aside. She always thought of Tante Frida when she wore it. While the weather was warm, it was a long journey ahead and she had to be prepared for anything.

She opened the four sea chests, starting with the armour Gunnar had collected on his raids. There were several sets of chain mail, vests, a helmet, and two swords left to sell. She placed those in the bottom, topping them off with Carraig's sword.

After digging up the treasure trove, it was reassuring to find the cross and chalices still wrapped in their pouches, and the sack of silver untouched.

Next, Fiona folded her clothes into the third one, adding the blanket Thorkell had given them as a wedding present and all Aoife's dry cloth pads. Finally, she went through her herb chest, assessing the ointments, bandages, salves, and tonics. She had no idea if Ragnar's family had any at all.

By then, Lilja was already up, rekindling the fire under the oatmeal pot. Fiona gave her a hug. Lilja's constant quiet presence was part of the fabric that held the family together. Runa's household had accepted her, taken her in like family, and once again, she was losing them. It was a strange journey she was on, but this choice had been hers. *I fervently hope Torfi's household will be like Thorkell's, not Ottar's.* Lilja handed her a bowl of oatmeal topped with honey, her favourite meal.

Runa stayed in her bed that morning, too weak to go to market, so Olrun took the boys and girls with her, the boys manhandling the cart. Fiona hugged Olrun, a sister, another talented, reliable, hardworking woman.

She sat beside Runa, snuggling Aoife close, watching the light around the woman as she slept. It barely flickered. Occasionally, Runa opened her eyes but couldn't even raise her head. Mid-morning, she heard a familiar voice outside. Atli greeted Thorkell. *He made it back in time to see me.* Torfi and Ragnar were right behind him. Torfi had ridden his horse, a nice-looking bay mare, while Ragnar had driven the wagon. They presented as robust, clean, healthy, and well-dressed men, looking out of place in Poor Town.

Fiona put on her cape and bundled young Aoife into the shawl. She kissed Runa's forehead then gave Atli a hug. "Thank you for all you've done. Take care of your leg; it still hasn't finished healing, but you're doing really well. I'll pray to Eir for you all," she said.

"If you're ever back in Hedeby, come and see us. You'll always be welcome," Atli replied as he helped Ragnar load the trunks onto the wagon.

Torfi walked over to Runa, looking over at the motionless old woman, seeing her closed eyes, and her barely rising chest.

"Atli, your mother's running out of time. I won't disturb her. There'll never be another with her skills. I remember her as a young woman, so vibrant, so bold. When she wakes, tell her I have prayed the gods take good care of her," he said, handed Atli the bride price and turned back towards the door.

Meanwhile, Thorkell crushed Fiona in a bear hug.

"Did you have a good trip?" she asked, looking into the face so like Gunnar's.

"We surely did. The cousins are safely ensconced on their property. No trouble selling the two bulls. The king's army needs feeding. They kept the third one for themselves. Are you ready?"

"As ready as I can be. Please tell Astra that Runa's dying. I'm grateful for all you've done for me. Right from the beginning, you took care of me like a big brother."

Meanwhile, Atli quietly confronted Ragnar. "Fiona's a good woman and a special one. Treat her well," he said with an edge to his voice, the tone implying there'd be consequences if he didn't.

"Atli, be reassured, I care deeply for her. No harm will come to her. I promise you that," Ragnar replied, as he helped Fiona clamber up on the wagon seat, the baby tucked in the shawl.

She heard the comment, and looked at Ragnar as he swung up on the driver's seat, picked up the reins and slapped them on the rump of the sturdy buckskin horse. He'd stated he cared. While he'd never said that directly to her, the fact he'd said it to Atli was enough to spin her into emotional turmoil.

Torfi mounted his mare and the little cavalcade set off down the street, with all the neighbours hanging out their doors, waving goodbye. Thorkell and Atli stood on the threshold watching them.

Fiona was excited as they approached the town gates, the Swedish guards acknowledged Torfi and waved them through. She'd never been on the northern road and was immediately interested in everything beyond Hedeby's Danevirke. Many farmers were heading home along the rutted and potholed lane, their wagons empty of farm goods but full of tired children and bags of purchases. Ragnar knew most of them by name and spoke with them as their wagon passed.

The land remained relatively flat once they were away from the wetland, except for a rising ridge to the northwest. Rich farmland abounded in the valleys. She caught glimpses of the sea behind low, forested hills to the east. Farms were large, with multiple houses and animal sheds; it was far more extensive than she would have imagined. Fields were green with wheat and oats, heads of grain rippled in sweeping waves as the breezes blew in from the sea. Stone fenced pastures marked boundaries.

"How big is your farm?" she asked Torfi, when he reined his horse beside the wagon where the width of the path allowed.

"We have more than two hundred acres, some in crops and some for pasture, leaving a good portion for the woods."

"There's more than one house on these farms. Is it all one family?"

"We have two main houses, mostly my immediately family and their children in the main building as well as cousins and their families in the other. About thirty of us all told. We also have one for the thralls where they live and weave, as well as the smithy and the livestock sheds. Most of our farming community raise sheep, cattle. and horses, with a few pigs, chickens, and geese."

"Someone mentioned sail-making. Is that what your thralls are weaving?"

Ragnar answered her question this time. "The thralls weave the coarser yarns into sail panels. It takes fifty panels to make a sail for a knarr or a longship. Up 'til now we've been selling them in Ribe further up the coast but we could do it in Hedeby on Ottar's ship. The finer yarns are used in the main house by the women and girls for our own clothing. It's got to the point where we'll need to get more sheep soon, just to keep up with the demand for wool."

"Torfi, you've got cattle to sell as well, don't you? Are they like Ottar's?" she asked.

"Yes, same breed. The Reds are good hardy animals—good meat and lots of milk. My wife's made a name for herself, making cheese but we never have enough of it to sell. All of us eat it," he said, laughing. "I've caught the grandchildren sneaking into her cellar on many occasions."

"Like you don't do that yourself!" Ragnar fired back at his father, with a grin.

Fiona sensed the rapport between the two men. "Are there many beekeepers around?"

"Only two of us that I know of, producing enough to sell. I can't keep up with that either. That's one area where you can help me."

"How would I help? I know nothing about bees."

"I'll show you when we get home," he said.

In many aspects the farms reminded her of home but on a much bigger scale. Aoife awoke and howled until Fiona shyly fed her, draping the baby with the shawl so her bare breast wasn't exposed. From the corner of her eye, she caught the smile on Ragnar's face as she held the baby over her shoulder and patted her back until she burped.

"What are you thinking?" he asked.

"I'm nervous about meeting your family. Astra said your mother, Gunnhild was a good woman. Mor Signy didn't like me because I was Irish. She treated her Irish thralls badly. Your mother might not like me, either," Fiona whispered, having trouble even looking at him. *What was his opinion of the Irish?*

He frowned. "Fiona, you haven't even met her yet. Mother's nothing like Mor Signy. That woman's got a reputation. We have twelve thralls. Most of them are Irish but a few are Finns. They work hard at the weaving, but we don't treat them badly. We're not beating them unless they deserve it. Mother's in charge of them."

"What did they do to deserve a beating?" she asked.

"Two of them ran away once but we brought them back. Listen, Far discussed bringing you here with everyone. They'll accept you as my wife," he said confidently, smiling at the wide-eyed baby peeking over Fiona's shoulder, sucking her fist.

Fiona remained silent, trying to dispel the cloud of doubt.

Seeing her withdraw, Ragnar said, "Torfi chose you for a reason. You're fluent enough in our language, you're an accomplished weaver, an experienced healer, and you have connections of value to us. You're a good-looking woman, too. Besides, I care for you, so stop worrying. We're almost there."

She took several deep breaths, closed her eyes, seeking her mother or Runa. Nothing came, so she prayed to the gods for strength and courage to endure whatever was coming, for the baby's sake as well as her own.

Fiona opened her eyes again as the wagon slowed to enter a tree-lined lane with houses and barns in the background. Torfi was leading the way, his horse pricking her ears as two large, black dogs approached, barking and snarling.

One word from Torfi and the dogs changed into tail-wagging, bouncing beasts, welcoming their master.

From the larger of the two thatched, planked houses, people poured out—men, women, and children, all clustering around as Ragnar brought the wagon to a halt at the door.

A tall, imposing woman stood there, scrutinizing her and smiling.

Fiona looked at her. "Is that your mother?" she asked. Ragnar nodded and lifted Fiona down. Together they walked to meet her. Torfi had dismounted, leaving the horses for a young lad to tend to, and joined them.

"Mor Gunnhild, this is Fiona and her daughter, Aoife," Torfi announced.

Gunnhild smiled and welcomed them in. "I'm glad you've had a safe journey. We've been expecting you. Come sit by the fire. Ragnar, bring her sea chests in. We've cleared the bench beside ours, for you both," she said.

Being able to see the light around people was a gift. Gunnhild's field was strong, Fiona could feel it. The cloud of doubt slowly dispersed. "I'm honoured to become part of your family. I hope you will help me look after my daughter, Aoife. She's only two weeks old. I have very little experience with children."

A girl brought over mugs of mead and pastries. Curious people milled around, getting a look at her and the baby. To Fiona, it was a sea of faces. She smiled back. Aoife began to cry.

SUSAN K. KEHOE

"She's probably wet," said Gunnhild. "Let's get her changed," she said, taking her over to the bench where Ragnar had stacked the sea trunks.

Fiona placed the baby on the bed then opened up the trunk to find a dry linen pad and changed her, disposing of the soiled one in the bucket of water, thoughtfully placed at the bedside. She watched as Gunnhild gently picked up the baby and began crooning to her.

"Ah, they are so delightful at this age," she said. "Once the men have finished their mead, we'll have the hand-fasting ceremony. I will stand for you. After that, we'll have your wedding feast."

"Oh, I almost forgot. Please ask Torfi if he will take Aoife as his ward, to protect her in case something happens to me."

Gunnhild thought for a moment. "That would be wise," she said and they returned to the table.

Fiona took the baby back and sat beside Ragnar. She watched her future in-laws speak quietly in the corner. Torfi finally turned and nodded. Meanwhile, pleasant smells of baking bread wafted through the room, and several women continued to turn a ram carcass on the spit, the fire flaring from the dripping fat, emitting the delicious aroma of roasting meat. She sat quietly and waited.

It was time. Everyone got up and formed the circle. Gunnhild stood behind her, holding the baby. Torfi called upon an elder to officiate. The wizened, stooped old man took their hands in his.

"My name is Sven," he said. He was thin and frail, wearing a long dark garment that hung to the floor. His white hair and beard hung unfettered down to his waist. Despite his physical look of fragility, he oozed strength and vitality. She looked at the light around him, not expecting to see the broad band of bright sparkling lights. *He had power! It was deceptive. He didn't look that strong.* He looked her over and smiled. He was reading her just like Runa had.

His voice rang out over the gathered crowd as he addressed the goddess. "Goddess Frigg, wife of Odin, we bring Ragnar, son of Torfi and Gunnhild, and Fiona before you to be wed. We ask they share a long and prosperous marriage and produce fine children, continuing the family line. Torfi has agreed to take the child Aoife as his ward, as her father Gunnar, son of Ottar, was killed in the Hedeby raid. She, like her mother here, will now be part of our community." With that, he released their hands.

No blood-bonding here, she thought. Looking into Ragnar's face Fiona saw desire, want and need, but it was very different from Gunnar's.

He put his arms firmly around her and kissed her, whispering "I've been wanting to do that for a whole year."

She blushed. Cheers and congratulations were in order. A pleasant evening followed with Fiona trying to put names to faces: Cousin Eric, tall, and bald, had a gold cross around his neck proclaiming him a Christian. He introduced his wife and three daughters. Tova, Ragnar's sister, was married to Gorm, the blacksmith husband, and Halvden was their eight-year-old son. Fiona lost track of the rest of them.

Ragnar pulled her aside at one point and gave her a slow, sensual kiss. That caused a lot of table thumping and lewd comments from the tipsy cousins. He just laughed, holding her at arm's length and eyeing her with a genuine grin, and a twitch of his head towards the bed.

"I need to feed Aoife first," she said quietly. For some reason, she wasn't nervous or afraid. *I can't believe I'm looking forward to this. Maybe because I know what will happen, it was my choice, and he didn't murder my family.*

They retired to their bench, where she fed the hungry baby. He sat quietly, watching everything she did. Gradually, the rest of the family wandered to their beds. Fiona was very aware of Torfi and Gunnhild, just a wooden partition away.

Ragnar ran his finger down her neck and onto her breast as Aoife was nursing. When the feeding was over, Fiona rocked her over her shoulder until the child was sleeping, then rolled her in a blanket, placing her against the back wall, out of their way.

Alone now in the darkened bench with only flickering fire light, they faced each other. He undid her braids and ran his fingers through the wavy tresses that draped her curves. She took off her dress, while he slipped out of his clothes. His body was lean and tight. He ran his hands over her slowly, then pulled her down on the bed.

Unlike Gunnar, Ragnar moved slowly, sliding his hands over her. He groaned but held back, touching and kissing. She slid her fingers over his muscular chest and arms, felt his wiry, tight muscles. Thoroughly aroused, he teased, giving her sensations she'd never felt before. *What was this? Oh, she throbbed for him.*

"Are you ready for me?" he whispered, lying between her legs, propped on his arms. A moan escaped her lips and she pulled him to her. Afterwards, as they lay drowsy and comfortable, Torfi and Gunnhild stood at the bedside and agreed that the marriage had been consummated, then went back to bed.

"Did I please you?" Ragnar asked, as she nestled in his arms.

Fiona ran her fingers gently over his face. "I've never felt sensations like that before."

"Never? Really? Why not?"

"Gunnar made love like a warrior, always in a hurry. Sometimes it felt more like rape. You obviously have more experience and took your time. It made a huge difference for me. I remember my parents coupling like that." Not only had he been gentle, but she had wanted it. "You let me enjoy it, too." *Now she understood. Both had felt the pleasure.* She drifted into sleep, content.

CHAPTER 44

Life on the farm

The next morning, a hungry Aoife woke her early. As the child happily suckled, Fiona listened to the awakening household and wondered what the day would bring. Ragnar was still sleeping, his bare body sprawled face down in the bedding.

When the baby finished nursing, Fiona got dressed, tucking Aoife in her shawl. She looked out the door as always. The sun was just breaking the horizon, lighting the undersides of the clouds, and outlining the dark shapes of grazing sheep, cattle, and horses in the pasture. A faint spiral of smoke rose from the thrall house. There were no pigeons, just ravens cawing as they circled just above the oaks, elms, and yews of the nearby forest. *Perhaps ravens are my guides now.*

Suddenly a pair of strong arms were around her. She froze.

"What are you doing?" Ragnar asked, kissing the nape of her neck.

"I'm reading the day," she replied.

"Meaning what?" he asked, looking puzzled.

"It's something my mother taught me. The gods show us what the day will bring. Look at the sun. See the colour of the sky and the shape of the clouds; they're long, low and fluffy. No sign of rain or storm. Look at the trees and the smoke from the thrall house. The treetops tell you the strength and direction of the wind. Watch the animals; they are grazing quietly. They're spread out, not bunched together, so nothing is threatening them. Look and listen to the ravens. They are circling their nests. It's going to be a good day.

"Do you do this every morning?" he asked, turning her around to face him. He was barefoot and bare-chested, clad only in his trousers. He looked down at her with a smile on his face. Raising her chin with his fingers, he gently kissed her.

"I do. It tells me what clothes to wear, what work can be done outside, and alerts me to danger. The pigeons and the hawk warned me of the raid in Hedeby before the horns were blown," she said.

"Today, I'll show you around the farm so you can meet everyone," he said, walking back to the bench to get dressed.

"I'd like that. Are there streams nearby? I need to find some plants, so I can make my ointments," she said as she braided her hair and pinned it up.

"There are several streams and one marshy area on the northern edge of our forest, that borders the fjord. We do have access to the sea."

"Could raiders land there?" Fiona asked, thinking of Gunnar's raid on her village.

"They have in the past, but Hedeby's a much better target, more plunder. Ten years ago, my older brother was killed during a Swedish raid. At any given time there are ten men here and all of us can use a stave or an axe.

"What about the women? Do they get training, too?"

"There's never been a need. I know the Swedes sometimes have women in the crews. Runa told me about your sword training. You defended her in that alley fight, too. Thorkell said you killed a warrior before Gunnar captured you. Is that true?"

"The warrior killed my father. He had his back turned, so I jumped him, and slashed his throat."

There was a very long pause. "I'd better behave myself then, hadn't I?" he said, leading her over to the table. She couldn't read his expression.

Three older women were working around the fire pit, fanning the embers until the kindling caught, and stirring the huge cauldrons of oatmeal. Two younger ones were grinding wheat for more bread. Fiona asked them their names, repeating them over again in her head.

The activity in the house was similar to Runa's home, but even more like Ireland. The men were preparing for the hunt or working in the fields. The girls were helping their mothers with their younger siblings, while the older boys were sharpening knives and restringing fishing nets.

She watched Torfi and Gunnhild as they organized their day. Gunnhild directed several young girls to work in the gardens or do the laundry, while others were assigned to weave or spin. Bags of fleece were piled against the walls. Fiona focused on Gunnhild and was pleased to see a warm glow around her. Not so for a few others. Tova, Ragnar's sister, greeted her pleasantly enough, yet her aura was cloaked. Several other women kept away. Time would tell.

Eric and his family kneeled beside their bench and prayed to the Christian cross above. She considered joining them, but decided to wait for now and watch the reactions of the pagans.

Two mature women brought in pails of fresh milk, then everyone lined up for breakfast. Fiona savoured the fresh, creamy milk that was still warm as she poured it on her oatmeal and drank it down, licking off the milk around her lips. Runa's family never had milk.

She quickly looked over each person for ailments, but on the whole, most of the clan looked healthy, except for a few elders including Sven, whose feet were grossly swollen; he was short of breath when he walked to the table. The shimmering light around him was still strong.

Torfi was intent on rounding up part of the flock for shearing and separating a few ram lambs for market day. He had selected three older boys to help him and were heading to the pasture. Gorm and Halvden were walking to the smithy. Eric and another man named Wulf and their sons were forest-bound, carrying staves, axes and fishing poles.

Ragnar led her along a faint trail, following the road they'd driven on the previous day. Deep beneath the trees were rows of wicker beehives and stacks of willow branches drying in the leaf-mottled sunlight. The air was full of droning bees flying to and from the fields. He seemed amused by her amazement.

"How many hives to you have?"

"There's about thirty here, and another dozen or so wild nests in the forest."

"Aren't you afraid of getting stung?" she asked, shrinking back from several bees buzzing in her face.

"I have been many times, but they don't bother me. In the autumn, when I collect the honey, I build a small fire and the smoke makes them drowsy, so I don't get stung much."

"Do you get bears? I've heard they like honey."

"The dogs keep them away most of the time, especially closer to the house. Out in the woods, I lose a few hives every year. I'll teach you how to weave a hive for me, using the willow. It's not hard, and it's a good winter chore."

"How on earth do they survive the winter with all the snow you must get?" she asked, looking at the three-foot high woven, round beehives, wide at the base, tapering to pointed tops. The entrance hole at the bottom was quite small but busy with hundreds of little bees buzzing back and forth.

"There's one queen bee. She never leaves the hive. During the winter, the other bees cluster around her in a large ball, keeping her safe and warm. I think the snow insulates them. I have to leave enough honey for them to feed over the winter."

She walked beside him as they circled back towards the house. He pointed out the huge vegetable gardens set back from the houses, where women and children were pulling weeds from the rows of dense greenery. She recognized the leaves of cabbage, turnip, onions, mallow, celery, and several herbs. Laundry was being washed and hung out to dry on lines strung between the nearest trees. Chickens were running free, digging in the dirt, opposing roosters strutting and claiming their patches of dirt, fat hens trailing behind. A gaggle of geese were waddling along the stream banks a little further to the north.

The two guardian dogs who had been with Torfi now trotted over to be petted by Ragnar before they checked her out. Inquisitive noses thoroughly examined her and Aoife in the shawl, and after deciding she was no threat, permitted her to gently touch their silky heads. They looked half wolf, but the tips of their ears hung over. *Ireland didn't have wolves.*

By that time, the boys had rounded up the sheep into a fenced pen and Torfi was busy rooing them, pulling shedding fleece from their coats. *This was different from the breed of sheep she was used to.* Fiona's village had to shear their sheep. These looked similar and were mostly light grey, brown, or black. One of the boys was collecting and sorting coarse outer fluff and fine under-fluff into different bags. The recently plucked sheep were released to scamper back to the flock.

Next came the smithy. The open door revealed young Halvden, steadily and rhythmically pumping the bellows, keeping the coals glowing as Gorm in his leather apron fiercely hammered a piece of red-hot steel into a curved, wedge shape. The man's shoulder-length hair hung limply on his shoulders, as sweat poured down his face and arms. The smoke, dark shadows and fierce glowing metal made the small workshop truly hellish.

"What are you making?" Fiona asked.

Gorm paused to raise the tongs, revealing the whole piece. "It's a new plowshare," he said.

"Where do you get the metal come from?"

"Ragnar usually finds some in Hedeby on market day. Much of the tin, copper, and iron comes from Britain but a lot comes from the eastern Franks, when we're not fighting them," he said, resuming his hammering.

Ragnar led her back out into the sunlight.

"How long would it take to make a plowshare?"

"By the time he makes the handles and the blades and rivets it to the frame, it might take three or four weeks. He should have it finished before fall plowing. The old one's worn down with the constant sharpening."

As they were walking toward the thrall house, the thought crossed her mind that if Torfi died, Ragnar would be first in line to inherit—if the family council agreed. That would relegate Halvden to second place in the family hierarchy. Ragnar's other married sisters had sons but they were younger than Halvden. If she and Ragnar ever had a son, he could again supplant Halvden. She was quite aware of the threat those situations could pose if Tova had ambitions. *That might be the reason for her standoffish attitude.*

Fiona had felt a holding back, a reserve when Mor Gunnhild had introduced them, although outwardly Tova had welcomed her. The light around the woman was tight and dark. *Every patriarchal clan had its power struggles*. That had gone on in her family, too. The squabbling at Ottar's house was even more complicated with multiple wives. So far, she she'd only seen couples, no concubines. *Perhaps they didn't practise that custom here.* Did Ragnar recognize the potential threat? He had such a calm demeanor that it was hard to tell.

The thrall house was a substantial building, almost as big as the main house. Fiona followed Ragnar inside and her jaw dropped. The three looms were huge, much larger than the ones in the main house where clothing was made. These frames were six feet wide and tall enough that the weavers had to stand, one passing the shuttle through the vertical threads, and the other tamping them in place. It would be exhausting to stand all day.

The place was dim, the only light came in through the open door with only a couple of reed torches bracketed to the wall. Burlap bags of raw fleece were stacked from the floor almost to the ceiling beams, not leaving much space for the six women standing at the looms. The benches were crammed in at the other end, the usual central fire pit with smoke rising to the small opening in the thatched roof.

Six other thralls were either spinning wool or plucking bits of hay and grass from the fleeces. On a smaller bench there was a stack of finished four by eight panels, which Fiona examined. They hadn't been soaked yet to tighten and felt the weave. The panels were woven in the two over, two under pattern. She could imagine them all sewn together to make a huge sail for a knarr or longship. No flaws were visible. Most of the wool was a shade of grey and coarse in texture, quite different from the fleece used for clothing. None had been dyed the bright red she'd often seen on her voyage.

Looking at the women, the first thing she noticed was how thin they were. No one had even looked up to see who had come in. Then she noted the strap shaped bruises on two of them. Gunnhild was in charge of these women. *Had Gunnhild done this? Were these the girls Ragnar had mentioned before?* She decided to discuss it later with Ragnar.

She watched an older woman spinning fleece and went over to examine the wool. She felt the texture of the fleece and compared the two spindles; one had been spun clockwise, the other counter-clockwise. "So the coarser, stronger wool is in the vertical warp and the softer wool is the weft?" she asked in Gaelic.

The woman's head jerked up, surprise on her face. She nodded, but seeing Ragnar was right behind her, dropped her eyes down again.

"We don't encourage them to speak Gaelic," he said, pushing her towards the door.

"Why not?"

"They should learn our language, just as you have," he said once they were outside, and promptly changed the subject. "This is just the beginning of making a sail. We sell the sail panels to the boat owners who soak them either in the sea or on their dock so the tides do the work. That felts them and tightens up the weave. When it is ready, they paint it with fish oil so it repels water. Then they sew the panels together and make a sail. Thorkell's longship would need at least fifty to make a sail; their knarr even more. A good sail can last for the life of the ship."

Walking back to the house, Fiona challenged him on several things, determined to understand what was going on. "I saw bruises on the weavers. Were they the ones that ran away?"

"Yes, that was them. Far found them a couple of miles down the road and brought them back. Mor made an example of them. She wasn't happy having to do that but couldn't let them get away with that either."

"I see," Fiona said, mulling that around in her mind. "My next question is about the use of Gaelic. "If you want them to learn Danish, someone has to teach it to them. They'll never learn it isolated in that house. Gunnar, Thorkell, and Runa helped me, even the men on the ships did. So did our customers. It's taken over a year for me to get this far, and I get by but I'm not totally fluent either. If you like, I could do that, if you and Gunnhild agree," she said, looking up at his face. "Ragnar, I need to know how I fit in. What work do you expect of me? I'm used to doing everything on a farm and all the healing part of it, too. That's what I grew up with."

"I'll discuss it with my parents. For now, look after Aoife, do some weaving, help me with the bees and the gardens, and don't worry about the thralls. We can work it out as we go along," he said, a serious and somewhat stubborn expression on his face.

She finally took the hint and dropped the subject, at least for the time being. When she was changing Aoife's wet pad, several of the women in the main house came over and were interested in the baby. The child was active and alert, grasping their fingers with little hands, happy, cooing and smiling and kicking her feet, her bright blue eyes crinkled with laughter. The baby was a good way to meet people. Gradually, Fiona was fixing names to faces and readily accepting the suggestions of the more experienced mothers who had brought their babies, too. She was thankful for having had the experience of meeting strangers at Runa's booth; otherwise it would have been daunting.

"Who is your midwife?" Fiona asked.

"That would be Hallis," one of them said and called the woman over. Hallis was an older woman, strong and stocky, and one of Tova's small group.

Fiona decided to be direct. Moving beside her, she explained to Hallis that while she was proficient with the plants and medicines, she had very little experience with birthing. "I worked with Runa for a year, making all the ointments and tonics, but I never got the chance to deliver a baby. If an opportunity come up, would you be willing to show me what you do? Could you teach me, so I can learn those skills as well?"

Hallis seemed a little reluctant but agreed. "There are several pregnant women in the other building, but they aren't due for three or four months yet," she said.

"Even if I just watch, that would be helpful, thank you," Fiona said.

Everyone was curious about her healing abilities, too, so she brought out her ointments and tonics, selecting an older woman named Inga with knobby arthritic fingers. "Here, let's try some of this and see if it helps. It's made from the root of the yellow cowslip, one of the goddess Freya's favourite plants. It might make the swelling go down."

Clustering around her, they watched as Fiona gently smeared the fatty, fragrant ointment on the swollen joints. Another woman named Thera showed her a cut on her leg that wasn't healing.

Fiona thought for a minute, then opened the jar of mallow root ointment. "Try this one. Sometimes it works when other ones won't."

By then, Aoife was sound asleep, and after washing the baby's pads and hanging them out to dry Fiona felt it was a good time to talk to Gunnhild. Ragnar had left to help Torfi with the sheep.

"Good morning. Ragnar showed me around the farm. It's so big. What would you like me to do? I don't want to intrude on anybody's work."

"Well, you can take over weaving this for me," Gunnhild replied, getting up from her loom. "Tova and I usually work in the gardens and with the thralls."

And so it went for the rest of the week. Each day she mingled with her new family, carefully sorting out the nuances, the rivalries, the issues. Sven, Torfi, and Gunnhild held the power, but there were undercurrents. Fiona felt blessed that she could see the light around people. Sometimes a smiling face was deceptive, covering a darker side. Tova was still shutting her out.

One day, a messenger arrived from Atli via Thorkell with a message to Ragnar.

"Runa's dead, isn't she," she stated quietly as he walked towards her.

"Yes, she is. How did you know?"

"I felt as if a part of me went away," she said, holding him close. He held her for a while, then they walked back to the house.

Ragnar had broached the subject of teaching the thralls to speak Danish with his parents, but so far nothing had come of it.

Still concerned about the thinness of the thralls, Fiona periodically kept an eye on the amount of food they were given. Two full buckets were prepared for them twice a day from the same pots as everyone else's, so the quality was good. Not like the slops served at Ottar's. The pails were delivered to the thrall house by the hired stableman, Jovik.

That particular evening as she washed Aoife's pads outside the door, she caught a glimpse of Jovik scooping food from the pail and stuffing it in his mouth before he entered the thrall house. *He's stealing their food!* No wonder they were so thin.

For the next two nights, she deliberately kept an eye on him. Jovik did the same thing. There was no doubt in her mind now. Going back inside, she sat beside Gunnhild as she nursed Aoife. When Ragnar and Torfi were in a long, complicated discussion and not paying any attention to her, Fiona leaned into Gunnhild, so they were head-to-head and whispered, "I need your advice."

"Oh?" Gunnhild said, putting her knife down.

"For the last three nights, I've seen Jovik eating some of the thralls' food before he brings it to them. He takes quite a lot. Why would he be eating theirs when he eats well in here?"

There was dead silence. Gunnhild looked shocked. "What exactly did you see, Fiona?"

"He took the two pails, looked around to see if anyone was watching, then scooped out handfuls and ate before he went in. I don't think he saw me. It doesn't seem right when those girls work so hard."

There was a long pause. "Leave it to me. I'll deal with it." The expression on Gunnhild's face was a combination of anger and disgust.

Later, when Fiona was getting Aoife settled for the night, she watched Ragnar, Torfi, and Gunnhild sitting at the table, heads bent together in deep discussion. She knew what they were talking about.

Leaving them to it, she made her rounds. Inga's hands were still gnarly but she was moving her fingers better without the pain, and Thera's cut was healing. She felt a sense of relief. *The remedies are working.*

One of the youngsters had fallen, and his mother was washing the large abrasion on his arm. Fiona offered some ointment, but the boy refused. Old Sven was sitting at the other end of the table. He admitted he sometimes used foxglove to strengthen his heart.

"Runa told me it was too powerful for me to give until I had more experience and another teacher," she said as she massaged his swollen ankles.

He nodded. "There are some things I might share with you."

"I'd like that," she replied with a smile, then walked back to her bench. She put her arms around Ragnar and gave him a hug. He was so busy with the bees and the animals that she hadn't see much of him during the day when he was either in the forest or the sheds, only coming in at mealtime. He looked tired.

"Problems, always problems . . . " he said.

"Did I do the right thing, telling Gunnhild about Jovik?" she whispered.

"Oh yes. Those women are her responsibility. She won't tolerate it. I thought we were feeding them well." He pulled her close and just held her.

"You're exhausted. What were you doing today?"

"Digging up old stumps in the south woods along the edge of the field. The horses finally pulled the them out. The boys will have to chop up the wood. There should be enough wood to last a good part of the year. We'd rather not cut any more mature trees just yet. I see Sven enjoyed his foot rub. Why don't you give me a back rub? I'm pretty stiff."

She was quite delighted to slather the cream on his broad back and loosen up the tight muscles as he sat there, his head bowed.

"Feel any better?" she asked when she was done.

He grinned and pulled her down on the bed. "I think so, but we'll have to see what I can do." She smiled.

The next night, Torfi and Gunnhild were unusually quiet and serious at the evening meal. Fiona always washed Aoife's pads after supper and was about to start that when Gunnhild caught her eye and motioned her away from the door. Several of the older boys had been sent on an errand and had not returned yet. *Something was brewing.*

Suddenly there was a commotion outside with a lot of shouting, and two strapping sixteen-year-olds dragged a fighting Jovik into the room, forcing him to his knees before Torfi. The whole household were on their feet, chattering, and gawking. Jovik scrambled up and stood before his master, blood running down his face from his smashed nose.

Gunnhild stood up and faced the boys. "Did he eat the thralls' food?"

"More than that. We were hiding in the trees. We saw him eat from both pails before he took them in, and he wouldn't give it to the thralls unless one of them had sex with him."

"What?" yelled Torfi, jumping to his feet, flabbergasted. "If you wanted a wife, you just had to ask. We'd have found someone for you." Gunnhild, for once, was speechless.

It was Sven who pushed his way through the throng, emerging as a menacing, powerful man despite his age, now pointing his finger. "Your family and ours have been on good terms for decades. That is why we took you in, to work for us. You have lived here for five years. Five years! There have never been complaints about your work. We've clothed and fed you. You have served us well. Why would you do such a thing? Has the god Loki bewitched you?"

Jovik visibly shrank as Sven pressed forward, his arm raised, his cloak making him look like a malevolent raven. Jovik fell to his knees and the circling crowd closed in on him.

"Wait, Sven," yelled Torfi. "We cannot sacrifice our relationship with his family because of his actions. Killing Jovik would destroy a treasured friendship. He isn't worth it. No, we'll not touch him. We'll return him to his family, and they can deal with him. Come, we'll lock him in the shed 'til morning. Three of us will ride to Ribe and hand him over," he declared. That will probably be a death sentence for him. He slapped the two boys, Ivar and Hrolt, on their backs for a job well done as the three of them marched their captive to the shed.

Gunnhild loaded up a basket of bread and fish for the thralls. When she returned, she sat beside Fiona and said, "Why didn't they tell someone?"

Fiona looked at her for a moment. "How could they? They are your thralls. You are their master, and Jovik is, or was, from a wealthy family. They couldn't tell you even if they wanted to. They don't speak Danish." Fiona wondered if anyone would have believed them anyway.

CHAPTER 45

Growth and change

Ragnar awoke with little hands tugging on his hair and beard. He opened his eyes to find four-month-old Aoife unwrapped from her blankets, kicking him in the chest, an impish expression on her face. Gently, he tucked her into the curve of his arm, smelling the sweetness of her skin. She lay there cooing and grabbing everything within reach, including his hair and nose.

He lay there for a moment, gazing up at the forest of greenery around him. Drying plants of every kind were hanging in bundles from nails and hooks in the end walls of their bench, and were even dangling high overhead on filaments of twine tied between the beams. They were testament to Fiona's visits to the forest, meadows, and streams with her flock of young helpers.

Surely she has enough to make her medicines. He felt like he was up a tree in a large nest.

Time to get up. Ragnar needed to prepare the wagon for the next day's drive to Hedeby to deliver honey, beeswax, two rams, and some flax.

Fiona was still sound asleep, the curves of her growing belly promising another child. He fervently hoped it would be a boy, but even a healthy girl would be a treasure, company for Aoife. He gently nudged his wife, who rolled towards him and gave him a sleepy smile and a gentle kiss as she caressed his face.

She snuggled Aoife to her breast, and when the child was content, got dressed. As usual, she stuck her head out the door to look at the day. "No rain. Should be good for harvesting. Will you still go to town tomorrow?"

"I must. Gorm needs tin, copper, and lead. With so many of the neighbours getting repairs done, he's running out of metal. Torfi's given me a list of things he needs and the lambs are ready."

"Will you stop at Runa's booth?" *I still think of it as hers.* "I'd like to know how everyone is."

"I will. I want to talk to Thorkell about shipping sail panels to Tynemouth. The buyers are always asking for more panels, but we don't have enough land to feed more sheep. We're at our limit now. It's all we can do to feed everyone on our holdings as it is. Too many of us here."

"Is there more land available?"

"Not really, unless something changes," he said. "There is another farm up the road that might become available. The male side of the family is dying off, and the women want to move to Ribe where their daughters live. Torfi's been talking to them, but I'm not sure we'd have the money to buy it."

"Ragnar, I could help you buy that property. I still have some of Gunnar's hoard that could be sold. How much would it cost? I know Gorm and Tova would like to move. If he moved, would he still be your blacksmith?" she replied, thinking of the gold chalices under their bench.

He paused for a moment, looking at her. "It might be as high as four hundred pieces of silver. That would be a huge investment for my family."

"I could possibly contribute, but how would that be handled legally? Would I become a part owner?"

"I'd have to ask Torfi and the elders. As far as the smithy, if Gorm and Tova wanted to move, he could always build a new one there and train an apprentice here. It is certainly an idea for us to consider. I thought you and Tova would be friends, but that doesn't seem to be happening."

"I still think it's Halvden's position in your family's hierarchy that's the crux of the matter. If we have a son, Halvden's position changes," she said, watching his reaction. "Family or not, ambition and jealousy can be dangerous. I'm watching your back."

"I aware of that, Fiona. I try to defuse any problems in the family. Someday it will be my responsibility. I will talk to Far later about the property," he said, knowing she was right, but it a path he really didn't want to go down. Obviously, her days of selling and bartering had made her a canny trader and she seemed to be aware of the undercurrents in the household. He would never underestimate her.

Six men were already out in the oat field, walking about ten feet apart in a line, their scythes slashing the grain stems in a steady, falling golden wave. Women and older children followed, gathering up armfuls of gilded stems, bundling them with string, then propping eight to ten upright together to dry, out of the reach of rats. If the weather held, the seed heads would be ready for threshing.

Ragnar quickly checked out the wagon, ensuring the wheels, axles, single tree, and shaft were in working order, as well as the harness for the horse.

"Eric, can you help me lift this crate?" he called as his cousin came out of the shed. Together, they hoisted it onto the wagon and tied it in place.

"Thanks. I see you've got the ram lambs separated in the shed already. Now we'll just have to load them in the morning."

"Who's going with you tomorrow?"

"I could take young Ivar or Hrolt. They're big enough to drive the horse, help me unload and fend off thieves." *It was never safe to drive alone, not even for him.*

"You might take Ivar. All he's doing these days is mooning over the thrall," Eric said with a laugh. "He'll be teaching her more than Danish, if he gets his way."

They both laughed.

Thoughtfully, Ragnar asked, "Eric, Fiona's joined your prayer group. Is that causing you any problems?" After supper, when her evening rounds of care were finished, she had joined Eric's small group of Christians. Christianity was rapidly spreading in the bigger towns on the peninsula. It didn't bother him much, but some family members didn't like it.

"She was baptized as a Christian, she knows the prayers, she knows some of the teachings. Folks are a little suspicious of her, especially since she's a healer, too, but it's more that she was a thrall and she's Irish, that folks are having trouble adjusting to. Having said that, she'd help anyone and she's a hard worker. Sven likes her, so she must be alright. He's no fool."

Later, Ragnar started smoking a couple of hives for winter honey and beeswax. Fiona didn't like working with the bees for fear of being stung, so he often had one of the younger boys help him.

She was keen to learn how to weave the willow fronds into beehives, though, and was very good at making taper candles. All in all, he was pleased with the way she'd settled into his family, except for the situation with Tova. They all got along reasonably well.

After Jovik had left and his bench cleared out, cleaning had revealed a bag tucked right at the back, half full of small items such as cloak pins that had gone missing from various benches around the house. *A thief, pure and simple.* The items were returned to their owners.

Young Ivar had expressed an interest in one of the thralls, a quiet diminutive red-head named Maire, who was looking a lot more attractive since the thralls were getting full rations. Gunnhild and Fiona had changed the routine. Now, some of the younger girls from the main house were washing fleece and plucking burrs, freeing the thralls to do more spinning. They'd made seven panels last month. Torfi was very pleased.

There were ongoing discussions among the elders about boys in the family marrying thralls, but no decisions had been made yet. Any thrall who married into the family would lose their thrall status, just as Fiona had. She was quietly encouraging that.

"I think it would be better if you kept out of it," Ragnar cautioned her, and to her credit he noticed she had avoided those discussions. She somehow managed to navigate the politics in the household and had aligned herself with his parents and Sven, the most powerful people in the clan.

Everybody loved Aoife. The child was bright, alert, and active. Quite often, Fiona left the baby with one of the other mothers when she was out in the woods or worked in the gardens and she returned the favour, becoming part of that group.

Gunnhild had finally agreed to let her teach the thralls Danish. Ivar willingly volunteered to help her with that, since it would have allowed him to spend a little time with Maire, but Gunnhild had put her foot down on that idea and said "nej" to that. Every two or three days, Fiona spent time with them, naming items in Danish and answering simple questions as they worked.

Everyone helped out with the harvest. The root cellar was filling up as the women picked onions, cabbages, turnip, and herbs. The hunters were bringing in wild pig carcasses to be smoked and, occasionally, deer. A lot of the meat was dried. The stacks of hay and straw were growing steadily, and the grain bins were slowly filling. Flax was being soaked after the seeds had been removed, but it took about two weeks to soften it. There was a huge market for it in Hedeby. They didn't keep much linen for themselves.

Ragnar watched as several large barrels were being scrubbed out in preparation for the annual making of the mead, although there was still a partial barrel from last year in the root cellar. How much mead they made depended on the amount of honey he could get from his hives.

That evening when darkness had fallen and the children had been put to bed, he lay on the bench with Fiona, his arm around her. Aoife was sound asleep beside them. "Are you happy here?" he asked, nose to nose, staring at her eyes.

"I am. I'm starting to fit in. Your family are gradually accepting me. I'm enjoying being back on the farm. I love the outdoors, the gardens, the plants, and the animals, even your bees. Runa's family were very kind, but I never was a town person. I'm enjoying being your wife. You are good to me. Did you make the right choice?" she asked, a thoughtful look on her face.

"I do believe I did. I've got a hard-working wife who has the uncanny ability to get what she wants. Sometimes I think you trick me into thinking something was my idea in the first place, and all along it was yours," he said, pulling her closer. There was total silence for a moment then they quietly started to laugh. Their love-making was mutual.

CHAPTER 46

Museum in Hedeby,
Germany, present day

Professor Jorgenssen stood in front of the museum exhibit, dressed in his good suit and tie, together with reporters, photographers, and university staff. After two years of preparation, the grand opening of his Viking exhibit was finally here. Jon's wife Elsa stood beside him, looking elegant as usual. Their sons were off playing soccer that day. Miles and Helga stood to the left, obviously delighted with the culmination of their hard work. Gina was in Peru, working on Inca sites, and Lars was in Mayan Belize, both unable to attend. Photos were taken and congratulations extended by the town mayor and the Dean of the University. Finally, the doors were opened to the long line of spectators and enthusiasts who flocked in.

The glass wall case showed artifacts from the grave of Hedeby Man—sword fragments, the board game, armour, the full skeleton, pendants, helmet shards, the bearskin cape, linen and wool fragments, and the lock of hair with its herbs and silk. In the bottom corner was a replica of the tombstone painstaking pieced together. The original was in a protective case at the grave site. It had revealed Hedeby Man to be "Gunnar, warrior son of Ottar" in Old Futhark. Each artifact had a document explaining what is was and its historical significance.

On the opposite wall was their ultimate success—the diorama. The background painting showed Hedeby as it would have been in 900s CE. The view was from inside the house with a backdrop of the shops, the harbour, the ships, and the fjord to the east through the open door. The Danevirke was clearly evident in the background. A longship was docked and being loaded by seamen.

The house was post-and-beam construction with plank walls and had a thatched roof, just like the other houses. Standing in the door way was a young warrior, five-feet-ten-inches tall with long, blonde braided hair and a beard. He was turning, as if saying goodbye to the young woman at the loom as she accepted a bag of coins from his hand. The sea chest was at his feet. He was wearing chain mail over his linen shirt, and the bearskin cape across his shoulders was anchored with a bronze pin. Hedeby Man was well-muscled in the upper body and was fully armed with a sword on his hip and a knife on his belt. A gold Thor's hammer pendant hung around his neck. His facial features exemplify his Danish descent—the straight, narrow nose, high forehead, and square chin. A tanned and ruddy complexion marked him as an outdoors man.

The woman had been Helga's creation, based on the DNA of the dark hair in the silk bow. She was pure Celtic—light skin, smaller frame, and refined features. The braided hair visible under her cap was a rich, dark auburn. She was clothed in a plain woollen dress with a linen overdress, typical of the era. Around her neck was an amber-bead necklace. A drop spindle hung from her belt, as well as a small knife. The wooden loom beside her had stone weights for the warp threads, and beside it was a woven willow basket containing spun yarn. Bundles of balm, meadowsweet, yarrow, and borage were drying on the walls. Over the corner of the loom hung a blue silk scarf, proof of the trade in exotic foreign goods. Documents provided interpretations of the historical evidence from many ongoing projects at the university.

Elsa looked over the exhibit, seeing for the first time the results of her husband's labours, the artifacts that were all-consuming in his world, resulting in his perpetual absence from home and family life for months on end. Essentially, she was a single mother, not seeing him for more than an hour or two a day. Yet here she stood, feeling very proud of his accomplishments. The diorama looked so real, the protective glass almost seemed to melt away. The detail was exquisite.

The DNA results had shown Hedeby Man to be Danish but also confirmed earlier Germanic background dating back to earlier Eastern Euro-Asian peoples. He had been raised on a mixed diet of meat and fish.

Jon had personally paid for the facial reconstruction of the skull. Gunnar, son of Ottar was as authentic as current science could make him—a strong, vigorous and dangerous young Viking. Elsa hadn't been too happy with that expense. She watched Jon congratulate Miles and Helga. Meeting them for the first time now put faces to the people he'd spoken about. This group of students had been difficult for him. Even here, she was picking up vibes. Regardless, their talent was undeniable. Fortunately, their joint paper written by all of them was being well received in the scientific journals.

When all the official presentations were finished, the couple wandered around the exhibit together with Jon pointing out specific items of interest and giving her the background story. They sat watching the throngs of people in the gallery.

When the flow of people eased and the noise level dropped, Elsa opened her purse and handed Jon an envelope.

"You've spoken many times about the DNA of Gunnar and the young Irish woman and you expressed an interest about your own as well," she said. "So, I sent a sample of your hair for testing."

"What? How did you get a sample of my hair?"

"From your hairbrush, just like CSI," she replied. "You're not the only one interested in history, you know."

He quickly ripped open the envelope and pulled out the charts, scanning the results. "This chart says I'm seventy-four per cent Danish, fourteen per cent German, and twelve per cent Irish. I don't believe it! Twelve per cent Irish! My great-great grandfather was born in Ribe. Do you think it is possible that I could be related to that young woman in the diorama or someone like her?"

"That would be wildly improbable, Elsa said. "What's next on your agenda?"

"I wanted to get this completed before I decided what else to do. I could easily become part of another local dig or just continue teaching. I haven't decided yet."

She knew him well enough to see he wasn't done with the DNA angle yet. "Well, maybe you might consider taking next summer off so we can do some travelling."

"Where would you like to go?"

"Quite frankly, anywhere—New York City, or Paris, or Rome, or somewhere where we lay on the beach, sip fancy drinks, and not get dirty.

Jon burst out laughing. "Okay, I get it. You're right, we haven't had a holiday in years," he said, but his mind was still buzzing. *Twelve per cent Irish was huge. There had been an influx of Irish slaves in the late 800s and early 900s CE. The chance that he could be related to that woman was so remote as to be improbable. But he had her DNA in the lab. He could get his tested and compare it to hers. What if I'm one of her descendants! And if there was a positive match, I will compare it to Gunnar's too.*

Printed in Canada